Who is Mr Satoshi?

JONATHAN LEE

WINDMILL BOOKS

Published by Windmill Books 2011

2 4 6 8 10 9 7 5 3 1

First published in Great Britain in 2010 by William Heinemann

Windmill Books
The Random House Group Limited
20 Vauxhall Bridge Road, London SW1V 2SA

Addresses for companies within The Random House Group Limited
can be found at: www.randomhouse.co.uk/offices.htm

The Random House Group Limited Reg. No. 954009

www.randomhouse.co.uk

A CIP catalogue record for this book
is available from the British Library

ISBN 9780099537687

The Random House Group Limited supports The Forest Stewardship
Council® (FSC®), the leading international forest certification organisation.
All our titles that are printed on Greenpeace approved FSC® certified paper
carry the FSC® logo. Our paper procurement policy can be found at:
www.randomhouse.co.uk/environment

MIX
Paper from
responsible sources
FSC® C016897

Typeset by Palimpsest Book Production Limited,
Falkirk, Stirlingshire
Printed and bound in Great Britain by
CPI Cox & Wyman, Reading, RG1 8EX

For my parents

I do not doubt interiors have their interiors, and exteriors have their exteriors, and that the eyesight has another eyesight . . .

'Assurances', Walt Whitman

The punchline of the story relates to an American academic saying of Beckett, 'He doesn't give a fuck about people. He's an artist.' At this point Beckett raised his voice above the clatter of afternoon tea and shouted, 'But I *do* give a fuck about people. I *do* give a fuck!'

Beckett Remembering: Remembering Beckett,
ed. James and Elizabeth Knowlson; words of Lawrence Held
(Bloomsbury Publishing)

1

ONE AFTERNOON last October, on the concrete of her patio garden, my mother had a fall.

The event replays itself in my memory like an old reel of film. The picture wavers; the perspective shifts; the quality wanes. At the time, I had a clear-eyed view of her. She was so distinct from her surroundings. But not now. Now, watching the film my mind has made, my mother's features blend with everything behind her: the shadows, the lawn, the sepia sky.

She was out there because, at the age of eighty, she woke each morning with one ambition: to keep that patio clear of weeds. Weeds kept growing between the slabs of concrete, and she kept pulling them up. Responsibility for the upkeep lay with the warden, but this made no difference to my mother. The warden was shooed away and, when I offered help, I was told to stay indoors. So that's what I did. I sat in her front room at Finegold Mews, drinking. Outside, it was a crisply lit autumn day. A sliding glass door stood between us and a thin beam of light lasered its way through, falling into the tumbler in my hand, making the ice cubes tremble. The only sounds I could hear were low-level corridor noise: the hum and whine of other residents shuffling along, dropping things, picking them up.

It was the thud, the first of two, that caught my attention. I was watching the light melt the ice when I heard it. I looked up, and immediately saw the danger she was in. The palm of her hand was squashed against the glass door. Her whole weight seemed to be behind it. Her fingertips, first dark grey, then light grey, slipped and squeaked. I stood up and shouted, 'Mother!'. For decades I had addressed her as 'Mum', but it was the word 'Mother' that knotted in my throat and unravelled in the room. Since her death, it's become the thing to say.

The seconds that followed form a series of staccato, black-and-white shots. She is drifting. Narrow shaken shoulders. Raised brows and fallen eyes. Neck delicately twisted. And the veiny hand. Only this disembodied alien, shrivelled and pockmarked, holding her up. Fingers, inching downward, until she seems certain to fall.

But then the scene changes. The hand stops sliding. Improbable, but it is off the glass completely, dropping, like a weathered stone, into the front pocket of her apron. She regains her composure and balance. She swallows, turns her face up to the sky, takes a big breath. It's a proud, defensive posture. Only the blackbird overhead can see how thin her hair is.

By the time the second thud came, she appeared almost safe. Looking back now, it is this moment, in which it seemed crisis had been averted, that was the crucial one. I stood in her front room looking through the glass door, the drink still in my hand. I could have walked five yards, slid the door open and brought her inside. Or, if she wouldn't be reasoned with, taking me for some troublemaking stranger, I could have reached for one of the little orange triangles dangling from pull cords. One of those, or that emergency button on the wall. A forty-one-year-old man can lunge for a triangle or a button without breaking a sweat. For an instant, I could have done any of these things.

I linger there, in that still moment, because it is the last time I really had any options.

How did I even get there, in a position to watch her suffer? Minutes before it happened, I was in the kitchen. I was clinking ice into a glass.

She walked in and took her gardening gloves from a drawer labelled 'garden things', but was oblivious to me downing two glasses of butterscotch schnapps, the only drink I could find, and swallowing three pink pills. Since the dementia set in, she was oblivious to most things.

She took her gloves into the front room. I poured a final schnapps, put the bottle back, and started looking for a snack. There was nothing useful to be found. You could tell that she had built a life for herself in the post-war years. The 'remedies' cupboard was packed with Milk of Magnesia, Vicks VapoRub, Fynnon Salts, Friar's Balsam, Germolene. There was a section of the fridge labelled 'rationed', stuffed full of butter, lard, margarine, cheese, eggs. A little storeroom off the hallway (labelled 'storeroom') housed precarious columns of tinned goods – fish, tomatoes, meat, soup, vegetables, treacle. Alongside the tins, sugar (caster, icing, demerara), flour (plain, pastry, self-raising), lentils, pasta, rice. Then there were the latticed jars of fruit preserve, the boxes of Braeburns and Bramleys, the bottles of squash. My mother had been acquainted with shortage, and she didn't forget it.

As I settled down on the leather sofa with my drink, the smell of meals on wheels in the communal corridor drifted in. I remembered that I hadn't eaten all day. I was so anxious about leaving my place that morning, about facing the dangers that crowd the world outside my flat, I couldn't manage any breakfast.

'Why don't you let me do it?' I said. She was hobbling across the carpet in the direction of the glass door. 'Why don't you let me pull up the weeds, if you're that bothered?'

She didn't respond. Instead, apparently remembering something crucial, she took a sidestep toward the television set in the corner. It was a clunky old thing, a throwback to a time when pictures didn't matter so much. She steadied herself on one of its blunt corners, reached around the back, and pulled out a shoebox. She placed the shoebox on top of the set, gave it a friendly pat and made her way over to the patio.

I said, 'What's in the box, Mum?'

She slid the door open with a colossal effort, then paused for a long time, considered my question. Cold air riddled the room. Then she responded. I remember the exact words she used. In the time that has passed, they have echoed through my mind with greater and greater resonance.

She said, 'The plan is to deliver it to Mr Satoshi.'

'Who's Mr Satoshi?' I said.

And she said, 'Most of all, the package is for Mr Satoshi. For when we get an address for him.'

Her voice was soft, but I heard each word quite distinctly. Then, her grip on the door handle suddenly fierce, as if someone unseen were dragging her outside, she said, 'And if you've got any influence around here, you'll see to it that the warden keeps off my back.'

She slid the door closed behind her and I sank back into a clump of cushions. The gardening gloves lay dejected at my side.

A heartbeat later, as I was swirling my sickly schnapps in the beam of afternoon light, I heard it. The thud. The air was clubbed flat by it. I was surprised that someone so tiny could generate such a sound, and for a second I thought the window might give. I stood to attention, but it stayed in place, her hand still suckered to it. White and sticky and pressing hard. Her head dipping, her body crumpling, her hand sliding downward. And then the recovery – the miraculous recovery – the straightening up, the chin to the sky, the hand off the glass.

One tick of a clock is all it takes for your options to evaporate.

The crucial moment. I felt my heart beating hard in my head. My mouth was suddenly dry, the corrosive fizz of a pink pill charring some hidden tract or tissue in my throat. But I ignored these signs. I wanted to believe that the scare was over. In that empty second, that blank space in time, I knew I had choices. But I convinced myself, I must surely have convinced myself, that there was no need to act. Why else would I have stood there, so rooted to the spot, as she – confident in her own recovery – leaned in again, determined to get it, determined to pluck the rogue dandelion from a gap between two concrete squares?

She wiped her hands on the front of her apron and dipped

lower, much lower than before, attacking the perennial scourge of her nice, neat, paved grid. In murky greyscale, as I see things now, she is hunched over a huge chessboard. And then it comes. I see it. I see that the stalk she is clutching isn't lifting. The dandelion's roots, wide-spreading and thick, won't budge from the hard-packed soil. The unsteadiness is all hers.

This time the thud was not from her hand, but her shoulder. It hurtled into the glass door. It slid. Her knees buckled as she succumbed to the gravitational pull of the weed. It drew her into an irresistible downward trajectory.

I doubt she had time to notice, as she accelerated toward the ground, how beautiful the bulbous seed head of the dandelion looked. Its fine, snowflake strands were spectacular. At first those strands held firm in one tight ball on top of the stem. Then they disappeared from view completely, obscured by her shadow spreading across the patio. But, on impact, the seeds burst out from the darkness. They exploded. A firework of bright white atoms, a magnesium flash that burns the image onto film.

And I didn't hear her head strike the concrete. I heard silence punctured by my own short, horrified laugh. I waded toward the window. I dropped my glass along the way. Instead of cracking, it bounced absurdly. Outside, thin wisps of October cloud thickened in the lowering sky. They drew a veil of grey across the garden. She lay there in a craggy heap. Her hand twitched mechanically and I let out a stupid whimper. The apron had gathered around her neck, and her spent face peeped over the top. Black blood drizzled from her one visible ear.

I stood there until I was sure that she was dead. I pressed

myself right up to the glass. My forehead flat against it, my hands too, eyes shuttered, and I stayed there for a long time, collapsed against the cold surface, let it take my weight completely. At some point, it started to rain. I went back to the sofa and sat there, watching translucent drops randomly merge and run jerkily downward. A pool of murky water formed around the body. If I close my eyes now, I can still see that water, a drama of reflected cloud, channelled into the soft grey glow of a camera lens.

Eventually, after taking more medication, I called the emergency people. When they came knocking I felt, just for a moment, that it was Mr Satoshi at the door.

It wasn't, of course. All that was waiting for me was the thick green rush of paramedics. Pretty soon I couldn't see my mother at all. The tightly assembled strangers put her on a stretcher and covered her with a cotton sheet.

Her face has remained veiled ever since.

2

THE FOLLOWING Monday, standing in a shaded row at the back of Longcross Church, I watched her neighbours slow-mouthing hymns. My hair was plastered down with sweat and I felt half choked by my tie. The joints and striations of the high windows trapped and shaped the light, illuminating the pews ahead with arcs of yellow, red and green, but the black-clad crowd didn't absorb any of the colour. Each mourner looked like a shadow of the next.

I was the sole representative of the Fossick family, but the residents of Finegold Mews had come out in force to hear the organ notes stir in the pipes. It was difficult to make my lips move in unison with theirs. Looking at the guttering candles and the flower arrangements and the way the white of the stained glass shivered like mother-of-pearl, a thought kept recurring, a question that had the effect of hardening my jaw: was a few years in a care home the way to get a decent turnout at my own eventual funeral? I wondered if my father would turn up, keen to play the estranged yet grief-stricken parent. Or old friends, just one or two, from when I was married.

In a break between hymns the priest said something

about shepherds and the fact that death is a great leveller, a reminder that we are all the same under our clothes. I was only dimly aware of his homily. I was thinking about the seeds of my mother's death, and when exactly they had been sown.

Number 17, Virginia Road. The house in which I grew up and Alice Fossick became, quite suddenly, old. It was there that, on one of my visits more than a decade ago, I first noticed the little white labels.

'Red napkins', 'White napkins', 'Red and white napkins'.

Initially they raised no alarm. My mother had always been one to write things down. Birthdays coming up, recipes mentioned on television, the next WI meeting.

But before long the labels had multiplied across the house, one stuck on every drawer and cupboard: '2nd best plates', 'washing tabs', 'broken china'.

Why not just throw the china away, Mum?

'Broken china (for bin men)', read the amended note, sandwiched between 'dishwasher salt' and 'pamphlets/warranties/manuals'.

The labels were just labels; there was worse to come. She wrote a letter to the local paper complaining that the post office had been closed down. 'It is a disgrace,' she wrote, 'that basic services on which the local community has come to rely are being withdrawn without proper consideration of, and consultation with, the villagers themselves.' She showed it to me in draft, to see what I thought. I knew it was a good letter, but I also knew that the post office was still open for business. When I walked her there to prove my point, she started laughing. 'Just winding you up,' she said. 'I haven't lost my marbles yet.'

It was hard to know what to think. She still harboured a wealth of information that most minds would struggle to contain: the names of everyone in the village, the order in which all sixty-six monarchs had ascended the throne, the brands of weedkiller suited to different soil types. She could remember the names of photographers I admired, the places my pictures had been published and hung.

It got to the point where I would come round at lunchtime and find her getting ready for bed, or I'd get calls in the middle of the night because she was confused about the darkness. At least she remembered my phone number, I thought. When neighbours found her standing on familiar streets consulting an A to Z, she said that she was getting her bearings.

'It's just age,' she said. 'In your seventies you get confused sometimes, that's how it is.'

I asked if she knew the name of my wife.

'Chloe,' she said, affronted.

I shrugged and laughed. She'd always liked Chloe. Years later, when Chloe died, it was my mother who cried the most, who gave in utterly to the grief.

'So what's the next test?' my mother said.

I asked her if she remembered the Prime Minister's name. I took care to frame the question as a joke.

'Ha!' she said. 'The old Chinese Commie. A.T. Lee! Bring back Churchill, I say.'

'A. T. Lee' was her name for Clement Attlee.

'He left Downing Street a while back, Mum.'

'I'm pleasing. I'm please. I'm pleased.'

'Could it be her heart medication?' I asked the doctor. His face wore the same look of apologetic vacancy, of familiarity tinged with confusion, that my mother's did.

'Hmmm,' he said, plucking a thermometer from his breast pocket. 'On occasion the symptoms your mother demonstrates can have other causes – thyroid problems, vitamin deficiency, even depression. We'll explore all avenues. We won't rule anything out.'

On the walk back from the surgery, I stopped at the Green Shop to pick up provisions. I left my mother waiting outside. When I re-emerged, she was stroking a dachshund with an uneven tan.

Mum said, 'Did you remember to get the paper for your father?'

I said, 'Dad left years ago Mum, you know that.'

'I remember my father,' she said.

Finegold Mews was the perfect choice. She already lived down the road from it, so in her lucid moments she knew the area. And there was the fact that all of the residents had the option of their own flat, rather than just some poky room. I even managed to reserve her a spot on the ground floor, with a view of the gardens and her own square of patio.

The patio sealed it. In December 1999, just before humanity in all its different shapes and sizes entered a new millennium, I moved her in. I remember thinking, as I drove us over there in a rented van, that her face looked suddenly different, the corners of the eyes and mouth drifting downward, as if past hopes were gradually subsiding. I remember wishing I had taken her picture more often, before her features acquired that downward aspect.

The Christian hymn medley finished and I made a dash for the church doors. In a quiet corner of the cemetery, hiding behind a silver birch tree, I lit up a cigarette.

Through a patchwork of stubborn shoots and triangular leaves, I could see my mother's weedy little memorial hole. No body in there yet, just spade-split stems and turned earth. All around it were tilted, mottled stones with barely legible names and dates. The mourners, all bone in the bleached light, navigated their way through an assault course of heel marks and tufts, arriving at her space in the ground.

I turned away, but into the vacuum of my ears came exaggerated shuffles and coughs and the sound of the coffin squeaking slowly downward. A few minutes of this before I managed to temper my own listening and, with the eyes of a child, see remembered things. The low lilac hedges at number 17. A porch filled with lemony squares of sun. Tidy rows of cut roses. I finished smoking and lit another and made the roses vanish.

An old man I had never seen before came scuttling across the grass, taking me by surprise. He grabbed my cigarette arm and squeezed it hard.

'Aha,' he said, gazing into my eyes. 'It's you! The reclusive photographer!'

'Indeed it is,' I said, baffled.

'Lovely service! Keeping well?'

'Well enough, thanks.'

'Smashing,' he said, storming off.

The coffin had been planted, everyone had moved to the car park, and I watched him join the crowd. I smoked intently, greedy for the cigarette's anodyne fug. Surely it would disperse soon, the muddle of walking sticks, Zimmer frames, bifocals, trifocals, dark grey coats with yawning shoulders. The apparatus of old age. Overhead, the sunlight present during the service was being hazed by clouds. The milky sky curdled and wobbly shadows spread and steadied into a general gloom. I decided to count to twenty-five. If the mourners hadn't disappeared by then, no matter. I would stroll past them, saying nothing, board the London train, lock myself away, re-engage with the routine. I counted to twenty-five. There was still a flock of mourners ruffling their black feathers on the pavement, parping frenziedly about grief and death and who would be next. I counted to twenty-five again, slower than before, shoe-screwing my cigarette butt into the grass, promising myself that this time I really would step out from behind this tree, head to the train station, and, if someone talked to me, I'd exchange pleasantries and move on, confident and sweat-free, because only kids and psychopaths rely on counting as a means of making things appear and disappear. And when I got to twenty-five once more, and then once more again, I just squeezed the pill bottle in my coat pocket and peered through the camouflage until people receded into the distance.

Off they went: to use the toilet, to drop tea bags in hot water, to tap dusters in dark corners, fortified by the knowledge that everyone else was doing exactly the same.

I picked my moment, but I picked the wrong one. As I tried to cut through the church car park, a lanky old woman scampered towards me. She swung her walking stick like a demolition ball. Her limbs flailed about with indistinct, fuzzy energy, a daddy-long-legs tumbling across a carpet, drunk on dying summer light. I was cornered against a tomato-red bonnet.

She said, 'You must be young Robert, Alice's son.'

'Rob,' I said. 'Or Foss.' I stared at the ground, hoping she would understand that I was pressed for time and energy.

When I looked up a few seconds later she was still standing in front of me, most of her weight resting on the thin wooden walking stick, the rubber ferrule not quite flush with the concrete. Her face reminded me of my mother's: swathes of sagging skin, so pale it was almost green. She was stranded somewhere in her eighties.

I said, 'Can I help you in some way?'

'Oh no. No help required.'

There was a Home Counties twang to her voice, the tongue strumming each 'o' like a plectrum over the rosette of a guitar.

'Were you at the funeral?' I asked.

'Oh yes, yes I was. I thought it was an excellent service. Don't you agree?'

'I thought it was fine, yes.'

'I was a friend of your mother's. I'm Freddie.'

'Hi, Freddie.'

Her hand felt rough and dry.

'You're a resident at Finegold, Freddie?'

'Oh I am, yes. Oh yes. Although I'm perfectly "with it". I knew your mother for quite a long time. She may have mentioned me, but I suspect . . . So I live down the hall from her neck of the woods. I believe you still have the flat? I mean to say that you haven't relinquished the lease?'

'That's right.'

'You haven't cleared her things out, I suppose?'

'Well . . . no. It hasn't been very long.'

'But you'll do it soon?'

'Fairly soon, I expect. I've got quite a lot of stuff on, though.'

'On what?'

'You know, just *on*. Stuff on. But I'll be clearing the flat out soon enough.'

'Oh, I see.'

I studied the pink bags under her eyes. 'You look concerned.'

'It's just, something has played on my mind, since your mother died. Something she said. A kind of request. Perhaps we could head back to the Mews and discuss things?'

'I really must get home, unfortunately. I live in London.'

'Of course, you'll have photographs to take.'

'Indeed.'

'I used to take photographs once. Not quite sure why I stopped. I suppose I no longer had very much to photograph.'

'Freddie, I really should be getting back.'

'Oh, I quite understand, I do, but this is rather important.'

'How so?'

'Well,' she said, leaning forward on her stick and glancing left to right, somewhat conspiratorially, 'it's about a shoebox.'

'A shoebox?'

I could see her scalp through sparse swirls of white hair. The skin was lunar grey and pitted, peppered with tiny silver and pink freckles.

She said, 'I believe there is a shoebox that contains something your mother wanted delivered. To a Mr Satoshi.'

The name sent an electric surge of memory fizzing through my veins.

'You know who he is?'

'Vaguely,' she said, 'vaguely. At least I think so. Satoshi sounds foreign, doesn't it? But unless I'm going senile it's just a nickname your mother used for an English chap, a

Bristolian we used to know. Why don't we head back to the Mews? I can drive.'

'You drive?'

She drove. She took me to Finegold Mews in a Citroën so frail its back doors were sealed with duct tape. A windscreen wiper had been reconstructed with a length of coat-hanger wire. Every ten metres felt like a triumph of substance over form. The car smelt like a biscuit tin, crumbly and sweet, and the speckled mud pressed into the floor and dashboard gave it an earthy atmosphere, the warmth of decay and petrification. I felt an odd sense of security, rarely experienced outside the walls of my flat. I felt it even as I glanced down the murky lanes and shady avenues that we passed, taking in their anonymity and the way that, like a rambling thought, they dallied this way and that, without a clear sense of limits and boundaries, of purpose and direction.

3

FINEGOLD MEWS, declared the copper lettering above the front entrance.

I followed Freddie through the reception area, making small talk about everyday ailments, banes and woes. The space was cluttered with lamps, chairs, rugs and coffee tables. These furnishings were new when I moved my mother in. The newness was a problem for her. It placed Finegold Mews in painful contrast with her old house, a home full of ancient objects tangled up with family memories. She had watched me leave number 17, to go up to university. She had watched Dad leave too, after he fell in love with the City, and later into a lusty embrace with his secretary. But some good ghosts must have remained.

'I'll just ask the warden to let us in,' I said, but Freddie was already pressing a piece of svelte plastic into the slot. 'You have a key card for my mother's flat?'

'Oh yes. We were great friends. Bad luck that I never managed to catch you on one of your visits, really.'

'Yes, well. I didn't get over here as often as I would have liked.'

The motion of opening the door unsettled a lot of dust

inside. I didn't know it at the time, but the dust would be the first of many things in my mother's world to be disturbed by my interference; soon nothing would remain settled, nothing would stay still.

'Take a seat, Freddie.'

'Oh, thank you, I will.'

My mother's high-ceilinged front room had an eccentric feel to it. The vaulting walls were out of proportion to the minuscule floor space, so that the room seemed to have been tipped on its end, less a room and more of a cereal box. There were photographs hanging everywhere, painstakingly spaced. The photos were the result of a strange project she launched in her seventies. It involved accumulating a photograph to represent each year of her life. I shot some of them, for example the one made up of tiny squares which, if you squinted at it long enough, cohered into a grid of identical human heads. It was a sheet of commemorative stamps her father had put aside for her on the day she was christened; she had me dig it out and snap it as a reminder of her first year. The one hanging in the top left corner of the far wall, a picture of a rugby ball, was another of mine. Any old rugby ball, but a reminder that in 1936, when my mother was seven years old, her father spilt beer on his lap when the wireless announcer declared that Alex Obolensky had scored a second try. England had beaten the All Blacks for the very first time.

I scanned these and other pictures, mesmerised by the polished glass in the frames. It undulated in the lamplight like fine skin, a living barrier, a human presence in the room.

Freddie said, 'Do you know which year each of these represents?'

'No. I don't know what most of the pictured things mean, which memories they connect to.'

She seemed to consider this very carefully.

'So,' I said, 'about this shoebox.'

'Oh yes,' she said, as if she wasn't expecting the shoebox to come up in conversation at all. 'How about I get us some herbal tea and a biscuit?'

'If you like. There might be something in the cupboard to the left of the cooker.'

She got to her feet with a croak and a groan, the attendant sounds of transition, and pressed her walking stick in the direction of the kitchen. It struck me as unusual to see an old person who was thin and tall, as opposed to thin and small.

She shouted, 'The one labelled "powders/granules/bags"?'

'Exactly.'

I got up, walked to the television, and peered over the top. Sure enough, beyond the scarred black surface, wedged at an awkward angle between the wall and the set, was the shoebox. It must have slipped back there, the victim of a paramedic's stray elbow or the corner of a stretcher. 'The plan,' she had said, her words crowded by silence, 'is to deliver it to Mr Satoshi.' And now this Freddie woman was suggesting that he wasn't just a figment of my mother's imagination, a name torn from a cereal packet or stolen from the *Afternoon Play*. I took the box over to my chair.

'Oh, that's the one!' she said excitedly, eyes fixed on my lap.

Shakily, she handed me a mug. The porcelain was embroidered with the tesserae of some liquefied flower.

'So,' she said. She lowered herself back into the leather sofa and leaned her stick against one of the nickel-studded arms. 'Mr Satoshi. It goes back to my schooldays in Bristol with your mother.'

'You knew her then?'

'Well, of course. Oh yes. Bristol. It's been a long while, but I know that city like the back of my hand.'

She studied her knuckles, white and shiny against the dark cotton of her skirt.

'Our favourite part of the city, your mother's and mine, was Cotham. Clifton was more elegant, but the bonus with Cotham was Mrs Cummings, a teacher at our school and a very dedicated philatelist. Regularly managed to obtain rare stamps that your mother and I had only ever read about in the latest Stanley Gibbons catalogue. The Nyassa ten reis was my favourite.'

Freddie started reciting the poetry of stamp collecting: magnifying glasses, perforation gauges, tweezers, gummed mounts, the hidden watermarks and their revelation in little grey trays filled with spirit.

'I don't mean to interrupt,' I said, 'but you might need to start from the beginning.'

So that's what she did. Her eyes widened and wobbled as she spoke, as if all kinds of memories were bubbling behind them. Freddie's mother was a German-born woman, Luisa, who had lived in England for most of her life and was naturalised. During the First World War, Luisa fell in love with a Bristolian accountant. 'They married after the war ended,' Freddie said, 'and settled down in Bristol to have me.' When Freddie was seven, Luisa died of sudden heart failure, no warning. Her father had just begun a posting to the British Central Africa Company in Blantyre, Nyasaland, so he sent Freddie to a boarding school in Bristol.

'That's the school your mother attended. And that's why that ten reis I mentioned was my favourite stamp. It had a giraffe on it, which made me think of Africa, and my father.'

'And you and my mother became close friends?'

Yes. The best of friends. For the first of the school holidays, Freddie stayed in the boarding house until the new term started. She had no family in England to stay with. After a while, my mother's parents started looking after her during these breaks.

'I did what her family did. Christmas and Easter in the Clifton house, and part of the summer holidays spent in a rented cottage by the seaside, usually in Weston-super-Mare. Your mum and I used to play on the beach for hours. We'd race each other up and down the seafront, heads down, watching tiny white crabs disappear into punctures in the sand.'

'And by coincidence you ended up in here, with my mother?'

'I had been living nearby. And when my son decided that it was time for me to move into a home, Finegold Mews was recommended as one of the best. I came to look around, and I found to my delight that your mother was here . . .'

'And was she pleased to see you, when you arrived at Finegold?'

'Pleased?' she said, the folds and lines of her face turning mauve. 'Oh, you know how it is.'

I told her that I did, that I knew exactly how it was.

'Do you have children, Robert?'

'What? No. My wife, she passed away but . . . There was an accident, while we were on holiday. Greece. That's where I got the scar on my cheek.'

'Oh, I can barely see it, actually. You know how these

things are, magnified a hundred times by the imagination. You would know that, as a photographer.'

'I haven't taken a decent picture in a while.'

'No?'

'No. I suppose I'm lucky. I can live off the money I make from reproductions. Two or three well-known photos that get wheeled out every now and then. It's not a lot of money, of course, but then I don't need much.'

'I understand you used to photograph writers, artists? Very successfully, by all accounts. I read about you in the *Telegraph* once. Or was it *The Times*? I get both, you see. The article described you as "brilliant and handsome". A picture of you with some tubby novelists.'

'Perry, my agent, pretty much wrote that article. I used to photograph artistic types, but you have to seek them out. There came a point where I didn't want to do it any more.'

'I see, yes. I had heard about your . . .'

'Weariness?'

'Oh,' she said, 'I was going to say remoteness. That's the word. It conjures a sense of grace. Inaccessible things, places. They are sacred, I always think. Like the past. Romantic. Somehow more whole than the present. The hard-to-reach things, they're the most beautiful, aren't they?'

'I wouldn't know. It's tiresome, really. But these last few years I've struggled to shake myself out of it. My flat, my routine, has become a kind of second skin.'

I scratched my ear and wondered why I was telling her all this.

'Tell me about Satoshi.'

'Dear God, he had slipped my mind completely! Having such fun chatting over tea. Yes, Mr Satoshi. He was a boy we knew in Bristol. We didn't always call him that, of course. He was plain old Reggie for a while. He wasn't foreign, he was English, but for whatever reason it was this Satoshi nickname that stuck. I don't know whether your mother coined it, or was just its greatest advocate. She spoke of him every now and then, in these last years, and still used that name. Since she passed away, I've tried to recall his proper surname, I really have. But he was just Reggie or Satoshi to me. Whereas for your mother . . . well, they were childhood sweethearts.'

'Sweethearts?'

'Yes. He was one of the reasons Cotham was exciting, because he lived there as a teenager. To start with we were all just a group of friends. It was long before Alice met your father. When was that?'

'I forget. Fifties. They married in the late fifties. Had me very late, in '68. Trouble conceiving, I think.'

'It was girls only, the boarding school we went to, but we knew a few of the boys who went to a nearby school. Reggie was one of them, and a rather good-looking lad he was too. We met him at a dance in the early forties. Him and his friend Geoff, who I took a bit of a shine to. The war was in full flow and we were all too young to join up, so we just ploughed on with our studies and lives as best we could. It was difficult, of course. Everyone had a brother or father out there fighting, and doing our homework and turning up for lessons on time didn't seem to have quite the same importance it once had. You know about the war, I suppose?'

'Studied history at university. I can't remember my mother talking about her wartime experiences much. I didn't get the impression that the war impacted on her a great deal.'

'Oh, perhaps. Anyway, in the early forties, when we met

him, Reggie's father had just been killed. One assumes Reggie took it pretty hard, though I didn't discuss it with him. Your mother probably did. They became quite close. Indeed, by the summer of '45, she was joking about them getting married.'

'Married?'

'Yes,' she said. 'Probably just joking. But then Alice always said she'd marry young. It was a thing of hers. Why hang around? she'd say. A sort of war philosophy, I suppose. Would you like some more tea?'

'Not really.'

She said, 'As the war progressed, Reggie felt he couldn't continue with school. Shame. He was a very bright, imaginative sort of boy. He moved to Surrey in '45 and stayed with relatives. He went to help build planes. I think he was a sheet-metal worker – well below his capabilities. Wing fillets for the Wellington bombers, if my memory serves me. It was once he was there that things with your mother got serious. Of course, with the distance, they only saw each other occasionally. One weekend every couple of months, usually him coming back to Bristol. Me, Alice, Reggie and Geoff were all huddled round a wireless the day Churchill announced we had defeated the Germans. But there was still work to be done. Reggie wanted to be part of that work. He had this uncle in Japan, mother's side I think. The Allied forces occupied the country, of course, for years after they dropped the atom bombs. The Americans mobilised all kinds of experts to go over there, to see how best to prevent the Orientals waging future wars. Reggie's uncle was one of the first to go. He was a well-known academic, an anthropowhatsit.'

'Go on.'

'Well, the uncle was with the occupation forces, and

needed an assistant. He offered his nephew, seventeen-year-old Reggie, the chance to join him out there.'

'And Reggie went to work for this anthropologist uncle?'

'He did,' she said. 'Went to Tokyo. While he was in Japan, your mother wrote to him often. From that moment on she talked about him only as Mr Satoshi. They were very much in love, I think. Making all sorts of plans for when he returned. Or so I believe, anyway.'

'I know nothing about this. The first I've heard of any of it. Did he come back?'

'I . . . Who can say? They certainly never married. Something must have got in the way.'

'You don't know why it didn't work out?'

'No, I don't know.'

Freddie and my mother saw each other less often after the war, their friendship eventually reduced to oddly polite exchanges, the kind of street-corner summaries in which whole decades are condensed into phrases like 'not too bad', into questions like 'how about yourself?'. By the time Freddie turned up at Finegold Mews, my mother seemed to have only a fleeting awareness of who she was. Slowly, they became friends all over again. A patient friendship, full of repetition. That's when my mother started talking about the shoebox.

'That one,' Freddie said, nodding and pointing a finger at the box on my lap. 'She showed it to me. She said the contents needed to go to Mr Satoshi. That he was in Japan. That she had an address for him, but it was out of date, words to that effect.'

'She said nothing else?'

'Nothing else. Except . . . she did say to make sure it got delivered, if anything happened.'

'She said that?'

'Yes,' Freddie said, almost whispering, as if she was telling me the most rare and private thing. 'She said it must get to him.'

I looked up at the photographs on the walls. The neatly ordered evidence of my mother's life. The flatness of her history. Then I zoomed in on each corner of the room, noticing which little white labels were still in place and which lay curled on the carpet.

'I'm terribly sorry, dear, but I might just have to use the toilet.'

'Be my guest.'

It took her a while to get up. I had to stand at her side to make sure she didn't fall. 'Oh, don't fuss,' she said, flailing out of the room. Something about the doggedness with which she moved, her sense of the effort required to achieve motion, made my breathing shallow. Funny that: if someone's mind rots, you get irritated with them, as though the deterioration is somehow down to a lapse in their own judgement. But if their body has the decorum to follow suit, tight sympathy swells in your chest.

We took the lid off the shoebox and peered inside. It contained a slim package. It was about the same size as a paperback. Taut brown paper tied with white string. Perfectly bland, no gloss, no distortion. It bore a label.

Reggie / Satoshi
Roppongi World Plaza 9–39,
Roppongi 1-chome,
Minato-ku,
Tokyo 106-0032

The address was crossed through with a diagonal line in a different colour ink.

'How did she know the address was wrong?' I said. 'There are no stamps on this. It's not like it was returned to sender. It was simply never sent.'

'I don't know,' Freddie said. 'But *she* knew. She said she knew it was wrong.'

And, soon after that, Freddie left. She didn't see me lift the package out of the box. She didn't see the folded leaf of paper that lay beneath it.

I stared at the letter in my hands, looking past the page into another moment somewhere, inexplicably reading the text aloud. The words sounded clean and smooth in the empty room.

The Berries
Constitution Hill
Clifton
Bristol
England

My own darling Alice,

I am writing this on the train to Uncle George, in a white-streaked carriage marked 'Allied Forces Only'. The only ticket you need to travel is your Western skin.

For miles and miles at the start of this journey I saw nothing bright – endless grey fields littered with shabby shacks & singed things, dark clouds that seemed determined to make me sulky & low. But then, just now, I closed my eyes for a minute & thought of you. I blocked out all the ash & weeds (how you'd hate the stubborn weeds!). I imagined the silk of your lips forming a smile, the scent of Coty Muguet in your hair. I counted your eyelashes one by one – and then I opened my eyes afresh & the landscape was changed.

The sun is a clean white behind black Shiba trees as Tokyo unfolds in the window. Lost mud paths are overridden in places by energetic patches of green. Not just weeds, but flower stems, long grasses, full-grown leaves. A hunched man with a pageboy haircut is cultivating a garden plot on a dusty roadside. You said there'd be no garden plots but there are! And between glances I find myself scribbling an awkward haiku for you, trying to keep my pen still as the train carries me, then pulls me back.

> *Bright young vegetables*
> *are growing in the light*
> *along the burned street.*

Stay smiling, my love, even if it's at the clumsiness of my poetry. You have no idea how much I depend on the memory of your smile.

    Ever your
    Reggie

4

AFTER A dream-lit night, I woke with a familiar liquid moan in my veins. The package was resting on my stomach like a needy pet. I had intended to go back to my flat the previous night, but here I was, crumpled on my mother's sofa. The television buzzed gently in the corner of the room. The usual headlines: terror, bombs in cameras, suspicious tape recorders, the narrative of disaster.

I searched for something else to watch but got lost among half-tuned channels. Somehow the sight of swarming dots reignited the images that had flickered through my sleep. It's a condition of middle-age that you end up swapping dreams for reality, but of late I seemed to be bucking the trend. When I was dropping off or on the edge of waking, I saw flashes of my own birth. I was inside the womb, struggling to get out. My chubby, compact little body was squeezed like a hunk of lime, acidic juices consuming me. My eyes, as yet untainted by any sight of the outside world, were encased in a foul-smelling sweat. I was practically a contortionist, legs and arms tied in party-balloon knots, and in these dreams my mother was always crying out, her explosive shrieks reverberating through the dark corridors of gore. And then, of course, there were the other dreams. The old Chloe dreams, the smoke-filled scenes, the blurred visions in which she drifts away.

I was awake and I was in my mother's flat. It made sense to use the time to sort through her belongings. There were a lot of them to sort through.

I had spent a week formulating the plan. The plan was this.

Step one: cluster. I would put all of the movable furniture in the front room up against the patio door. Not only would this give me more space to move around, but it would have the added benefit of meaning I didn't have to look out at that little square of poorly scrubbed concrete.

Step two: categorise. I would split my mother's belongings into three categories, each of which would form a pile in its own corner of floor space:

A) monetary value but no sentimental value;

B) sentimental value but no monetary value; and

C) rubbish.

Later on, I could subdivide pile A into things that I should give to charity shops, things that I should keep, and things that I should sell. As for pile B, I could already sense the difficulties it would cause (what single thing is there in the universe of things that doesn't have some sentiment attached to it?), but no system is perfect, and I was determined to be ruthless.

Step three: remove and terminate. I would get everything out of the flat and terminate the lease.

When executing step one, I moved not just the furniture but the photographs. It took a long time to get them off the walls. I boxed them up and decided that, with the exception of three photographs, I would put the collection into storage. The first one I kept was the picture of the commemorative stamps. The other two were of me as a newborn baby at St Peter's Hospital. Clearly 1968, the year of my birth, was deserving of two images to jog the memory. In both photographs, my mother was upright in the hospital bed. You couldn't see her face, only her shoulders, arms and the bed sheet tucked around her waist. I was in the middle, wrapped in a blanket. The two portraits were almost identical, except that one was in colour and the other in black and white. I put the three photographs in a leather satchel, next to the letter that I had found in the shoebox, and moved to the next phase of the plan.

After a couple of hours of piling, category B had already become unmanageable. It was an enormous great toppling mountain of sentimental paraphernalia. And I had, on finding a few bits of familiar jewellery, been forced to generate a category D: a pocket's worth of things that bore sentimental *and* monetary value. Category A was straightforward – it consisted of one television and one radio. My mother's last will and testament, a WH Smith one-pager, had not expressed any preference for where these or any other objects should go. Since she was a divorcee and I was her only child, they were mine by default. Even though I didn't want another television, even though I already had three radios. It was tempting to squeeze them into category C, a bin liner half full with scraps of newspaper and sea-coloured tea towels.

After working my way through the front room and the bedroom, I started on the storeroom off the hallway, boxing up huge quantities of tinned food, packets, bottles. I'd see if Freddie could find a home for these things. She had mentioned that a couple of charities ran regular collections at Finegold Mews. Perhaps they'd take the clothes too.

Last of all, I turned my attention to The Snug, a little attic room above the hallway. Access was through a panel in the low ceiling. When pressed, the panel clicked and swung downward, bringing into reach a fold-down ladder hooked to the inside. The ladder wobbled as I trod on its rungs.

There were abandoned objects everywhere, coated with dust, seeming to create their own weather system among the exposed beams and posts. A carved wooden poodle; a broken Doris Day record; seven HB pencils; half a dozen empty bottles of perfume; a mosaic trinket pot that opened to reveal a small mirror; a light brown synthetic belt buckle. It was strange to think that these items were signifiers of sentiments now inaccessible to me. She had chosen to preserve them, presumably because of their value as memory triggers, part of her strategy for keeping a foothold in the past. But now their associated meanings, if not already long-forgotten, had been buried with her.

For what seemed like hours I knelt in The Snug, combing through all of the random debris that my mother's life had washed up. Some things, like the loose photos I looked through, I could shore against my own brittle memories. Me at the seaside, learning to walk. Me with my father after I won the Most Improved Player Award for Longcross Rovers Under 13 B Team, a bittersweet trophy because it tacitly acknowledged my lack of basic coordination the previous season. As I flicked through these pictures, my throat became sore. Perhaps it was the dust, or the onset of a cold. Probably dust. How can you catch a cold when you hardly ever come into contact with people? A clean bill of health was a fringe benefit of my seclusion.

I needed water. Hunched, I staggered past slabs of foam insulation and swivelled myself round to descend the steps.

That's when I noticed it: a metal box in the far right corner of the attic, half covered by an old bed sheet. There was no particular reason why it should grab my attention, but it did.

I approached the box cautiously, inhaling a cobweb on the way, coughing as I held it up to the light. It was obvious that it hadn't been disturbed in a very long time. I used the sleeve of my sweatshirt to wipe away the dust: a thick, grey dust from a different era, made of tenacious fog, of dogged dirt. The metal beneath was scratchless, pristine.

The lid popped open without difficulty. Inside were a dozen tiny nested boxes and several neatly arranged tin canisters. I removed one of the boxes. It contained what seemed to be multicoloured lumps of liquorice. On closer inspection I saw that they were handmade flies, used for fishing. The bodies had been created from finely blended dubbing. The undersides of the flies varied in colour – yellows, reds, greens. The wings also varied; some were made of thin white yarn and others from carved foam. The canisters were full to the brim with hooks of different shapes and sizes and each canister was labelled. 'Dry Fly'; 'Heavy Barbless'; 'Nymph'; 'Salmon Double'; 'Bass Bug'. I hovered over them, spine arced, head cocked. I felt tense and light. Never knew that my mother or father liked fishing. Thought I'd know a thing like that.

I was about to resume my search for refreshment when I

realised something: the little canisters were resting on a wooden shelf a few inches off the floor of the box. The top right and bottom left corners of the shelf featured hollow spaces the size of thumbnails. Slipping the tip of a finger into each, I lifted the shelf up, taking care not to unbalance any of the containers still resting on it. I was surprised by what lay beneath. The more I stared, the more I was surprised.

I suppose I expected more fly-fishing gear. Reel perhaps, or the raw materials for making flies. But what I found was paper. Not an instruction manual, not *The Fisherman's Almanac*. No: thick, creamy paper, coated with neat blue ink, folded flat, crisp as starched handkerchiefs. A yellow satin ribbon, water-stained and earth-spotted, held the pages together. I pulled an end and the bow unravelled.

As I unfolded the first sheet, it rustled and creaked, enlivened by its emancipation. I appeared to be looking at two letters, both a few pages long. Both bore a date on their first page, both a day in 1946.

The handwriting was familiar, but it took me a blank second to realise why. The letters were from Mr Satoshi. First the one in the shoebox, now these. I seemed destined to inherit his collected correspondence.

I heard noise from downstairs. Importunate knocking, loud and unexpected, followed by Freddie's voice. 'Robert!' she shouted, the name whistling through the letter box. 'I have the warden here! I thought we might hatch a plan for your mother's belongings!'

Once the letters were safely in my pocket, I went downstairs to talk charity shops, refuse collection and the market for ancient televisions.

* * *

After making arrangements with Freddie and the warden, I caught the London train. I was travelling light. I had decided it was best to put most of the category B stuff, the sentimental belongings, into storage. I didn't want these things cluttering my flat, but I wasn't ready to throw them away either. My satchel contained the three photographs saved from my mother's walls, the package for Mr Satoshi, the letter from the shoebox and the letters from the fishing gear. It felt odd that most of these mementos related to a man of whom I knew next to nothing, not even his real surname.

On the journey to London, a favourite saying of my father's popped into my head: 'There's a whole world out there, Robert.' He had started telling me that during my teenage years. Some things change with time, some don't. At the age of forty-one, as the train bumped me along in the direction of Waterloo, the words sounded as off-key as they always had. A *whole* world: as if the enormity of the thing was its main attraction.

We pulled into Clapham Junction to pick up some more travellers heading into the city. It was a Tuesday, but most faces were creased with the Monday blues. One quick glance at the mob on the platform demonstrated that the 'world out there' can be far from empowering. Beyond the drizzled window was the unmistakable heave and whir of an urban universe too fast and large to offer the average citizen anything. It made me anxious, watching the way the city, hungering for its crowds, swallowed them up so voraciously. A panic sweat gripped me as I observed people elbowing their way into the coffee shop on the platform, or engaging in brisk business at the news-stand. They were all at the mercy of the city's appetite, they just didn't realise it. Soon enough the coffee cup was binned and the sodden newspaper was the only thing between their heads and the salivating sky. When they finally swarmed onto the train, it was as if they were fleeing some great catastrophe, as if Clapham was on fire. That's the way with crowds. They have a mad, terrifying energy, a power that is not their own.

I closed my eyes. Sometimes, in a metropolis like London, brimming with over seven million people, the only way to survive is to retreat into your own world.

As I stepped off the train, I felt my legs wobble and my scrotum tighten. The cold indifference of the November air wafting through Waterloo Station sent a shot of adrenalin screaming through my veins. I was out of practice when it came to London life. Recent training hadn't gone beyond opening the door to delivery men from the supermarket, or postmen bearing parcels of books and discs and camera film, or international restaurant staff carrying tin foil trays from India, cardboard from Italy. I slipped my ticket into the slot and shivered as I passed through the barriers. My satchel trailed behind me and was momentarily stuck there, two grey wings beating the leather. Before moving through the station I opened the satchel flap and checked that the parcel, letters and photographs remained undamaged.

I took a bus to Chancery Lane and walked the length of the Gray's Inn Road. It was throbbing with human traffic, a crowd of mingled faces and breathless voices, but I coped by employing a technique a doctor once taught me, a trick for preventing an attack. It involves visualising the place that panics you as a familiar object seen from on high. I conjured up a picture of the Gray's Inn Road as an old book that I had read many times. I scanned it from mid-air. There was a 'me' down there, but it was just an empty shell dressed up in skin, flesh, hair, clothes. The real me was floating overhead, surveying the names of the side streets, the language by which this part of the city defines itself. To the left: *Theobald's, Northington, Roger*. To the right: *Baldwin's, Clerkenwell, Rosebery*. Gray's Inn Road was the central spine of the open book, and these myriad lines of text drew out from it. There were marks, creases and folds in unexpected places: the roundabouts, mews and murky grasslands; the places where life escapes the script.

At the intersection with Guilford Street, I thought about Chloe. We used to live there, in a small flat overlooking Coram's Fields. From our bedroom window, which looked out on the Brunswick Square side of the fields, you could see four sheep – never more, never less. Even now, after all that's happened, I remember their spiralled horns and crimped wool. I remember how they shimmered exotically in the early evening light. Chloe loved them. A little bit of rural romance in the middle of the city.

Just before I turned into my side street, I saw a woman who looked like my mother. She sat on red-brick steps twirling a waxy leaf in her hand. A crocodile of schoolgirls zigzagged past her, blowing bubbles with fluorescent gum. Rain started to spit down, drawing blood from the ground at her feet, and when I looked again she had disappeared.

It wasn't until that evening, shut away in my flat, that I read the second letter. I managed to stop myself reading the third, but I think I knew – even then – that this exercise in restraint was both token and temporary.

Civil Information &
Education Section
GHQ, Supreme Commander
Allied Powers
Tokyo
Japan

7 May 1946

The Berries
Constitution Hill
Clifton
Bristol
England

My own darling Alice,

Here I am in a beautiful room facing the moon,
writing to my gorgeous girl. I can't wait for your
mail to come in. I suppose, by all the rules of
separation, I should feel sunk in dismay. But I feel
buoyed when I put pen to paper, blessed that I have
someone so special on whom to lavish my love.

Finally I've met with Uncle George, or Dr Harvey
as my new colleagues in the PO&SR Division call
him. He welcomed me off the train like a father, all
thick arms & hot breath. He looks more round-
headed & beetle-browed than I remember, and it
feels strange to be face to face with the whole
reason I am out here. Without George, I might still
be a panel beater at Vickers-Armstrong, shut off
from the world in a dim old factory full of outworn

models & textbook patterns. He says he has high hopes for me, & I've placed my hope in him.

George is already getting me involved in his work & has appointed a Japanese assistant, Watanabe, to show me the city. I thought blitzed Britain was bad, but Tokyo's citizens would be grateful for the worst of London's slums. Here there are no Victorian terraces, no suburban semis, no prefabs. My first impression of urban life here is wood. Wood every-where. There are clustered shacks, delicate yet surviving, made of wooden beams all interlaced. They could be from any age. And then there is the collapsed wood – charred, mottled, in steaming heaps all over the place. George says that, just before the Emperor surrendered, black smoke filled the skies as his minions burned up wartime documents. Well, there is still a grey shadow of that smoke in the air, miles & miles of flurried secrets encircling the city. You look at the landscape & it's hard to imagine a whole society ever lived here, that it hasn't always been flatlands, veiled & dark & unbuilt. Lone chimneys here, iron shutters there; hospital hulls & bathhouse rubble. Reminders of a distant Tokyo stick up like scorched thumbs from the ashes.

At first, just for a minute or two, I felt a guilty kind of excitement at seeing the effect of things I helped make back in Weybridge – B-29s & their bombs. I told George as much over lunch. All he said was, 'We should remind them every day it's us that won.'

In our headquarters downtown, living standards are excellent. My moonlit room is in the eaves of a former hotel. It's luxury compared to Mum's house in Cotham, my cousin's place in Weybridge – even your parents' Clifton castle. The food beats the rations back home: steak twice already, chicken whenever I like, your favourite roast beef, veal cutlets, meat loaf, potatoes, salad, vegetables, always some cake or other, always ice cream with the dessert. You worry that I might be getting thin, but I'm becoming bigger & stronger by the day.

It's not like this for most Japanese. This afternoon I went out doing a survey for George on starvation & malnutrition. I took Watanabe with me. He called me 'sir' at first & I pressed him to call me Reggie. He looked nervous but grateful, then started saying 'Mr Reggie' this, 'Mr Reggie' that!

One of the first Japanese we talked to was a seven-year-old girl wandering on her own through ashen beams in the Azabu neighbourhood. She was dusty & dry in a half-rotten blouse, a doll made of earth. No shoes or socks on, the eyeballs somehow empty as bubbles. I noticed a mud-seamed white box hanging by a sash around her neck. We asked the girl if she had enough food & she said not since her family died. It's a Buddhist custom to carry the white box around the neck. It contains the ashes and bones of the dead.

Her name is Kazue. She took us inside Ueno Station. It's a vast shack clogged full of homeless, & she isn't the youngest to live there. There are

41

toddlers with awful deformities, their features waxy and misshapen, the facial structure melted. Many of the A-bomb survivors who have made their way to Tokyo live in stations like this. They grope sense-lessly at the walls, their personalities soft & edgeless. The smell inside is unbearable. There are 'honey bucket wagons' everywhere, holding human waste collected from floor toilets. Civilians are so desperate for fertiliser that they level dim patches of dry earth with the waste & attempt to grow crops with it.

On our way back to HQ, I told Watanabe I would try & do something for Kazue. He laughed, then went quiet. It took a lot of persuasion to get him to say more. Eventually he mumbled that there were three million in Tokyo who needed me to do some-thing. I pointed to a little vegetable patch sheltered by bamboo grass. Potato plants were growing, just starting to flower. I told him there was still life in his city, found myself coming out with the lines I wrote for you on the train. He just looked at the plants, at the little purple buds. Then he said, 'In English your name is Reggie, but in Japanese the best name for you is *Satoshi*. Clear-thinking, wise. A fast learner. But maybe optimistic.'

After dinner Watanabe gave me a poem of his own on a piece of torn grey paper.

> *Only the weeds*
> *seem to receive*
> *the new sunshine.*

Do you ever resent my optimism, Alice? I have every reason to be miserable. I am sitting in a room that is empty of you. I'd do anything to breathe in your hair, dream beautiful dreams with your head on my chest. But I refuse to lose sight of the reason I'm here. I am bettering myself every day, unfolding a new future for us. I find myself going round the city, cutting through the smoke, pulling up the weeds. I make sure that only flowers remain. If I stop & picture you for the briefest moment I can love everyone & everything more than I dreamed possible. Bombed-out areas seem to hold an energy. The dirt is hopeful, somehow. Delicate, yielding, full of life.

Each night I take one of your old letters & I kiss the words. I remember our last afternoon together. I hold that saffron scarf & wrap it around my neck. Then I stare at your picture, tacked to the wall above my pillow, & wait for sleep.

Post just going, my love.

Write very soon.

Yours forever,

Reggie

5

IN THE middle of the night, I did a strange thing. Waking from the usual juddering dreams, I climbed out of my soggy bed. I staggered into the hallway, picked up my satchel and took out the parcel. I found myself carrying it into the living room, where I stood in front of the television, pressing the brown paper to my forehead. I held it there, against my skin, eyes shut, and I kept it pressed to me for a seamless, transparent moment, nearly collapsing against its cold face, abandoning myself to it completely. Then I put the parcel on top of the television and went back to bed.

I was preparing lunch when the phone in the hallway started ringing. The saucepan of drained pasta was warming on the hob and I had a jar of pesto in my hand. It kept ringing as I spooned the pesto onto the pasta, added the fried onions, and stirred it all together with a wooden spoon. Eight times, ten times, twelve times. Sometimes the determination of other people leaves me breathless.

Defeated, I picked up.

'Foss? Finally. Jesus fucking Christ. Fuck me.'

'Perry? Perry, listen, I'm —'

'I'm your *agent*, Foss. And your *buddy*. We go way back. And you don't pick up for months, *months*.'

'Listen, Perry, I'm –'

'Don't tell me it's a bad time, Foss. Just *don't* tell me it's a bad time.'

After the accident in Greece, people invariably rang and said, 'Have I called at a bad time?' What they meant was: are you busy coping, are you busy going crazy, are you busy being medicated? You start by saying no but you end up saying yes. Yes, it's a really bad time. Then you make a curt promise to call them back, and never do.

'Perry, I'm sorry. That's all I was going to say.'

'Fucking hell.'

We kept going like this for a while, him swearing and me apologising, until the tone of cultivated anger in his voice gave way to something soft and enquiring – the voice of a man who seeks earnestly to understand the decisions of someone less world-wise than himself.

Perry said, 'You sound bad, worse than before, I'll come round.'

'OK.'

'I don't know where you live. You won't give me an address. Where do you live?'

'Not far from you, Perry.'

Perry unleashed a throaty laugh that snowballed down the line, adding layers of static as it rolled.

He said, 'Foss, when I couldn't get hold of you I . . . well, you know I call that Finegold place when you go off the radar. And when I called yesterday the warden told me about your mother. I'm sorry. You should've got in touch, at least to tell me the funeral details.'

'I wanted it to be a small affair. You know how I feel about crowds.'

'The warden said there were loads of people there.'

'There were. All nursing-home types. A big day trip for them, a chance to ward off death by sheer force of numbers.'

'And since then? I get sick thinking of you in some secret little bachelor pad, groping the walls.'

'I've just been here, watching the odd bank transfer come through online. It's a living.'

'It's living in the past, Foss.'

'It pays the bills.'

'*New* work pays *more* bills. Pays for houses, pays for holidays. Keep it arty if you like. *Dazed & Confused*, *Vanity Fair*, they'd love some fresh shots from you. You're one of the most important photographers of your generation. Do some new work. A few years ago you had everyone posing for you. You remember that shoot you did of the YBAs? And the Caulfield shots. The Caulfield shots were beautiful. And the writers. Updike, DeLillo, Roth, Bellow, McCarthy. You shot them all, in one room, at the same time. Shame about Pynchon, shy old bastard. But even so, you snapped the Jackson Five of American literature!'

'That was then.'

'And this is now, Foss. Your isolation. It generates hunger in the market. It grows the myth, deepens the appetite. But only for so long. As far as the market is concerned, you've been invisible for the last few years. Well, that's fine, right? God's invisible, and people worship *him*. But soon enough, absent a miracle, the congregation starts to doubt your existence. The fan base dwindles. At least put together that book we talked about. Your greatest hits, it'd go down a storm, convert the non-believers. The interest I've had from publishers, it's fucking *ridiculous*.'

'I'm still going through the contact prints, Perry.'

'Course you are,' Perry muttered. 'Course you fucking are. Would you just choose some fucking pictures, Foss? Or send me the negatives. I'll sort the proof sheets. I need those photos.'

'I'm selecting, cataloguing, identifying. It's a laborious process.'

'*Life* is a laborious process where you're concerned. I'm not being unsympathetic, Foss. I know you've been through stuff. God knows, I know. I understand what your isolation these last few years is about. You think, after what happened in Greece, it's somehow your fault, that you deserve to suffer. She was your wife and your muse, I know that. But how many times have you left your flat in the last six months?'

'Plenty,' I said. 'How's Pedro, by the way? Still working on that Chilean project?'

He said, 'How many?'

'Are you still growing that ridiculous ponytail of yours?'

'How many?'

'A monthly visit to my mother. Plus the doctor. Everyone needs to see a doctor every now and again.'

'This solitude thing. It's gone far enough, Foss. It's borderline agoraphobia. Get up off the sofa, stop stewing in your own juices. If London's bogging you down, go explore. Go to China, somewhere like that. Take your camera somewhere new, lose yourself in something a bit bigger than your own routine. Create some photos with a sense of community. Think about China, a new world to picture. I could place your shots with any magazine. *Any*. We could probably find you an exhibition space. What do you think of China?'

'I think of crowds. Too many people to count and measure. Helplessness, collective hysteria. I think of a negative, a unique image, reproduced a thousand times, each print the same as the last, until the force of its original meaning has been crowded out completely.'

'Jesus Christ. I'm glad I can't take a holiday snap to save my life. It's a blessing, being predisposed to cut people's heads out of pictures. None of this burden of talent rubbish. Fuck China then. Somewhere else.'

'I'm fine here.'

'God, somewhere, anywhere! Name a place that interests you. There must be some place beyond that front door that holds a little intrigue?'

'Well . . .'

'Well what?'

'Japan is interesting, I guess. But it's still going to be crowded and —'

'Japan! Do a shoot in Japan. Shrines, high-rises, Snoopy dolls, Hello Kitty, electric toilets, manga, karaoke booths, zen, all that bento shit. Japan, a photographer's paradise!'

'Electric toilets?'

'Oceans of them. Japan. It's all about Japan, Foss. For once you've come up with a commercial idea. The future is Japan.'

'The future is terrorism on a TV screen.'

'Whatever. I've been, and the future is Japan.'

We drifted into silence. It put Perry at an advantage to talk about air travel and foreign climes. There were times when he seemed to use terms like 'jet lag' as tools of attack.

He saw the lack of stamps on my passport, the self-imposed travel ban, as a symptom of some deeper flaw.

I said, 'I'm not going, but I admit Japan is probably an interesting place. In fact, I ordered a book on it last night, online. About the occupation, after the Second World War.'

'I'll come round now to discuss, then you'll give me the greatest hits prints. I'll teach you about Japan. Trust me, follow me. A student walks seven feet behind his teacher, Foss, lest he step on his master's shadow. What's your address?'

'Listen, Perry, I've got to go. Smells like my flat's about to burn down.'

'And I bet you'll burn down with it rather than go outside. I want those photos, you fucker.'

Strangely buoyed by a conversation with an old friend, I returned to the kitchen. A fog of incinerated pine nuts instantly deflated my mood. It seemed I had failed to turn off the hob before taking the phone call. All moisture had evaporated from the saucepan and a raft of penne pasta had run aground on the Teflon. A small pool of pesto had bubbled and hardened around its corrugated form, fire-bombing and fixing it. Worst of all was the onion. It was completely seared, its little veins all scorched and blackened, carbonised and killed.

I couldn't recall what I'd been thinking about before the phone rang. Wooden spoon in hand, something had been on my mind. But it was gone. That was the way of late. Thoughts and feelings evaporating before they were fully formed. Perhaps I was thinking about last night's letter. My heart was beating fast as I read it. My mother's life. Flat and settled and still. That of a clever, homely, outward-looking woman with a bracing sense of the tangible, a trust in the particular powers of cooking and cleaning and tidying. Born in '29, married in '59, mother in '68, divorced in '88, dead in '09. Did I know the shape, the shade, the texture of the life stretched between these dates? She probably changed her mind about Mr Satoshi, about her feelings for him. If someone wrote her biography, Satoshi would probably be a mere footnote in her eighty-year history, one that her failing mind referenced by chance on the day she fell.

With the pasta destroyed, takeaway seemed to be the best option. I hunted for the Chutney King menu, but it was nowhere to be found. All I came upon was a flat in need of a makeover. The once white walls in the bedroom were greying, and the double divan looked bowed and weary. Most of my life was lived in the living room, with inanimate objects: an old leather chair with spindly legs and curvaceous arms, a pockmarked oak writing desk that doubled up as a dining table, a second-hand sofa, a tired television. The only vaguely expensive things were the laptop and a floor-standing anglepoise lamp. The lamp dipped over the back of the armchair like a snow-laden branch. Two bookcases were pressed up against the back wall, the thin shelves sagging under the weight of novels, plays, poetry and history.

In case of house fire – an eventuality that often crossed my mind – I felt I would probably save Wordsworth for poetry, Shakespeare for drama, and Amis for prose (Kingsley or Martin, depending on my state of mind). There had been a time when I would have saved my cameras.

The evening brought dark thoughts.

I opened the bathroom cabinet with unhelpful hands. The interior looked less varied than when Chloe had lived with me: no face wipes, no moisturiser, no cotton buds. Just bottles of pills. All with names like fictional planets, their own synthetic sci-fi language. The reality relievers: OxyContin, Vicodin, Demerol. The nerve deadeners: Nembutal, Valium, Xanax. The sight stimulants: Ritalin, Adderall, Strattera. Plus the nasal decongestants, muscle relaxants, skin steroids, anti-fungal creams. I selected my medicine carefully, already soothed by the ordering, the choosing, the mixing, the pushing and twisting of squeaky bottle tops. There wouldn't be a biography of my life, but if there was, the writer would need to capture the plastic colours, the bitter powders, the thick carpets of mucus rolling down my throat. These were the shades, the flavours, the textures of my days.

By the sink I kept a yellow radio in the shape of a duck. As the drugs did their soldierly best, I tinkered with it. Eventually Bach bounced off the bathroom tiles. It sounded like *The Art of Fugue*, a piece I remembered from my child-hood. My mother used to put the Glenn Gould recording on Dad's record player on Sundays; the vinyl spun as she cooked us both a roast beef dinner. It was always beef on Sundays. She took great pride in the fact that the weekly hunk of meat was 'made in Britain' and provided by the local butcher. In fact, she took comical satisfaction in the whole beef-buying ritual, from the orderly queue for it on the Saturday, the non-metric units by which it was weighed, right through to paying for it with what she insisted on calling 'a few bob'. A satisfaction in the sense of national history, however trifling, that came with it. Each Sunday, the beef formed the centrepiece of an elaborate meal completely unlike anything we saw for the rest of the week.

It was as if, every Sunday at 7 p.m., my family was celebrating some unspoken event, marking somebody's arrival or somebody's departure.

As the night deepened, there was a kind of chemical force field around me, muffling out the frenzied street sounds of drinkers, hawkers and taxis on the Gray's Inn Road.

To the neutral observer, I was watching a news feature about a French equity derivatives trader who had thrown himself off a bridge in La Défense. But it could have been a programme about anything. My mind was being drawn elsewhere. It was being drawn to the package. I didn't know why I had put it there, on top of the television. In the darkness of my flat, the screen flickered messages from the outside world as it always had. The change was in me: that night, I found myself averting its electric gaze. I sat on the sofa, obedient as ever, but in my dilated state I was trying to imagine what lay beneath that brown paper. I decided to get up and open the package. I decided to sit down and not open the package.

I turned off the television, not to help me think but to put an end to all thoughts. I reached for a book on my shelves and, since I couldn't face whole sentences, chose a volume of poetry. But the volume in my hands came burdened with memories.

I read a Wordsworth poem that had been Chloe's favourite.

> *No motion has she now, no force;*
> *She neither hears nor sees;*
> *Rolled round in earth's diurnal course,*
> *With rocks, and stones, and trees.*

I remembered Chloe reciting the verse in our flat on Guilford Street, chair leaning back against a window spotted with sheep. I remembered her smoking recklessly as she did so, a weightless ashen cone dipping off the tip of her cigarette. She smoked like that to generate an aura of suspense, to engender stimulus through risk, and it worked. As she finally tapped the ash into an ashtray, all sorts of thoughts would start smouldering in my head. Did being alive mean being sealed within time, presence, motion, earthly events?

In the days following my mother's fall, I had thought about putting the Wordsworth verse on her gravestone. But the stonemason wanted a fortune for the work. My mother would never have approved of me spending money on words. She never bought a book, always went to the library. She never bought a greetings card, always wrote a note. 'Words should be free,' she would say. 'If words aren't free, something's wrong with the world.' She was a product of her time, my mother. She came of age in the forties, the era of make do and mend. She wouldn't have spent money on words. So I decided that all that was needed to mark her spot was a clear label. No fuss, no poetry.

Alice Rebecca Fossick
1929–2009
Beloved mother of Rob Fossick

'Beloved' is the only word that she might have taken issue with. An indulgence, adding nothing.

I re-read Satoshi's first two letters in bed. It was a peculiar feeling, being immersed in his words. I could feel his thoughts becoming my thoughts, our memories fusing together. But nothing quite cohered, not his picture, not mine. There was this rising sense of my own ignorance: a grey dust cloud through which I could see only glimpses of real things, fragments of buildings and people and places that might have meant something to my mother. I found myself overwhelmed by that fog. It left me sad and weary.

Part of me was determined to abandon her past there and then, to find – at this late stage – some respect for her privacy. But I didn't. Instead, I got up, opened my satchel, and took out the third letter.

Civil Information &
Education Section
GHQ, Supreme Commander
Allied Powers
Tokyo
Japan

3 June 1946

The Berries
Constitution Hill
Clifton
Bristol
England

My darling,

The mail has just come in and I have eight letters.
Among them, my gorgeous, were four from you.
One was addressed to the base in Kure. They've
been painfully slack in forwarding it.

When I sit & read your words, I find myself
amazed that someone absent can have such a power
over my senses. It frightens me a little bit, the fire
you can spark up in me with just a word or a thought
or a blank space on the page. I fear sometimes that
it will burn me up, that it can't be healthy to love
anyone this much. The memory of that last afternoon
consumes me – you were at your most beautiful,
you listened so carefully to every awkward word that
tumbled from my lips, & holding you tight I realised
that without you my life would be absolutely empty.

My darling, from your last letter it seems that you like my new Japanese nickname, so you'll be pleased to know that Watanabe is calling me 'Satoshi-sensei' all the time now. It has caught on among the Yank researchers too. Clearly I'm becoming more Japanese by the day. George seems to find it hilarious that my 'little Gook friend' has christened me. I challenged him on using that word, but he flew into a rage. Unexpected & odd. I suddenly saw a side to him that might explain why he & Dad didn't get on so well.

No matter. In other ways George shows kindness – take his reaction to my story about Kazue. Do you remember her, Alice, the girl with the white box? I managed to convince George to give her a go as a servant in our living quarters. He already has the ideal roster (cook, boy, maid, gardener, nursemaid, laundress – where else can you live like this?) but he showed sympathy & said Kazue could help with cleaning & simple tasks. So that is what she's been doing. Watanabe seems concerned by the arrangements. Maybe he thinks it is not our place to interfere with Tokyo's homeless, picking just one to save from Ueno's filth. Kazue certainly isn't complaining. I've never seen someone so grateful for food.

In the streets, I see seven-year-olds like Kazue scraping roadsides for pumpkin stems & seeds, occasionally joyous if they lay their hands on an insect or rodent. The other day I came upon a black marketeer with a bucket of live frogs. He was selling some to kids as food, taking potato powder as currency.

An angry customer kicked over his bucket as I passed, and suddenly the ground was dotted green. I was reluctant to help a spiv, but I did my good deed & lent a hand catching the warty things. It took forever. Every time I thought I'd trapped one, it slipped through my hands.

After a visit to the squalid black market it's a relief to get back downtown. The area we all live in has been nicknamed 'Little America' — very comfortable & completely unlike the rest of the city. SCAP has put up road signs, & there is now a MacArthur Boulevard, constantly crowded with gleaming military jeeps. I can walk from one end to the other without being out of sight of an American or British face. It gives a sense of familiarity in the charred city. We shop at the PX, & it's there that the locals & the Allies come closest to mixing. Japanese loiter at the windows with open mouths as we come out with mustard in litre jars, meat in fifteen-pound chunks, veg & fruit in mess-size tins. Alongside the beggars are the *panpan* screaming 'yoo-hoo' to the GIs, hoping for business. And then there are the Japanese children. George says we are here to turn the Orient into a Christian, capitalist democracy. That's all well and good, but then you see the children & the games they play. Always the same games: *yamiichi-gokko* and *panpan asobi* — holding a make-believe black market, playing prostitute & customer. Is this the new Japan?

I hope I'm not boring you with all these details. I suppose I'm trying to capture Japanese life, not just for you but for me down the years. I'm taking photographs for the same reason. Even so, when I go around doing surveys & research & taking pictures of the people of Japan I feel like a bit of a carpet-bagger. George says an anthropologist, like a journalist, needs to take advantage of his 'free-wheeling role' and that therein lies the secret of pros like Mead & Bateson. But when I flash my Brownie Reflex Synchro at a street family it doesn't feel right. How do you take a picture of a life without completely violating its privacy?

Enough depressing reportage – I mustn't forget that this is a new beginning for us, an opportunity. I'll come back soon enough & you'll be with a man who has a bit of real experience behind him. We can live like kings in London. I could take that job with Mass Observation – George says they pay well & would be glad of my experience.

On the subject of London, I hope you still intend to try for work at the agricultural college. Will you stay with Freddie while you get on your feet? The company of a friend is probably just what you need at the moment. I bet she is still keeping Geoff on a tight leash. He has my fly-fishing things & wrote me the other week to say he has failed to impress her with his angling expertise.

My love, I have to run – a dreary public opinion survey awaits. George, Watanabe and I may do a field trip to a rural community in the coming weeks. That promises to be better experience. No doubt I'll spend most of my time wondering what you're doing at home.

Alice, I miss you & love you so much. You keep asking if I am safe & well. The truth is I am very safe & very well – the only thing I am lacking is you. One day soon we'll be together for good. This period of separation will disappear into the past like a distant coastline.

Longing for that day.

Ever yours,

Mr Satoshi

6

LIKE A distant coastline, he said, and it struck me as a good analogy for the past lives we leave behind. It felt like I'd spent the last few years, since Chloe died and my mother faded, watching old territory recede. My GP had repeatedly said, 'There are millions of others in the same boat.' He had said, 'You're not alone, feeling this way.' And I had routinely given him reassuring nods, but only so that he kept autographing my prescriptions. Whatever he claimed, I knew there was one ocean over there, crowded with life, and a paddling pool imitation closer to home, just for me, the surface smoothed by stillness.

I tried not to linger on the paragraphs in which Satoshi declared his love. I was on safer ground reading about frog-eating, black markets, MacArthur Boulevard. Yet there was a particular line in the letter that caused my curiosity to hurdle self-preservation: 'One day soon we'll be together for good.' He had so much faith in the direction their lives would take. Something must have set them off course. That something, for me at least, was now out of reach. The letters had been exhausted. If there were others, they were probably lurking in some ornament or apron or book on the charity shop shelves.

* * *

There was a taut white quality to the morning light, a solidity and bravado. As it bullied its way into the living room, I sat at my desk sorting through negatives. Old photographs of the Gray's Inn Road, my way of bringing the city inside. They were taken at the point in my career when photographing pavements had become easier than photographing people. I found I could not look into another pair of eyes, even through my lens. I couldn't tolerate the sight of other people, especially the artists, the ones with the penetrating gaze. I started doing corporate shots to try and get back into portraiture, boardroom snaps to hang above mammoth teak tables. My subjects talked about structured products and collateralised debt obligations and mortgage-backed securities and exploding bridge facilities. I tried to guide the conversation away from the financial markets and towards hobbies and interests, but you could see the panic wobbling in their eyeballs. Most of them worked sixteen-hour days. Few free weekends, few uninterrupted holidays. In their youth they had done paragliding, deep-sea diving, white-water rafting, horse riding. In their retirement they would do wine tasting, poetry writing, pasta making, beach lazing. But right now, at this busy juncture, they worked. All their interests were in the past and in the future. And I got depressed for them, until I remembered that I wasn't all that different; a camera instead of a keyboard, rental debt instead of a mortgage. Smile. Raise your chin. I'll bounce light off this wall. Try to relax. Without really deciding to, I stopped taking photographs.

My book on the occupation of Japan arrived and I read it voraciously, stretched out on the sofa, sucking cigarettes, an ashtray on my chest. *Psychologies of Defeat: Japan, August*

1945–April 1952. I read about dissent suppression, food shortage, foreign labour, inflation, one-family rhetoric, banned slogans, sensuality control, thought police. I read about the Public Opinion and Sociological Research Division, the department that it seemed Satoshi and Harvey had worked for. The central pages of the book contained contemporaneous photographs, some banned by the Allies, others promiscuously reproduced to within an inch of their propagandering lives. I looked at each of them carefully, some slight variations on a single form, some radically different. Dark, melancholy, evocative pictures. Urban nightscapes, memory landscapes. Body shots of *panpan* girls, polyglot courtesans, leaning in the dark, gift-wrapped in light neckerchiefs. Gritty black-and-whites of bars, dance halls, hole-in-the-wall eateries, crooked streets, cluttered back alleys; posed stills of a Japanese model in a white two-piece bathing suit reclining on a grimy balustrade; a landscape shot of a mass of gelled American soldiers, smile-squinting in the sun and shape-shifting in identical uniforms; Emperor Hirohito's hardscrabble face peering out from above an accountant's suit and tie; the desolations of flash-banged cities, places without borders, limitless grey.

It was liberating, looking at these pictures. Many of them had a natural jitteriness, a tilted, skewed, restless quality that, rightly or wrongly, I associated with Japan. It made me think that Perry might be right, that I could take decent photographs out there. It might be interesting to explore modern Japan, to see how it compared to the landscape of Satoshi's letters, to set the current city against its ghost. But, even if I got over my fears, did I still have it in me to combine line and form in a particular way, darkening light and lightening dark, remaking a moment without distorting its truth? Was I still a photographer?

All in all, it was a busy Thursday afternoon.

On Channel 486, there was a news item about how unemployment would hit three million within six months. The consequences would leave 'lasting scars on modern Britain'. Channel 521 was running a report on new American plans to help Afghanistan embrace a fully functioning democracy. Channel 605 was re-airing frenzied camera footage of protests outside a courtroom in Baghdad's fortified Green Zone, a shaped swarm of bodies furious that an Iraqi reporter was to be locked up for hurling a shoe at President Bush. Cut to the man himself who, after spending the last nine months in prison, was reporting on his first few weeks of re-engagement with the world. His nostrils and ears looked inflamed. His tongue sought out a prominent gap in his front teeth. The news segued, seamlessly, into a feature about 'Sock and Awe', an online game inspired by his actions, and it was then that I reached for the mute button.

There it was, the package, the star attraction, lying coquettishly on top of the screen, begging to be touched. It looked strangely alluring, shimmering in refracted light, a golden-brown crown on a square-headed king.

I took a workable combination of pills and formulated a plan.

The plan was miraculous in its simplicity. It was a three-word plan: post the package. It had an address on it, neatly transcribed on a little white label, and that's the address I would send it to. That's what addresses are for, I told myself. To give parcels a sense of direction. If Mr Satoshi isn't there to receive it, then tough. The postal system is unforgiving like that. It has a rigid inner logic, the same as any other system.

On the Internet, between sips of bitter tea, I picked an international delivery company. I lifted the package from its pedestal and brought it over to my side of the room. I'd forgotten how light it was. Was it a paperback? Why did the contents feel padded, firm yet soft? I typed the crossed-out address into a box marked 'Tell Us Where, We'll Get There'.

Roppongi World Plaza 9–39
Roppongi 1-chome
Minato-ku,
Tokyo 106-0032

The best thing about the whole arrangement was that the delivery company would collect the package from my door. They could be with me by 5 p.m. that afternoon. £45.99, provided I had estimated the weight correctly. Not cheap, but it was fast. By five o'clock, I would know that I'd done all I could to deliver it. I'd wash my hands of Mr Satoshi. My mind would stop fidgeting. The temptation to open up my mother's past would finally subside.

I decided, just out of interest, to run a search for the address. When the Roppongi World Plaza website loaded onto my screen, I clicked a Union Jack button in the top right-hand corner. A wave of electric dots crashed over the text and translated it into English. A 'modern apartment block', according to the first line. If the pictures were anything to go by, the building was impressive in a blank, gimmicky kind of way.

It was only when I had finished my cup of tea that I felt

any quiver of uncertainty. How likely was it that this slab of brown paper was actually going to make it into Mr Satoshi's hands? There was an address, but it seemed my mother had doubted its accuracy. I needed a pen and paper. I needed to start thinking in sentences. There were some key uncertainties. I found a biro and scribbled on a blank page in *Psychologies of Defeat*.

<u>Mr Satoshi</u>
— What's his real name? Reg, Reggie, Reginald. Surname unknown. Unclear whether still uses the 'Mr S' nickname.
— Address? No apartment number. May not even be at World Plaza. If he is, why didn't M send?
— Job? Must be retired by now. Used to be junior anthropologist with British Occupation Forces in Japan, but no obvious qualifications.
— Blood link with G Harvey — but <u>mother's</u> brother, so Reg isn't a Harvey.
— Alive? Uncertain. Seventeen when wrote first letter, so now 80 yrs.

The last point on the list really got me: was I posting a present to a dead man? Plus, even if he was alive, and the package did find its way to him, there was the question of how he would react to receiving it. He would most likely assume that my mother had sent it to him. So he might send something back. Or worse, he might turn up at Finegold Mews.

No, that wouldn't do. I needed closure, boundaries, limits, not a million more doors creaking open. I would at least have to explain to Mr Satoshi that my mother was dead, tell him how I came upon the package. I'd write him a short covering note, a line or two to accompany the delivery. I dug around in a drawer and found some decent writing paper, then thought about what I wanted to say to him.

It proved difficult. *I think you knew my mother, and . . . I read your private letters to her, so . . . I'm not sure if this is your address, or even your name, but . . .* I abandoned successive drafts, crunching sheets of paper into frail, lazy balls ill-suited to flight. And then I started thinking about how, even if I *did* manage to write the perfect letter, its tone would be shaped by so many things outside of my control. What if the package contained something completely out of keeping with my words, a gift that transformed their meaning? Just suppose I wrote a beautiful letter. A fine, magnanimous letter of tribute and condolence. He would read it and weep. Of course he would – who wouldn't? But then he would open up the package, the sharpness of his blue eyes blurring to sea green, and find that it contained . . . cat food. Yes, cat food. It was entirely possible. Under the brown paper there could be two shallow foil pouches side by side, lightweight, expensive, the high-end stuff that comes in tiny portions. Michelin-starred feline fare. Mr Satoshi would assume, quite fairly, that I was some sick practical joker.

My mother was most likely in an airy space between old age and madness when she put the package together. It could contain anything. She didn't have a cat, of course, but once I'd thought this thought, this thought about the cat food, I couldn't write another word.

The watch on my wrist told me it was 3.30 p.m. The

delivery person would arrive at 5 p.m. Before then, I needed to sort myself out. My original plan was too simple. It was too well defined to work.

Men of the world, weather-worn men with savvy blood gliding through their veins, confident characters that blend in even as they stand out, don't get upset every time their phone rings. They deal with the threatening urgency, the anonymity of its beady cry, the bewildering array of possible words, hesitations, silences that crowd in from the other end of the line. They probably cope with the ringing of other telephones too, all the other telephones, ringing for all sorts of people and transporting all kinds of disembodied speech, ringing in the phone box that they walk past, in the house that they walk past, in the pocket of the person that they walk past. But I am not one of these men.

My shirt felt like wet cling film as the phone unleashed a third cluster of rings in as many minutes. With boundless reluctance, like a conceited doctor resorting to a medical encyclopedia, all remembered remedies exhausted, I fretted my way into the hallway and reached for it.

'Hello? Hello, Robert, it's Freddie. Is this a bad time?'

I said, 'It's fine, Freddie. How are you?'

'Oh, well, very well. Went to a lovely funeral earlier. A woman with cancer.'

'That's . . . nice.'

'Sad but fitting,' she said, apparently buoyed by grief. 'And speaking of departures, I was just wondering how you're getting on with the package?'

'How I'm getting on?'

I angled my head to get a clear sightline into the living room. Through the letter-box-thin doorway, the package's tanned poker face returned my gaze.

Freddie said, 'Yes, you know. How you're getting on. Whether you've delivered it yet, and so on.'

'Well, I'm probably going to get a delivery company to pick it up later, actually.'

'Oh. I thought the address was crossed through.'

'I realise it's not ideal.'

'And your mother indicated to me, that is to say I gained the inference, that the address was not accurate. It was not the right address at all.'

'Yes. Well.'

'Were it accurate, then presumably Alice would have posted it herself.'

I moistened my lips. A choking boom of traffic rattled the living room window.

She said, 'I just assumed that you would go over there and, you know, *find him*.'

'Pardon?'

She said, 'Find Mr Satoshi.'

It was unclear if this was supposed to be funny.

'I take pictures, Freddie. I'm not a detective.'

'Oh, it might do you good!'

'Look,' I said, 'I don't doubt that Mum intended to send the thing, once. But who knows? She barely knew what was going on, those last few years. It's probably not that important. There's probably nothing much inside. And the simple fact of the matter is, I don't have an up-to-date address for this Mr Satoshi.'

'You haven't managed to gather any other . . . evidence?'

'You're getting carried away with the detective thing. This isn't an Agatha Christie. Evidence isn't a term I'd use in this scenario.'

'You haven't gathered anything then?'

'I found a few things, when I cleared out Mum's flat. Letters. That's it. From Satoshi, written while he was working as a junior anthropologist in Japan.'

'Well, that's wonderful!'

Her tone was undecipherable, empty of inference, and three minutes later she was still talking. She gave me her phone number so that I could keep her informed of 'developments'. The digits tumbled into my ear with dream-like effect, a secret hypnotic code. I felt dazed, time and space closing in as it does in the rectangular universe of the viewfinder.

'Freddie,' I said, and I said it firmly, because it was becoming clear that she was trying to place me, obstinately, under her own jurisdiction, like an empire appropriating a vulnerable colony. 'Freddie, I'm going to have to put the phone down now.'

'It was important to your mother,' she said, and her tone softened as the sentence ran its course, the truth of her words shaped by a slow and certain fading of voice.

Half an hour later I was back at the telephone. I had a bubblejet-printed picture of a glass tower in my hand, and below it the scribbled switchboard number for Roppongi World Plaza. What if the address wasn't wrong at all? What if Satoshi still lived there?

'*Moshi, moshi.*'

The fact that a man in Japan was speaking Japanese

should not have been surprising, yet it completely threw me. Clearly I was in an unusually heavy chemical state.

'Oh, hello. Can I speak English?'

He laughed nervously in response to this, then began to speak in a hesitant voice punctuated by stifled yawns. It occurred to me it was probably pretty late over there.

'So you understand a little?' I said, gathering that he was a reluctant linguist.

'*Hai* . . . yes. *Sukoshi*. A little . . .'

'And this is Roppongi World Plaza?'

'Yes, sir. World Plaza.'

'I want to post something to one of the residents.'

'To post . . .'

'I would like to mail something, to a person living in the World Plaza.'

'OK. You need address for building?'

'Well, no. Sort of. I just need the person's flat number.'

'Flat?'

'Apartment. I need the person's apartment number.'

'OK. Apartment number.'

'Yes.'

'You don't know number?'

When he said 'don't', it sounded like 'donut'.

'No. I'm afraid not.'

He asked, 'You at least know name?' Then he yawned again. I hesitated before answering him. There was every chance my pronunciation would be wrong.

'Satoshi,' I whispered.

'Ah. Satoshi, huh?'

Was that a hint of recognition I could hear in his voice?

'You have . . .' he continued, searching for words, 'a family name?'

'You mean surname? Satoshi is a first name?'

'In Japan, yes. Satoshi is a pre-name.'

'The thing is,' I said, some realisation of the extent of the confusion I was about to unleash already dawning on me, 'Satoshi may be a nickname for this man, not a family name or a surname. It may be a sort of . . . pretend name.'

He stayed silent for a while, apparently giving this some thought. 'I can check,' he said, 'whether we have a Satoshi living in World Plaza. If you wait a few minutes.'

'OK,' I said, 'thank you. Please look for Reggie as well. First name Reggie. Or like Reggie.'

During the implausibly long interval that ensued, keeping an eye on the package all the while, I listened as a thin band of static crackled its way from Tokyo to London, then back again.

'Sir?'

'Yes, I'm here.'

'No Satoshi lives here. No one by other name either. Very sorry.'

I kept him on the phone for a while, the two of us going in semantic circles, until I felt dizzy, even mildly deranged, and had to hang up.

The digital reading on my laptop was 16:57.

I drew the curtains in the living room and the bedroom, snapped down the blind in the kitchen, and turned off every lamp and ceiling light. In a few minutes, the delivery man would arrive, a guy whom my confirmation email named as Chad. Chad would want to take the package away.

Sitting on the carpet in complete darkness, I heard footsteps. I didn't move. He pressed the buzzer numerous times, the intervals between buzzes getting shorter and the buzzes themselves getting longer. When Chad's frustration peaked, my ears were swamped with one long buzzing howl, an ululation of anger that pierced the silence in my flat long after he had gone. But, when he went, I felt enormously relieved. There was no point sending the package today. I'd wait until tomorrow.

Except, as the darkness of the November night got thicker, pouring through the cracks in my curtains, staining my living room a stagnant black, there was a problem. And the problem was this: if it was cat food, I needed to know.

I switched on one light after another, each bulb spurting into life like a derisory firework, and sat on the carpet under the glow of my anglepoise. There was a large glass of whisky at my side, but otherwise it was just me and the package, both of us knowing what was about to happen. Its angular folds were clean and precise, the string around it expertly crossed and tied in a double bow. I could tell that it was my mother's work, the product of years of experience in wrapping for birthdays, christenings and Christmases. I turned it over in my hands, attempting to memorise every line and crease. That way, once I'd had a peek at the contents, I could rewrap it and pretend I hadn't touched it at all. I found myself in a state of voyeuristic, silent enchantment, weak-thumbed with the sense that, at any moment, someone could burst through the door and reprimand me for my actions.

The double bow sat at the centre point where the diagonal and vertical lines of the string crossed. I held the central knot in place with one hand and picked at it with the other, slipping the nail of my index finger into its compact orb. Like an onion, each layer of the knot was the same. Undone, unravelled, the string was around two foot in length. I abandoned it in a spiral heap and started to carefully unfasten the thick, waxy paper. There was no sign of any sticky tape holding it together. The neatness was all its own.

There was a tight seam running lengthways along the underbelly of the package. As I lifted it, I saw that it had been formed by folding an edge of the paper down over itself in thin strips. The end result was a rigid spine but, with one flick of a fingernail, it uncoiled like a spring.

Before me was the expanse of unwrapped brown paper, flat against the carpet. The contents sat in the middle.

High-end meaty jelly was noticeably absent. Instead, a thick rectangular Jiffy bag. Typical of my mother: an excess of packaging, great importance placed on the surface of things. Never be too careful. Don't tempt fate.

A hot bright wave of intrigue hit me and I ripped open the Jiffy. I felt my heart pulsing, everywhere. Chest. Neck. Ankles. Wrists. I could hear its wild beat, a hundred marbles scattering on a hard floor. The intrigue became nausea; the nausea became guilt. It wouldn't reseal. Too late. So might as well take a look.

Three white envelopes. That's all the Jiffy contained. All three envelopes sealed. Two were wafer-thin, so thin they couldn't contain more than a couple of sheets of paper each. The third envelope was thicker; it probably held half a dozen folded leaves. Written in the top right-hand corner of each envelope, in my mother's upright script, little more than a series of rigid scratches in blue ink, was one word: 'Private'.

In the dead centre of each envelope, in the same hand, another word: 'Satoshi'.

I retreated to the bathroom and took some pills. There was too much to think about. I had to shut it all out. I didn't need it. I didn't need the paper and the string and the ink to tell me it wasn't my day. For the second time that evening, I ensured that everything in the flat that could emit light was burned out. I pulled down the duvet, slipped under the soft cotton, to rest for just a moment, to stop the dizziness, the overwhelming sense that my world was being emptied of meaning. I closed my eyes and I tried to remember things.

My mother. I found I could barely remember my mother. I summoned up childhood memories, but she was absent from the scene. There was just a mother-like outline chalked on the wall, or the car seat, or the bed. As in a police drama, all that was left was a cordoned-off area, an inaccessible space. Not a mother – just the edges of a mother. The only scenes I could picture fully were from her final years, the dementia years, when she was someone else entirely. These were the years when she would say her own name again and again, 'Alice, Alice, Alice,' as if trying to summon up her old self, to anchor the present in the past. Her features vanished into the grey walls of my bedroom.

7

FRIDAY BEGAN, and three cups of coffee later, feeling cheated that the caffeine seemed only to have thickened my tiredness, I found myself digging through the various cardboard boxes that filled my wardrobe. I chose a box to take over to the bed and I lay on my side rummaging through the contents: an album of childhood photographs that my mother gave me when I left for university, brimming with pictures of my younger self standing by birthday cakes and bicycles; a few crayon drawings of flowers headed 'For Mummy' and signed 'R. Fossick, 6 years' or 'R.F., 7 years', lawless abstract efforts that I stared at for a while and then threw in the waste-paper basket; a few well-thumbed *Just William* books that I put aside to transfer to my living room shelves; and then a fat notebook with a picture of an octopus on the front. I opened the notebook. A diary from my teenage years. Why had I kept this?

I flicked through the pages. There were few references to the wider world, barely any historical hooks and claws, just the ink of angst spilling all over the place.

'Alone.' That word came up often, which was strange, because I couldn't remember feeling alone *before* the accident in Greece, only in the extended aftermath. I kept flicking through the pages, but I remembered nothing. I tore out some sections, whole months crackling in my fist, because they left me annoyed at my detachment from the past, my lack of nostalgia for childhood. I returned the remains of the diary to the box, tucked the box away in the wardrobe, and paused to take a look at the photographs that I had taken from Finegold. Of the two pictures of me as a baby, I looked less wrinkled and greasy in the black-and-white shot, but it was spoilt by a slight chromatic aberration, different wavelengths of light coming into focus in front of and behind the film plane. By comparison, the photograph of the stamps had few technical flaws.

I swapped the bed for the sofa and watched spokes of sunshine slowly ride across the flat brown paper and the eggshell envelopes. 'Private'. The contents of the three envelopes were private. I sighed and squeezed the bridge of my nose, feeling a desire to climb into my wardrobe, between the boxes, in the furtive gaps between the present and the past.

Suddenly the air fragmented. A flurry of knocks on the front door.

It could only be Chad from the courier company. Chad wanted his money.

Body still in the living room, I peered down the hallway. The door's burnished wood seemed to be undulating torpidly between each knock. There were fine hatched lines and loops in the grain, as on the pelt of an animal. I tightened the belt cord on my dressing gown and twirled a chest hair between thumb and forefinger. I wondered if Chad would accept a cheque.

The letter box creaked open and a fat, crumpled finger emerged below the brass flap.

A voice said, 'I know you're in there, you cloistered old fucker!'

The finger shrunk backwards, looking embryonic as it receded from my world.

'Perry?'

I opened the door a crack and he pushed it the rest of the way. A sulphur light split the sky above his head, sending my eyeballs into spasm.

'I wonder,' he said, 'if you might oblige an old buddy with a cup of coffee?'

'I was in the bath,' I said, running my fingers through parched hair.

'Must have been a long bath. A wet dream of a bath. I tried to phone ahead, landline and mobile. Your mobile makes a weird sound these days.'

'I got rid of it. I don't need all that technology. Got rid of my digital SLR too. Sick of infinite reproducibility.'

'Ape. Caveman. And this is your cave.'

He hugged me and made a play of pinching my backside, which is a thing that Perry does. I took him through to the kitchen and spooned coffee into a cafetière as he berated me. He had aged in the year or so since I had last seen him. His hair, brown streaks now overridden by grey, was railed back in thin tracks. He was wearing a charcoal three-piece suit over a crisp white shirt. From a frontal view, he looked like a City professional. It was only when you considered him side-on, got a view of the ponytail running down the back of his thick neck, that he seemed more like an ageing rocker. His face, still as pitted and earthy as a potato, had grown squarer and fleshier.

'Foss, tough to think how long it's been.'

'I know, Perry. What is it with time?'

The kettle boiled and I turned the coffee granules into hot mud, bubbles breaking through dark spaces.

Perry said, 'You got a Bud to go with that?'

'No beer, I'm afraid. Whisky if you like.'

Perry frowned and his face, freighted by one thick long eyebrow, acquired an almost sculptural solidity.

'You're looking tired,' he said, taking off his jacket and folding it on the work surface. 'How are you coping?'

'Surviving nicely.'

'Definitely weary-eyed, but still quite muscular, fat-free. Where does a man get musculature like that? Do you work out in this shithole? Or is book-reading, TV-watching, the sum of your exercise these days?'

'You forget music-listening. Pretty much anything that involves sitting still.'

Perry blinked hard, as if trying to separate what was real from what was not. He said, 'I was hoping you'd shoot me today, buddy. Yes, me. The *Guardian* is doing a piece on my talents. The brains behind the artists, some shit like that. I don't trust those left-wing photographers. I want you to take the snap.'

'I'm left-wing, Perry.'

'You're not any wing, honey. You're dead centre, six feet under, deep in God's asshole.'

'Are they doing a feature on your facility with words? I used to be the one with pictures in the *Guardian*. How things change.'

'Well, more of that later. I've got some news for you. A proposal. An offer you can't refuse. A downright gift.'

'You're giving me an album of your best photos?'

'I'll have you know I've got an impressive body of work. Pics of tourists standing in front of Big Ben, the Houses of Parliament, that pissing cherub in Brussels. They're in private collections all over the world.'

'How did you get my address?'

'Some wrinkled chick. The warden at Slimegold Pubes.'

We moved into the living room, two puffed-up giggling old men. Perry sat on the sofa, sipping coffee and telling stories about faded friends. I set up my kit. The portable stand had grown a melancholy skin of wardrobe dust. I unwrapped my quartz light and screwed it into the top. He watched as I picked out a 55mm Nikon lens, eyes following my fingers carefully, not missing a thing, mimicking the photographer's strategy.

'So what's the offer I can't refuse, Perry?'

'Like I say, it's a gift. The greatest gift a man could give a dressing-gowned, porno-clicking, self-suffering cut-off cock jock like yourself. The gift of your career, returned to you with a fucking bow on it. The gift of freedom.'

'Artistic freedom, or physical freedom?'

'Both, sweetheart. While I was doing my journo schmoozing, I spoke to this *Guardian* picture editor. She's setting up a new magazine with a consortium. High-end, glossy. She'll buy up your photos of Japan in a heartbeat. Your take on the Tokyo craze, the Far East buzz. Twelve shots that capture modern Japan. A broad brief. Then I spoke to my guy at *Vanity Fair*, and he's on board too, anything with a human angle. Homeless fellas, blind accordian players, nude shows. Think Walker Evans. Robert Frank. Flights paid for, subsidised freedom. They'll struggle with accommodation, credit crunch and all that, but I'll make it back for you. A foreign foray would make a perfect closing section for your Greatest Hits book. In fact, it could be a separate book in its own right. Give me something by Christmas. It'll sell.'

'Lift your chin.'

'Do this for me, Foss. Do this for yourself.'

I fixed him in the viewfinder. My heart clenched and unclenched like a fist, exercising itself in the privacy of my chest. The light wasn't right, too olive-coloured. His zoomed face looked like a series of little tubes and boxes, each neatly set on a green canvas, like a circuit board. I got up and adjusted the curtains and the quartz light. My reflection in the window had the pallor of toothpaste.

'I'm just saying,' Perry said.

'Try standing against that wall over there.'

He did a drum roll on his knees and stood up slowly.

He said, 'What's all that shit on the floor over there? Brown paper, envelopes.'

'You were talking about China before. Why not China?'

'Because you sounded fucked off when I mentioned China. You made it sound like a fucking gulag.'

'I just said it'd be crowded.'

'Everywhere's crowded. Japan's crowded. London's crowded. For you at least. For you, three's a crowd. *Two* is a bloody crowd. How different can any two places be if you're intent on describing them as "crowded"? Greece was Greece.'

'It isn't just Greece, Perry. When I was in the press a lot, had that exhibition in Shoreditch, someone sent me a sheep's eyeball in the post. A sheep's eyeball. Remember? We had it checked out. It's enough to make anyone anti-social.'

'Whatever. A little ovine never hurt anyone. People send me bits of sheep the whole time.'

I took his picture.

He looked into the camera and said, 'We're all getting old. I'm getting old. I want to die knowing I've opened myself up to things. Histories, places, secrets. You know? I want to curl up in a chair in a warm room on some sunlit fucking Saturday. Have a happy ending. Don't you want that?'

I swallowed hard and adjusted my footing, shooting more quickly now.

'I think about it more and more, Perry. Keep your chin raised, that's it. I think about being old, of course I do. It's all a matter of cold arithmetic, I suppose. We're greying in accordance with some cosmic formula. I'm forty-one. Not that big a number, really. Hardly anything at all. But what if you double it, just for argument's sake? That makes eighty-two, which is a lot, a bigger score than my mother made. How long before I start sticking labels on every single thing? I get scared that I'll end up needing labels for every photo I've ever taken, even the ones I used to do of the city's signs and billboards, exposures of the Queen's Head, the London Stock Exchange. Pictures of self-labelling things. I'm worried I'll forget what they're about, that they'll slip away from me. I'm trying to bounce light off this wall, so turn, that's it, good.'

Perry's eyes gave a little mournful flash and I kept clicking, moving towards the end of the roll.

After we'd finished, he picked up his jacket from the kitchen surface and pulled out an envelope from a pocket. It was a brighter, crisper white than the ones resting on brown paper in the living room.

'A gift,' he said.

'I don't accept gifts from my subjects.'

He opened the front door and said, 'It's customary for house guests to bring things from the outside world. You want my gift. You need it.'

Then he pressed the envelope into my hand, squeezed my shoulder and turned away. The ponytail danced on his shoulders like an electrically charged squirrel. I watched it recede, dancing all the while, into the hectic thinness of the street.

Slowly, cradled by the sofa, savouring the crackle of paper, I ran my thumb through Perry's envelope. I had thought about doing this with the envelopes marked for Satoshi, but opening something expressly marked 'Private' would somehow drag my snooping to a new low. In chemical terms, it would be like swapping a pill bottle for a syringe.

The contents slid out of the ruptured pouch.

A plane ticket. London Heathrow to Tokyo Narita. Monday. 8 p.m. Open return.

I sat and watched the news and took pills and re-read Satoshi's letters. Just as the drugs started to perform their palliative tricks and effects, a name appeared emboldened on a yellowed page: 'Uncle George . . . Dr Harvey.'

I ran some Internet searches. A few hits came back. I printed an obituary from *The Times* that suggested Dr Harvey's illustrious career had been cut short. He died in late July 1946. I resolved to conduct a proper review of the document later, when the haze of druggy distortion had lifted a little. For now, I was fit only for the most basic manual labour, not brainwork, not detective work.

On the carpet, re-wrapping the three envelopes in brown paper, I failed to recreate my mother's neatness.

Did I want Perry's gift? Did I need it? The weekend came and went without bringing me an answer. Then, on the Monday afternoon, I found myself taking a taxi to Heathrow.

8

AT DEPARTURE Gate 12, queuing for the privilege of a numbered seat in an urban tube, the nausea hit me.

It was sudden, as always. The stomach-jolt sent me careering past confused travellers, helplessly skinning my shins against their luggage. They fixed me with glazed, uncomprehending eyes, knowing that my blurry, veering form didn't belong in this patient white-walled space. What was he doing, this ashen, unbalanced figure? What did it mean? Something in the world had gone awry.

As I bent into the cold basin, the drumming of my heart became one constant, vibrato blast. Bile spurted up throat. Electricity singed scalp. Eyeballs bulged. My insides were coming loose, a sensation lurching between diarrhoea and orgasm. A lightning flash of porcelain white. A technicolour blast. It was uncontrollable, and it barely seemed to be coming from me. I turned on the tap too eagerly. The pressure sent vomit-shrapnel into my face. My sleeve caught on the steel spout and water tunnelled up my arm. I rinsed, spat, drank.

Sitting on the toilet seat, studying my damp watch, I was heavy-limbed with a thought: the worst could still be to come. My first panic attack had been on board a plane. It was August four years previously, just after Chloe died. I was flying back from Greece. I spent a terrible hour in the brutally sterile cubicle, thinking my heart was exploding, staring at the blue liquid bubbling in the bowl.

In the weeks after landing in London, I sought help for my sickness. The psychiatrist looked elegant in a shade of green I couldn't name, but her opening gambit was rather blunt. 'Over the past few weeks, since the accident, have you experienced any of the following symptoms: rapid heartbeat, rapid breathing, feeling hot and sweaty, nausea, trembling, dizziness, ringing in your ears, feeling faint?' I told her, 'I haven't had ringing in my ears.' 'Have you ever had thoughts of taking your own life?' she asked, a propitiatory sparkle in her eyes. She was wearing a low-cut top and she scratched her tanned clavicle in a way that made me want to photograph her. I said, 'I've written a suicide note or two, but only to see how it would sound.' Later that day I was explaining to the chemist that, yes, I did pay for my own prescriptions. In the months that followed, my pill collection grew and grew. So did my symptoms. Every journey outside my own home became a cataclysm, a catastrophe.

In the pre-Greece world, I had a few established friends, people from school and university. I lost some through my behaviour at Chloe's funeral. Then, deciding I needed a few months of solitude to get my head straight, I got slack at returning people's calls. And that, it turns out, is how you lose people. A little carelessness is all it takes. Before long, you are too easily satisfied by things that require only the most sanitised forms of human contact: films, music, books.

Mediums that allow you to be safely voyeuristic, an outsider looking in. It starts to run under your skin, the fleeting footage and the sounds and the words that carry histories and lives out into the distance, out into the realms of other experience, into other stories, the stories beyond your own. You become addicted to these narratives of struggle. And, in a way, they help. But only so much. The struggles are always someone else's, never your own. It's the same with photography. You try to find your private agonies in the lines of someone else's face, but their loss is always different to yours.

I heard the final call.

In my economy seat at the back, knotted in the Boeing's bowels, I just about survived. Only once did I make the key error: between two Pink Floyd tracks, I dropped my Raymond Carver paperback on the floor, my earphones came loose, and I suddenly found myself thinking about the impossibility of escape. I flew to the cubicle. A thunderous vacuum sucked away the remains of my stomach, sending me stumbling into the door handle. Back in my seat, the other travellers didn't seem to care as I popped three pills. Their eyes were aglow with reflected light from tiny screens.

'Toothache,' I slurred as a woman with a pumpkin-coloured face handed me a sixth miniature whisky. She pouted and said 'yes' in a voice that sounded patronising and joyful, pleased with herself for having recognised a nervous flyer. I told myself that things could be much worse: Perry could have negotiated that I be on the other side of that curtain up there, in business or first. In a throne seat with five private stewardesses, my issues would stand out a mile. But not here, gummed to my cheap seat. Here my symptoms weren't distinguishable from those of the general passenger populus: I blended in with the fearful and the drunk and the drowsy.

I glanced at the video screen, showing various statistics about the flight. Exterior temperature minus 52°C. Altitude 10,051 metres. Local time at destination 09.32.

The Times obituary for George Harvey was folded in the back of my paperback. I read it, then read it again. Soon the rhythms of the journalist's words became part of the plane's movements – and gradually I felt myself being lifted, then dropped back, into sleep.

Obituary of
DR G. W. HARVEY
ANTHROPOLOGIST AND ETHNOLOGIST

Dr G. W. Harvey, Sc.D., F.R.S., died suddenly in Japan on 21 July at the age of 61. If he could not be said to have had two careers, he at any rate achieved two distinguished reputations: first as an anthropologist and ethnologist, then as the head of a specialist international team working under General Douglas MacArthur, the Supreme Commander of the Allied Powers in Japan. In each sphere he rendered important service at a critical juncture, and his remarkable generosity was an essential factor in his success.

George Winston Harvey, who was born on April 25, 1885, in London, was the elder son of Graham Harvey, head of a firm of typefounders and printers. He was educated at Christ's College, Cambridge, where he studied zoology and became a close friend of R. Jacob Dower (afterwards Harmsworth Professor of Naval History), whose cousin he married in 1906. His early publications included 'An Introduction to the Anthropological Analysis of Consumption' in 1917. The success of this and contemporaneous articles and essays led to his being invited to conduct research with the Department of Social Relations at Harvard. Whilst there, he became interested in Oriental and African studies and on his return home published many papers dealing with the Oriental mind. He advocated this subject in Cambridge (encouraged thereto by

A. M. Prichard), whither he came to give lectures at the Anatomy School from 1924 to 1928. During his tenure at the school, funds were raised to equip an expedition to Japan to make a scientific study of the people there. In April 1928, the expedition arrived at its field of work and spent over a year in Hokkaidō and Honshu, Japan, bringing home a large collection of ethnographical specimens, some of which are now among the glories of the British Museum.

By 1937, Dr Harvey had obtained an Sc.D. degree in recognition of his already significant achievements, and on his return home from a second expedition to Japan he was elected a Fellow of his college (Junior Fellow in 1937, Senior Fellow in 1938). In the spring of 1939 he travelled abroad once again, taking up a position as guest lecturer in the Department of Anthropology at the University of Chicago, and in the summer of 1940 led a project at the Kincaid site on the Ohio River in Southern Illinois. Soon afterwards, the United States government sought his assistance in teaching at the Military Intelligence Service Language School in Minnesota, which at that time was being organised in anticipation of an American occupation of Japan.

In the spring of 1946, Dr Harvey was appointed Chief of the Allied Powers' Public Opinion and Sociological Research Division, a crucial team within the Civil Information and Education Section. Based in Tokyo, he coordinated a group of five American and British social scientists, as well as over fifty Japanese social scientists, translators and clerical workers. He gained a reputation for continually laying aside his own work to help others with theirs.

Of his individual and attractive personality much might be written. Many found in this reserved, erudite scholar and leader a delightful companion and most loyal friend.

His widow and son survive him.

9

THE TWITCHY ceiling light injured me, and the mere act of looking at people was worse. It would have been better not to move my eyeballs at all, but they were darting around of their own accord, attempting to bring things into focus. Drops of condensation had formed on my irises, forcing me to observe the shops and desks and hordes through a pane of weathered glass. There was a storm brewing in my head, Narita airport pulsating to cosmic thunderclaps, an electrical clatter.

Small firm bodies were scattered everywhere, their compactness somehow threatening, as if they might explode. They ghosted past gleaming chrome elevators and a Citibank ATM. I could make out two Japanese girls in micro-miniskirts and knee-high socks. They sipped cloudy liquid from bottles with the words 'Pocari Sweat' printed on the side. What kind of name was 'sweat' for a drink? Maybe an entrepreneurial stewardess had got hold of my in-flight blanket, wrung it dry, bottled the panic juice.

I wheeled my suitcase towards the ATM, inserted my card, entered my digits, tapped a button that promised forty thousand yen. I had no idea how much that equated to, but it was in the mid-range of what the machine offered me. After a nervous wait, waves of gratitude crashed over me when the notes emerged. My whole presence in Tokyo had been authenticated by some higher computerised power. My short trip had been sanctioned. And it would be short, a day or two of frenzied photographs, a cursory search for Satoshi's current address, then back to London with a clear conscience. I opened my satchel and pressed the foreign currency into a gap between my camera case and the package. A transaction receipt parachuted slowly onto the cold blue vista of the floor.

I needed a hotel, any hotel, but the queue for the information desk was too long and capricious to bear. I stepped onto the tarmac outside.

The horizon was fairly bare, not the bustle of tall glass buildings I had expected, just sky everywhere, fading from afternoon blue into evening black, sparsely scored by the pale trails of sinking planes. Bracing air sieved through me as I dragged my suitcase and hand luggage towards a line of taxis. A dozen Toyotas and Nissans, most yellow, some navy, either new or polished daily, and no one waiting for them. Even in my state I took this as a hint that there were better ways of getting to the city centre, but the realisation didn't stop me parking up my belongings and reaching out for a door handle.

Before my fingers made contact, a Japanese man with a rotund face jumped out of the driver's seat, waving his arms at me. He wore white gloves that were too small for his hands and a chequered V-neck sweater. He looked all set for a game of golf.

'No no no!' he cried. 'No hand, no hand!'

I froze in position, bewildered, one arm extended in front of me, the other hovering above my suitcase. As I waited for his next move, my eyes settled on a gap between his two front teeth.

'I take,' he said. 'I take.'

He darted around the rear of the car, picked up my case, and put it into the boot. I managed to keep hold of my satchel.

As he jumped back into the driver's seat, I reached out again to open the rear passenger door. His face popped up above roof level. '*Sawaranaide!*' he said.

While I considered this, the door swung open without human intervention.

Inside the cab, lace doilies covered the seats. Like the driver's gloves, they were a pristine, freshly laundered white. The driver turned the ignition key and the engine started to hum, modulating slowly, searching for its tenor. He craned his thick neck to see me.

'A hotel please,' I said. 'A cheap one. Any hotel.'

Content that I had conveyed enough, I sank back into the seat. But he just looked at me and bit his lip.

'Somewhere central,' I added.

He frowned. A nervous sigh whistled through his front teeth. It dawned on me that the tourist information desk had been by far my best option.

'Shibuya?' I said hopefully. If *Psychologies of Defeat* was to be trusted, Shibuya was somewhere in the centre.

'Shibuya,' he said.

Whatever he was thinking, he looked worn out by it.

He swivelled back round, his upper body pitching forward as if he planned to throw himself through the windscreen.

He produced an enormous street map. He opened it and considered the pages gravely. He turned the book upside down. He looked at it sideways. Then he flicked to a new page and started the analytical process afresh. I sat looking at the outline of his rounded shoulders. They were sunk massively forward, carrying a great weight.

'Hmmmuh,' he said finally, the battle cry of a man resigned to his fate.

It took twenty minutes for Tokyo to come alive. I looked out of the window and saw my reflected eyes, laid like tracing paper over the scene beyond the glass. The wastes of the airport were behind us and the taxi was pulling through roads flanked by buzzing neon shapes. Glittering skyscrapers were randomly marshalled across the skyline, sheets of sunlight shattering across their glass walls. These crystal buildings looked so delicate set against the fuming road, freighted as it was with the rattling metal of cars and buses and lorries, that it was difficult to believe that they belonged in the same world.

No book or film had prepared me for the million-coloured veinwork of the city. Its lights blazed incredibly brightly, dimming only when the taxi was sucked down into a tunnel. When we resurfaced seconds later, I felt like a disgorged newborn unable to take in the world outside the womb. Fluorescence poured down from street signs bearing strange lettering, filling the porches of shops and seeping under the arches of alleyways.

I swallowed very hard. A traffic light blinked.

We approached a Starbucks. It towered over a six-way intersection that whirred with traffic. My ribcage lurched as we banked into a thinner street, jerking across unplumbed welts in the tarmac. We paused as a wave of spectacularly clad locals flooded a pedestrian crossing. A minute later, the taxi came to a stop outside a tower of triangular bay windows.

'Shibuya Grand Hotel,' the driver said. He looked nervous, his eyeballs flitting across the scar on my cheek.

I could tell from one glance that the Shibuya Grand Hotel was too grand for my budget. But, in my condition, a night or two of luxury wouldn't hurt. Perry said he'd make money from my photographs, and he was a moneymaking expert.

The taxi door opened automatically, cranking up Tokyo's volume: beeping horns, groaning cars, high-pitched chatter. The air smelt of petrol. My driver leapt out of the car and ran round to the boot. He removed my suitcase with great care, as if it were full of treasures, not knowing that the letters and the package were in the satchel slung across my shoulder. I thanked him and pressed a couple of notes into his hand. He dug into his pocket and gave me change, and when I signalled for him to keep it he looked humbled and appalled in equal measure. You'd think I'd offered him a kidney. I accepted the change and he gave me a deep bow.

In the lobby, a girl with perfectly manicured hands greeted me in staccato English. 'Sir – welcome – may I? – we do – yes – of course – one minute.' She bowed a lot too, pressing the palms of her hands together in supplication as she did so. I was treated like a medieval knight, returning from some great and dangerous quest. I'm just some middle-aged guy, I felt like saying. A recluse starting out from scratch.

10

I LAY sprawled on a foreign bed. The sun had risen before me — it was making a mockery of the flimsy curtains — but the television in the corner of the room, hanging in a brace, seemed not to have caught up with the passage of time. Its screen was full of the purple light of evening.

I woke with a startling clear sense of what I needed to achieve with my day. I needed to find Satoshi. It was as if thoughts of my mother's ex-sweetheart had, overnight, encased me in a kind of crust, a new skin. It was hard to sit up. My bondage to him seemed to preclude easy movement. I lay and waited for life to work its way through my body, seeping into my joints and muscles, rendering them pliant.

As I clambered under the shower head, my legs bent to the sound of a rifle shot. But as the water enveloped me, the harsh creaks emanating from my bones seemed to soften. I tackled each inch of my flesh with foamy diligence and rare determination. The plane's residue of fear snaked down into the whorl of the drain. After drying off and working on my teeth for a while, I studied the toilet's pallid enamel mouth. I wondered what Edward Weston, that great toilet-loving photographer, would have made of this equipment. What I was faced with was far from the functional simplicity that he had snapped in the twenties. The bowl in my eyeline was flanked by two disconcerting panels of buttons, each embossed with kanji script. Once seated in the cockpit, I experimented with a knob on the right-hand side. As I rotated it, the toilet seat started to warm my thighs. Not unpleasant.

Only after the event, zipped up and leaning over the bowl, was I forced to consider which button would activate the flush. A good deal of experimentation followed and, eventually, a burp of approval emanated from the toilet's glossy jaws.

Although it had been a long time since I'd last stared into them, the jaws of my suitcase proved less intimidating. A familiar selection of neatly folded clothes, taken straight from my bedroom drawers. I looked at the little cotton chambers of red and blue and grey, proximate but not mingling, divided by electrical cords and unfurled socks. The sight made me think of textbook diagrams of the human heart. I surprised myself by unpacking my SLR and taking a picture. I couldn't remember the last time I'd felt the urge.

I picked something to wear. For my bottom half, the choice was between faded blue jeans and unfaded blue jeans. I opted for the former. For my top half, I settled on a grey T-shirt and a thick black jumper. I went to the window and threw the curtains wide open. I was at least twenty floors up. An imposing mass of dark glass hung in the air to the right. To the left, a giant silver cylinder sprang up from a concrete slab like a futuristic chimney. On the horizon, reflections multiplied and merged on a labyrinth of cubes and cones and pyramids. The striking thing was the vastness of it all: office after office, shop after shop, tower after tower. From my vantage point, Tokyo did not end.

I emptied the contents of my satchel onto the bed: keys to the flat, Ipod, Carver paperback, several tubes of multi-coloured pills, notepaper with the address for Roppongi World Plaza, camera film, compact digital camera (even Luddites need a fallback), hip flask (emptied at Heathrow), Mr Satoshi's letters, Dr Harvey's obituary, banknotes and the package. I locked the letters in the safe next to the minibar, swallowed some pills without water, then grabbed my coat. The skin around my Adam's apple started to prickle as I returned the package, the notepaper and the pill bottles to my satchel, slinging the leather over my shoulder. The digital camera would do for this morning; I put it in my coat pocket. Having the SLR around my neck would be a burden. A necessary burden, but one I wasn't quite ready for.

Down in the lobby, the receptionist with pearl-plated fingernails looked deep into the ridge of my scar and confirmed that I was too late for breakfast. She handed me a few of the hotel's business cards for no discernible reason. I crossed the polished marble floor, fixated by my own quivering reflection, bracing myself for an exit.

I stood on the threshold, the electric doors flickering just feet away. No choice but to go. Thresholds are safe places to be, but you can't lurk on them forever, noticing without being noticed. Multicoloured tourists charged in with shopping bags and children, and those on their way out tossed scarves around their shoulders so casually you'd think their imminent adventure was no big deal. I watched as the doors opened and closed, opened and closed. Street sounds faded out and then intensified again, louder each time the glass screens parted. A bellboy asked if I was OK. 'Just thinking,' I said, and he backtracked with a ripple of bows, him in a permanent state of apology, me in a permanent state of fear. I tried to block him out. I tried to block them all out. I tried to block out absolutely everything as I lurched outside and, within seconds, leapt back into the lobby. It must have been a ludicrous sight, me hopping in and out, out and in, marble to concrete, concrete to marble, but I did it several more times, everyone watching as I tried to trick my mind into thinking it was the Gray's Inn Road out there. The Gray's Inn Road: its familiar signs and symbols, the central seam of an old book I could rise above, read, study, inhabit.

And I was momentarily free. My vision was blurring, but I was moving down the street. Almost graceful for a second, gliding where the crowds were thinnest, until a mob of shoulders barged my coat. I caught my balance but my insides started to bubble. A damp white man in a stupid hat blocked me and asked if I knew the way to a restaurant. 'I can't tell you how to get anywhere,' I said, pushing past him. 'Thanks for nothing,' he shouted. He kept shouting after me as, once again, not again, my mouth filled with bile. I swallowed it down as I weaved among throngs of vinyl miniskirts, purple tights and voluminous Afros. I stared up at spaces where there should have been street names – Harrison, Cromer, Guilford – but I couldn't see any. I thought of Walker Evans' photographs of Broadway signs, billboards and adverts. But there was no equivalent lexical reservoir to draw on here. Nameless, foreign streets. Nothing readable, nothing legible; no labels, no meaning. Fluorescent lights of shops and shards of glass competing for airspace. And, underneath them, the crowd. The crowd writhing nightmarishly through the city. Taking me. Taking me with it.

Satoshi, I told myself. Satoshi, Satoshi, Satoshi.

But no, he wasn't near enough, not then. My jumper was heavy with fluid, it couldn't be sweat, too thick, must be blood. Losing blood. My heart was stuttering, my brain softening, my lungs shrivelling. A swarm of compressed bodies hardened around me, sent me under, sunk me deeper, deeper, through waves of wheeling light. As my knees buckled it felt like slow motion, but it wasn't. Everywhere I looked there was an agony of twisted limbs and bloated eyes and straining knots of upflung faces.

And then concrete. Concrete rising up to smack me on the shoulder. On impact, I retched emptily. Up there, somewhere, a riot of shadows, heels like five-inch daggers, backlit hands, a yellow orb in a thin grey sky, neon symbols flickering like stars.

11

I SAT in the hotel lobby, clutching my throbbing shoulder, remembering something important. The crackle of my mother's voice in a kitchen filled with clouds that smelt of sage.

She was in her element on roast beef Sundays at number 17. The warmth of the kitchen seemed to sustain her. As a child I would sit on the washing machine in the corner, jigged by the drum's revolutions, watching her create pink ribbons of bacon, jagged rocks of potato, mounds of globular sprouts. The walls were heavy with shelves stacked with china, jelly moulds, jars and vases and scales, ancient shimmering things made of copper and brass, battered cookery books with walnut-stained spines. She had these oversized glasses with beige frames. My mother only ever wore her glasses for cooking and gardening. The details of foods and plants were the only aspects of everyday life that warranted close inspection. At around midday, when most of her flurries of preparation were over, the sealed oven pulsing out nourishing heat, she would turn her bug-like eyes onto me and start telling stories.

She liked to recall an anecdote once told by John F.

Kennedy to an expectant crowd. 'Kennedy's best story,' she'd say, as though her memory was chock-full of Kennedy's stories. She heard it on the radio on 21 November 1963. The president, suggesting the then-impossible idea of space travel to his audience, said there was once a boy who had a favourite hat. One day, the boy was faced with a wall he was afraid to climb. So he threw his favourite hat over the top. The boy feared losing the hat more than he feared climbing the wall, so once the hat had gone over, so did he.

My mother loved to recount that tale. In typical fashion, she omitted the context, neglecting to tell me that Kennedy was shot dead on the 22nd. The context spoke of the dangers of traversing barriers and boundaries, but that wasn't the point she wanted to make to her only child. My mother was always selective about what she kept and what she gave away. Perhaps that's why I grew up feeling I knew so little about her. She told me other people's stories but never her own. And then it was too late to speak of anything much at all.

She did say a strange thing to me one Sunday. One thing that, with hindsight, feels like it was an invitation for me to probe her past. I must have been twelve or thirteen years old. She said, 'There are some questions that lack answers.' I stared at her. She said, 'Often there aren't answers, but if you want to ask me anything, you should ask.' I considered her words. What sort of thing should I ask her? She blushed, she didn't know. Looking back, I half sense an unfocused yearning within her for interrogation, for a moment of reckoning, a time when she could unburden herself of some great niggling weariness.

* * *

Is weariness hereditary?

I padded across the marble lobby and resumed my position in front of the glass doors. Attempt one: fifty yards. Attempt two: one hundred yards. Attempt three: one hundred and fifty yards. This was my life, blurring the border between gravity and levity, measured out in heavy, farcical footfalls.

I brought my drugged eyes up from the pavement. First I saw sheepskin boots, then what looked like subway steps, and, higher still, beyond the blur of neon, vast television screens floating in the air, pointing down at me, full of global dots. The screens flashed adverts for fizzy drinks and blended whiskies. I kept walking and made it to an illuminated shop sign, a traffic-light mesh of green, orange and red. A 7–Eleven shop. The combination of colours seemed to flicker deep out of my own childhood, stirring up nostalgia for chocolate and football stickers.

As I walked in, all three staff members behind the checkout desks shouted something. Whatever the nature of their greeting or enquiry, it seemed to be rhetorical. They shouted the same thing to the Japanese guy who entered immediately after me. A comforting smell of fresh doughnuts hung in the air. I took a bottle of Pocari Sweat from a fridge, more out of intrigue than thirst, and inspected a stand of paperbacks and magazines. Most were manga booklets, the cover pictures broken up by thought bubbles that probably explained this character's frown or that character's smile. I had often wished photographers had recourse to the thought bubble, or the speech bubble for that matter. There was one book in English: a fat travel guide. I took the book and the drink to the till and paid a woman whose breast pocket was filled with felt-tip pens. A Western businessman to my left had made the fatal mistake of opting for the self-service checkout, busily charging himself many thousand yen for his own cufflink.

In the Starbucks next door, I bought an orange juice and a blueberry muffin without uttering a word. The bushy-haired barista probably spoke English, but I enjoyed the primitive freedom of ordering by hand signals. On the table opposite mine was a Japanese girl in her twenties. She had fluorescent pink hair. She reached for her frothy cappuccino, took a sip, then started rummaging around in a leather handbag on her lap. The leather was stretched into mounds and peaks that suggested the contents had been crammed in carelessly; the bag was probably a victim of rush-hour panic, stuffed with one hand as she flung her front door open with the other. She removed a small tin of lip balm, rubbed some on her lips, and took another sip of coffee. I persisted with my juice. It was too thick. A layer of it coated my oesophagus and refused to be swallowed. I held my travel book in both hands, but it was the pink-haired girl I was looking at. For the briefest of moments she must have realised this, because she met my gaze. There was a bright defiance in her eyes. I tried to imbue my face with affable qualities, then looked away, feigning serious thought.

The coffee shop was busy with lunchtime trade, but I was barely aware of the Japanese voices around me. When you don't understand a particular language, it's startling how quickly you can tune it out. Speech becomes nothing more than a low buzz. Conversely, in a foreign environment, recognisable language takes on a greater intensity.

'Doing some heavy research, huh?'

It was the pink-haired girl. I was bringing a ball of buttery crumbs to my mouth and it took me a few seconds to catch her meaning. I drew the book into my chest and reacquainted myself with the cover.

'On Japan,' she added. 'You look pretty engrossed. I have a few expat friends over here. They call the *Lonely Planet* "the Bible". Watching you, I see what they mean. You've got this super-serious look on your face. It's like you're thinking, if I look at this page long enough, I'll learn the meaning of life.'

Her voice was softer than I'd expected from someone with fluorescent hair. She used her tongue to push out her cheek, perhaps trying to detect some suspicious flavour.

She said, 'You're not a mute, right? Cos I've got nothing but total sympathy for mutes, but small talk's small talk, and I'm not into sign language or whatever.'

The air travel had desiccated my lips. I moistened them and said, 'I'm not a mute, but I suppose it's hard to tell. In those Paul Strand photographs the mutes always have signs around their necks saying "mute", don't they?'

'I've never heard of Paul Strand.'

Of course she hadn't.

She said, 'You're British, right?'

'Your English is good,' I said, nodding, finding in my own voice something weak and unpractised.

'Thanks. You're a real charmer. How's your Japanese?'

'Not so good, now you come to mention it.'

'First day here in Tokyo?'

'Yes. Well, I arrived last night.'

'I can kinda tell. From the panicked grip you've got on that book, I guess.'

She was right. My knuckles were white with stress. I removed a fragment of fruit zest from my bottom lip as a fresh crowd pulled up chairs around us.

'Are you a student?' I said, lowering my voice.

'Sure am,' she said, apparently not feeling the need to lower hers. 'How can you tell? Is it the silly hair? Because that's Tokyo, not a student thing.'

'I'm not sure it was the hair.'

'Maybe it was the hoodie.'

Her right hand disappeared behind her neck and re-emerged clutching the hood of her navy blue sweater.

She said, 'Last semester I took loads of –' There was a cough, a pause, a sip of coffee, and I sensed that the next word would be *drugs*. '– history classes, and this professor we had was an absolute Nazi. He had this thing about hoodies. He couldn't stand them. Banned us from wearing hooded stuff in his classes. He said it made us look like the worst kind of students. "Lazy reprobates," he said. "Obsessed with cool." Can you believe it? I used to get that kind of stuff from teachers at high school, even a little on my bachelor's degree, but I don't expect it now. I mean, I'll be twenty-five in a few months. Admittedly I *was* a bit of a pain at high school, always playing up and being super confident, always being loud so people knew I was in the cool set. But that's what everyone does, right? You know how it is.'

'Hmm.'

'What's your name?'

'Foss.'

'Want to know mine?'

'Why not.'

She broke her name down into its three syllables for me:

Chi. Yo. Ko. Chiyoko. Then she asked if she could join me at my table, and before I could say anything, she had.

'So. Foss. That's a kinda unusual name, right?'

'Yes.'

'And? Does it mean anything?'

'It's short for Fossick. It's a surname. My first name is Rob, but no one really calls me that. My mother took to calling me Foss. She seemed quite taken by it, for some reason.'

'I see why she likes it. It's different, it's right for you. Other names are as common as weeds. "Foss" as a first name makes you stand out. Are your mum and dad still alive?'

'No. I mean, my father is alive, not my mother.'

'Sorry to hear that,' she said, looking at me with some feeling. Sadly I followed her eyes, and I pictured what she could see. My puffy bags and heavy lids, the letter box of my mouth and the teeth lightly tanned by indoor spores. And the scar on my cheek, the skin pursed around it like a drowned man's lips.

We fell into silence.

'You don't say much, do you, Foss? A guy of few words. But I get the sense that there's some interesting stuff going on inside there.'

She extended an arm unexpectedly, tapping my forehead with an index finger, the nail painted black. She scrutinised my eyes and said, 'You're one of those guys that says the bare minimum.'

It struck me that Chiyoko was the sort of person who, given enough time, would say anything to anyone. Perhaps it was a desire to know what she'd say next that led me to ask if she wanted another cappuccino. OK, she said, but soon she would have to leave for classes. She was a student at Keio University, doing a master's degree in literature. After I came back with her coffee, we fell into politenesses for a while – the weather in Japan, the weather in England, the rise of Starbucks – but soon returned to talking about her life, then mine. When I mentioned that I was a photographer she sounded oddly interested. She rushed through all of the reasons why she thought photography was, next to poetry, the 'super-supreme art form'. I was happy to be the audience for her quick-fire monologue.

'Don't you have anywhere you need to be? Sightseeing in Starbucks all you've got planned?'

'Actually, I need to make my way to an address in Roppongi.' I leaned down, fumbled in my satchel and noticed a dim tremble in my fingers as I smoothed the notepaper over the tabletop. 'Roppongi World Plaza. Have you heard of it?'

'Uh-huh. The Minato Ward. I'm heading roughly in that direction. How are you planning on getting over there?'

'I was thinking of a taxi.'

'Mr Rich, huh? Well, you'll need a map for the taxi driver – otherwise you don't stand a chance.'

'Even though I've got the address?'

'Most of the smaller Tokyo streets don't have names, so taxi drivers like pictures.'

'There must be a map in this book,' I said, fanning the pages of the Bible ineffectually.

'Subway's quicker,' Chiyoko said, taking the book out of my hands with a confident swipe. 'We'll take the Ginza line to Tameike-Sannō. We can walk from there.'

I told her I'd be fine on my own, that there was no need for her to accompany me. She stood up, slipped on a baby-blue raincoat and said, 'Fossy, you need all the help you can get.'

I was too struck by the nickname to object.

Melodic bells chimed as the subway train arrived, on time, to the minute. My blood lurched when I saw how packed the carriage was, so I stared down at the ground with affected nonchalance.

The doors closed behind us and my eyelids tingled. The carriage seemed to house everyone in Japan, more or less. We pushed through a muscular twist of bodies and joined a network of arms jigging around a chrome maypole. I plunged my free hand into my jeans pocket, clenching my invisible fist. A trickle of sweat slid down my spine.

'What's London like?'

'Good,' I said, feeling a faint itch somewhere deep in my nose. I sneezed before I could free a hand from either the pole or the pocket. A swollen-faced man swaying in front of us brushed down his jacket and shot me a look. What would he do if I vomited? What would I do? 'London is nice,' I added.

'Nice, huh? I'd love to go to London. Spent a year in New York once, as part of my study programme. Made lots of friends, went out loads. I think the nightlife in London sounds awesome. Is it awesome?'

'Very probably,' I said, focusing on an advertising banner dangling above the welded crests of commuter hair, zooming in on a single piece of cereal tumbling into a bowl, imagining that I was climbing inside its honeycomb shell.

'If you're a photographer, shouldn't you be taking pictures of all of this?'

She waved a hand around the carriage. People ducked to avoid it.

'I like to get familiar with my surroundings first.'

As we travelled beneath nameless streets, Chiyoko rushed through a series of facts about the Tokyo transport system, pausing every so often to ask me a flurry of personal questions. In central Tokyo, she told me, there are three categories of train systems: subways, the 'JR' and privately owned tracks. Am I married? The subway is the fastest and easiest way to get around central Tokyo. Am I gay? There are thirteen subway lines, four of them called 'Toei' lines, the others 'Tokyo Metro'. What did I study at university? Each line has a name and a colour. Is my trip business or pleasure?

'Somewhere between the two,' I said, a popping sound in my ears reminding me that I was deep underground, feeling neither businesslike nor hedonistic. 'I'm hoping to find a guy called Satoshi who lives, or lived, in the World Plaza. And I'm hoping to take some good pictures too.'

'Interesting,' she said. 'An unmarried not gay history graduate photographer.'

The man I had sneezed on appeared to have fallen asleep, despite still being vertical. For the rest of the journey, I mimicked him.

12

I CLIMBED the escalator with desperate speed, Chiyoko struggling to keep up with me. Only when I made it outside did I turn around. A blurry flash of her blue raincoat emerged from the tunnel, a blob of minty toothpaste squeezed from its tube.

It was a relief to see, under a naked winter sun, buildings and sky taking shape around me. The area was less frenetic than Shibuya. The shadow at my feet, thin and slanting, had a vast concrete canvas to stretch out on. Its dark form suggested a crutch under my armpit, but this was the shadow's deceit. The crutch was my satchel, hanging low, carrying the package.

We walked in silence for a while, until Chiyoko cleared her throat. 'So you don't like being underground, huh?'

'What do you mean?'

'You were silent, pale as anything. I mean, don't get me wrong. You're a good-looking guy. What are you, thirty-five? Tall, kind of rugged for an arty type, in good shape. But down there you looked like a corpse. Am I wrong?'

'It's not a thing about being underground. I get anxious in . . . unfamiliar places.'

'Like, claustrophobia? I've always wanted to meet a proper claustrophobic.'

I shook my head and tried to explain, taking care to be vague as to where eccentricity stopped and illness began. Even so, she laid me bare by asking if I'd told my doctor.

'Everything's already diagnosed,' I said.

'Well, I'll look after you, Fossy. Until we find the building, anyway.'

'Thanks.'

'You must really want to track down this Satoshi guy, huh? What is he to you?'

Sunlight caught her cheekbones, emphasising the taut pink of the skin. The rays bleached her eyelashes a chromic silver colour. I felt a strange urge to stand still and watch those eyelashes, to bask in their moth-like shadows, but we kept walking.

'Old friend of my mother's,' I said.

'And will he be easy to find? Did your mother leave you all his details?'

'Not exactly.'

'Still playing the bare-minimum game, huh? Fair enough.'

'She died very recently, my mother. But she'd been ill for a long time. She'd been a different person. Does that make any sense? And then I found out that she'd known this man Satoshi and wanted to send him something, but for whatever reason she never could. So . . .'

'So you're here to do this last thing for her,' Chiyoko said. She said it quietly, the corners of her mouth suddenly down-drawn by some miniature sadness.

'You OK, Chiyoko?'

'Uh-huh, of course.'

She blinked heavily, the way a drunk person blinks to aid orientation, and after a few minutes of silent strolling we stopped outside a high-rise apartment block. The entrance to the building was a sleek affair: highly polished black and grey tiles framing glass, just like the picture on the website. Reflections from the street ran across the walls and windows – liquefied car doors and shivery trees, floating heads and unspooled bodies.

'This is it,' Chiyoko said. 'Roppongi World Plaza.' Then she added, frowning, 'I'll try and help you do this.'

She took off her raincoat and approached the stone steps. She was wearing a frayed denim skirt that rode up a little as she wiggled ahead. I noticed her slim, bare legs for the first time, the thigh skin paler than that around her calves.

Inside, a helmet of gelled hair was visible over the top of a high reception desk. Within a few seconds the helmet became a head, and then a whole upper body dressed in green uniform. As soon as the Japanese man was standing straight, he disappeared again with a severe bow.

They started talking.

When Chiyoko switched from English to Japanese, it was as though a thread in her larynx had been gently twisted. An urgency entered her voice, high-pitched and breathy. The man's voice found a much lower register – lower than the voice I had spoken to on the previous Thursday. Intermittently, the two of them pronounced English-sounding words: *manshon* could be *mansion*; *furonto* could be *front*; *manejya* could be *manager*.

'He's just the receptionist for this block,' Chiyoko said. 'If you need to know information about residents, he has to clear it with his boss, who's out. But he says they don't

113

usually give out personal information about a resident. Unless it's a police matter, that is.'

'I just want to know which flat Satoshi lives in,' I said.

Chiyoko conferred with the receptionist, who looked increasingly bewildered, and turned back to me. 'Do you know this Satoshi guy's surname? Because apparently he knows most of the Japanese residents in the block.'

'He's not Japanese.'

'He's not?'

'It's kind of complicated . . . Satoshi's sort of a nickname, I guess. His English name is Reggie. I don't know his surname, or which name he goes by these days.'

Chiyoko frowned, and the reception man started frowning too. A single hair on his head pinged to freedom. He quickly pressed it back in place with a raft of fingers.

I said, 'Something about the fact "Satoshi" means wisdom, or clear-sightedness? He was an anthropologist. He came here to help the occupation forces, following the end of the Second World War. And he would be old now, around eighty. But he's white, English. He came to Japan after the −'

I felt a sharp kick to my ankle.

'I think we might miss out the war part,' Chiyoko whispered. I looked over at the reception guy. He gave us a pregnant stare. Chiyoko started relaying my confused explanations, or apologising for my war comment, or both.

After a minute or two, their undecodable sentences shortened into the same solitary word, repeated over and over as a child repeats a half-learned lesson: *gaijin gaijin gaijin*. Then the receptionist started saying 'hai'. *Hai. Hai.* Even then, I knew 'hai' meant 'yes'. Surely so much affirmation was an encouraging sign. I moved forward a couple of steps and leaned my elbows on the cold counter. In a flesh-coloured room behind the reception man, a woman in a blue tunic and Lycra leggings was arranging chipped enamel pots on a tray.

'He does remember an old British guy. He says that most of the expats here are in their thirties or forties, working for investment banks and law firms. The occasional teacher or journalist. But this guy stood out because he was well into retirement age, and also because he spoke excellent Japanese. Still working, it seems, because he left the building at 9 a.m. every day, Monday to Friday, regular as clockwork.'

'And does he know which flat?'

'Somewhere on the first floor. But this is the bad news: your man Satoshi, if it was him, moved out of this building a few years back.'

'A few years?'

'Uh-huh, a few years.'

'No forwarding address?'

'None. Sorry.'

The tunic woman popped a breath mint and disappeared, a slight shuffle in her walk. My thoughts turned to what awaited me back in London.

'Nothing else he can tell us?' I asked. 'Any distinguishing features? Anything he can say about the way Satoshi looked?'

When Chiyoko finished translating the questions the receptionist shrugged heavily, his shoulders rising right up alongside his ears and then falling almost out of view.

'He says he remembers that Satoshi, if it was him, was old-looking, but that's it. Apart from that, he says all you guys, white Westerners, kinda look the same. No offence, of course.'

The receptionist let out a jagged laugh, then slapped a hand across his mouth, appalled by his own outburst. Chiyoko thanked him for his time; I nodded and turned. Then, just as we were exiting the glass doors, he shouted something.

'What's he saying?'

'Hang on.'

More Japanese.

'He says he's pretty sure the guy's name was Pickford.'

'Pickford?'

'Legend old,' the receptionist seemed to be saying, scratching his hair all the while. '*Hai*, Legend old.'

Chiyoko said, 'He didn't recognise "Reggie" when you said it. He remembers the guy's name as Reginald. Reginald Pickford.'

I clutched my satchel, fingertips welding to the leather.

Reginald Pickford.

I should have felt pleased to have a full name, but back on the streets my mind registered a bleakness and anonymity. I had a further clue to follow, and I felt swallowed by the prospect.

'You look miserable, Fossy.'

'I just want to deliver the thing.'

'Do you know what it is, the thing you're supposed to be delivering?'

'No,' I said, picking up speed. 'It's wrapped in brown paper.'

'Come on, Fossy!' Excitement pulsed across her lower lip, the tremble-mouthed expression of a cat about to pounce on fresh prey. 'You must have at least *thought* about what's inside?'

'No. Well, yes. But the contents are a mystery.'

'So you come all the way to Japan and it could just be, like . . . a Christmas card? Or a baby elephant?'

'Some theories are more random than others.'

'You've got no background, no idea who this guy was to your mother?'

I explained, in as few words as possible, how I had come across the package and the letters after she passed away, how I had found out that Dr George Harvey died soon after Satoshi's arrival in Japan, how I didn't know if Satoshi had come back to my mother. As I talked, I arranged my body into the stance that I tend to adopt when I'm outdoors: leaning slightly forward from the hips, head tilted down, chin pressed into neck. It's one way of fencing myself off from the anxiety pressing in from all directions.

She insisted on peering inside my satchel, muttering 'Wow, kinda crazy' as she prodded one end of the package. 'I've got to walk over to the university. Want to walk with me? There's a business hotel close by where you can hail a taxi, if that's how you're planning to get back to Shibuya.'

Incrementally, so that I barely noticed the change, the streets got busier. With each successive block, a thicker cacophony of electronic beeps and buzzes emanated from games arcades. Individual voices clustered into a collective hum drifting out of restaurants and bars. Men outside karaoke clubs barked news of special offers. Taxi doors creaked open and clacked shut. Two young Japanese men, one in a waistcoat and shirtsleeves, the other in a coat like mine, sat on the pavement outside a shuttered shop, smoking and watching passers-by. They looked up as we approached.

Through a thin film of cigarette smoke I met the waist-coated one's eye. He was probably drawing conclusions from our odd coupling, the middle-aged foreigner with scarred skin and the silken-cheeked Japanese girl. He looked down at my scuffed grey trainers. Can you tell from a man's shoes how much confidence he has in the ground beneath him?

'Which hotel are you staying at?' Chiyoko asked.

'The Shibuya Grand.'

The name flashed in my mind as my fingers explored the lining of my coat pocket. I'd already seen the sign above the entrance half a dozen times, what with all the morning's comings and goings. I stopped walking and offered Chiyoko one of the business cards I'd been given by the pearly-fingered girl.

'Pretty swish,' Chiyoko said, taking the card.

'I just arrived there by accident, really. If I'm going to stay in Tokyo for a few days, I need to find somewhere a lot cheaper.'

As we started walking again she said, 'You're planning to stay a few days?'

'I don't know. I really don't. I do want to find Satoshi, Pickford, if I can. And my agent is going to kill me if I don't take some photographs while I'm here. The Satoshi thing is just a side project really, I just want to get it out of the way.'

'Is it difficult, taking interesting photographs?'

'It didn't use to be. But lately my pictures haven't had any life to them, they don't bear witness to anything. Everything's stuck in the shadows.'

'If Satoshi's still alive, maybe you'll get a chance to take a good picture of him. What did you say the other one's name was, the dead anthropologist?'

'George Harvey.'

'You know how Harvey died?'

'No. I found an obituary. It said it was sudden.'

'Sudden death, huh? Doesn't that generally mean gruesome murder? In crime fiction at least.'

I shrugged, but she didn't notice.

'Listen,' she said, 'my university library has got a historical section of its catalogue, an online database thing with scanned images of loads of old papers. Copies of tons of government reports that were classified back then, during the occupation, but have now been released under American freedom of information laws. I dug through some of it once, for a paper on historical literature. It's all fully searchable – keywords and date ranges.'

'I could search it?'

'That might be difficult.'

'Don't worry then.'

'You give up easily, don't you? I was going to say that I've only got an hour or two of tutorials this afternoon. I can take a look later, if you like. See if Harvey and Pickford pop up anywhere. You got any dates I can search for?'

'Spring and summer '46. That would be a good start, if you really don't mind.'

'No problem. One possible route to Pickford, huh? Taking the road less travelled and all that.'

'Isn't that –'

'Yeah, it's just a line. By the way,' Chiyoko said, turning to me, 'this probably isn't fit for a famous photographer, but if you need somewhere to stay, somewhere really cheap

– and a *lot* less pleasant than the Grand – then give me a call, huh?'

She handed me a cream-coloured business card. In a wavy font it bore the name 'Hotel Villa Dolly', along with an address, phone and fax number. The edges looked like they had been cut with makeshift scissors.

'I work there, in the evenings. It's in Shibuya. About ten minutes from the Grand, towards the seedier end of town. There's a map on the back of the card.'

'Thanks,' I said, trying to look relaxed as I turned the card in my hands. Within seconds, I was picking it off the pavement. 'You know, you really don't have to spend your time on this. Most people in your situation wouldn't.'

'Most people in your situation would have thrown that parcel in a cupboard and forgotten about it.'

'Which is no way to treat a baby elephant?'

'Exactly! Elephant cruelty. Super uncool.'

We kept walking, smiling now and then at a muddle of insignificant things. From the main street we turned into a narrow, warped lane and headed uphill. After climbing a stairway we emerged in the middle of a busy avenue. Tall cubes of concrete peered down at us, their multiple eyes fidgety with yellow life. Skeletal neon lights adorned the outside of buildings, flickering between floors: it seemed different bars, restaurants and shops resided at each level. Eventually we reached a squat block set between two karaoke bars, a seventies monstrosity that looked similar to my old university's student union.

'This is the business hotel I mentioned. You can get a taxi from here. Tell them you want to go to Shibuya-eki. Got that? *Shibuya-eki*. It's the train station.'

'OK, thanks. I guess I'll pop round to the Hotel Villa Dolly soon, to see if you found anything on that database.'

She squeezed the top of my arm, and was gone.

I took a taxi back to the hotel, staring through the sun-stained window at a dizzy tumble of shopfronts and bars, scenes that were bright but not sharp. I picked up a Starbucks sandwich and took it to my room, then dozed off with damp bread in my hand.

What seemed like a split second later, I woke to a mess of door knocks. At first they were indistinguishable from the thumping that had got going in my head.

I must have looked bad, because the bellboy's face slackened with pity as I peered out from behind the seven-foot stretch of faultless wood. 'Fax for you from Miss Chiyoko,' he said, pressing a sheaf of papers into my hand.

I felt faint and feverish as I examined the fax cover sheet. A handwritten scrawl covered the printed data:

Fossy, I'm a fast worker.

U.S. Army Intelligence Section (MIS) Report

Date: July 23, 1946
Title: Investigation into the death in suspicious circumstances of Dr. G. W. Harvey on July 21, 1946
Document Number: RPVX-866-746372813-5532-GWH

The following transcript is of a taped interview with Watanabe Funakoshi (26), a research assistant in the Civil Information and Education (CIE) Section of SCAP. Materials related to this interview can be accessed using application number RPVX-866-SQ-117 (note: document missing — Lt A.R.G. 08/26/1946).

The investigation recorded here was carried out under the direction of Major Richard M. Banks. The field investigation in [*text redacted*] on the Chiba peninsula was conducted by Lieutenant Herbert Jameson with assistance from Sergeant A. Nakamura. The lead interrogator for this interview was Lieutenant Jameson, who also prepared the documents. The interview was conducted over a two-day period in [*text redacted*] in the Asakusa District.

Impressions of the interviewer: Mr. Funakoshi comes across as bright, articulate and mature. He is of a well-regarded Japanese family and his English is unusually good for an Oriental, no doubt a product of his time in the diplomatic corps. Toward the end of the interview, as he described the key events of July 20 and 21, his speech became noticeably halting and he looked uncomfortable. However, it was my impression, despite these signs of nervousness, that he answered my questions in an open and truthful manner and that his memory of events is as reliable as can reasonably be expected. (Lt. H. Jameson)

You understand that you are here to answer questions relating to the death of Dr. George Harvey, your superior in the CIE Section of SCAP. Please would you begin by describing your relationship with Dr. Harvey and the other members of CIE who joined your trip to the Chiba peninsula on July 20?

When the Pacific War broke out, I was studying anthropology at the University of Tokyo, and was lucky enough to obtain a position working for the diplomatic service in the staff of Shidehara Kijuro. After the Allied victory, this experience allowed me to secure a role with CIE as a research assistant. I have since worked under the supervision of Dr. Harvey, although day to day I have had more immediate contact with Mr. Reginald Pickford. He was a special research assistant and, as you know, the nephew of Dr. Harvey.

For the trip to the Chiba peninsula, I joined both Dr. Harvey and Mr. Pickford. The fourth member of our group was a servant girl named Kazue, who is seven or eight years old.

What was the purpose of your trip to the Chiba peninsula?

Dr. Harvey had received a commission from the Natural Resources Section of SCAP, a request to conduct some research on rural communities. The NRS was particularly interested in the organization of fisheries, for example the social and economic dominance of private boat owners and alternatives to the private boat owner system, such as cooperatives. So very early last Saturday, that is the 20th, I drove us out to the Chiba coast to the village of [*text redacted*].

As we got close to the village, we came past wheat fields and rice paddies. Then the road took us back to the coast, past offshore mudflats. It was low tide so the flats held some stranded boats. People were working in shallow water, *ama* and so on, diving girls collecting shellfish. We arrived at our destination in the middle of the afternoon. We were staying with an acquaintance of Dr. Harvey, a Japanese man who owns a small inn overlooking rocky water. I must apologize, but I cannot remember the exact address of the inn. I could draw a map?

We have details of the location and the proprietor's name. Please continue.

Of course. The owner – the proprietor – provided us with dinner that evening. It was an impressive banquet. We ate a good deal of sashimi, yellowtail tuna and salmon caught that day by the *ama*, and good sea urchin.

Did the group drink alcohol?

Yes. Dr. Harvey and Mr. Pickford had a number of cups of sake. Kazue ate in a different room close to the kitchens, but of course would not have consumed alcohol. I had three, perhaps four cups of sake myself. I would not say that anybody was very intoxicated, but we did drink.

At midnight, perhaps ten or twenty minutes past, we decided we were all tired. I had a small, shuttered room on the ground floor, at the back of the inn. Mr. Pickford and Dr. Harvey were sharing a large suite upstairs, simple but the best available. On my way to bed, I passed the servants' quarters, where the dirt floor was covered with sleeping mats. I looked in and saw Kazue sleeping on one of the mats. A few of the servants employed at the inn were also resting there.

I fell asleep very quickly that night. However, after a couple of hours, I woke. It was hot and dry in my room. I could hear a strange noise outside.

Please describe the noise you heard.

I thought I heard a deep voice shout something in English. It sounded like 'get us boy', or something similar. I still do not know for sure what was said. Part of me wonders whether I heard these things in a dream. But, at the time, I remember feeling very much awake – I could not get back to sleep. So I decided to investigate. I got dressed, put on some slippers, and took my trench knife in case there was danger outside.

I knew that I could access the veranda from the front of the inn. As I walked past the servants' quarters, I looked in and noticed that Kazue was no longer in there. This did not trouble me particularly.

Are you feeling unwell? You seem agitated all of a sudden. Sergeant Nakamura will get you some water.

I am fine, thank you. That will not be necessary.

I walked out onto the wooden veranda, which had a beautiful view of the sea in the daytime and led right up to the water's edge. But by night it was, of course, very dark. It was almost impossible to see anything. Over to my right, a mile or so up the coast, was the village harbor. The boats there were glowing silver in the moonlight. But in front of me, as I heard the second noise, it was almost pure black.

Please describe exactly what you heard. It is important that you omit nothing.

I thought perhaps it was the howl of a wild animal, and I was grateful to have my knife. It was coming from the water's edge. But the more I listened to the noise, the more human it sounded. I became convinced it was the howl of a person in extreme pain or grief. It was a horrible, terrible sound. Then my eyes started to adjust to the darkness. I could see a moving shape up ahead in the water.

I approached cautiously, until I got to a slight slope of stones where the water was lapping. I could see now that it was a man. He was slumped, kneeling. His head was on his chest and his knees and hands were in the water. The howling sound he was making grew fainter, then he went silent. I said something in Japanese, and he looked up, raising his arms as though terrified, or in order to surrender. I could see then that it was Mr. Pickford.

Sergeant Nakamura, would you be kind enough to get the interviewee a glass of water before we go any further?

Thank you, that is very kind.

When I saw that it was Mr. Pickford, I removed my house slippers and waded into the water to help him up. It was only shallow, it barely came halfway up my shins. The air smelt of copper and salt. Mr. Pickford, still kneeling, clung to my trouser leg when I got to his side. He was shivering, even though it was a hot night and the water wasn't cold. 'Mr. Pickford,' I said, 'have you been attacked?' Words to that effect. His chest was naked. His shirt was ripped so that it hung around his waist. I did not know what had happened. He looked almost drowned.

Mr. Pickford started weeping. I asked him again if he was all right. I used the name 'Satoshi', which was a name he liked me to use. It sounds strange, I know, but we had become friends and it was a Japanese nickname we grew to use. Anyway, he said nothing when I asked him questions. He stayed on his knees in the water. I tried to help him up, but he could not or would not move.

Then what happened?

He started rocking backward and forward, it seemed he had no control over his body. Something about the shape of his hand looked strange. I reached down to take it in mine, and he flinched when I touched it. I examined it as best I could in the darkness. The skin on the knuckles was cracked and weeping blood. He could not stretch out his fingers. After I let his hand go he kept it raised. Then he said, 'Over there,' and pointed to the right of the inn.

From what I now know, I realize that he was trying to point to where it had all happened. But at the time, all I could see in that direction was firewood.

I did not know what to do. I thought it best to get help from inside the inn. I left him and went to wake up Dr. Harvey. I kept knocking on Dr. Harvey's door, but there was no answer. I wondered if I had got the wrong room, so I went to wake the proprietor. In the ten or twenty minutes that followed, neither of us could find Dr. Harvey or Kazue.

Was that when you contacted Dr. Eddington?

Yes. I felt very strongly that I should contact one of my supervisors in the division as a matter of urgency. I knew that Dr. Eddington was in the village of [*text redacted*] only five or six kilometers away. I asked the proprietor to send one of his servants as a messenger to this village, to inform Dr. Eddington that something bad had happened, and that Dr. Harvey was missing.

While I waited for help, I waded back into the water and stayed with Mr. Pickford. I tried to get him to talk about what had happened, about whether he had been attacked and whether Dr. Harvey had been hurt too. He did not say anything. He kept rocking backward and forward. Sometimes he wept, sometimes he just looked blank.

Then, only an hour or two later, Dr. Eddington arrived with a number of Japanese assistants. He split us into two search parties to try and find Dr. Harvey. My party carried Mr. Pickford inside first, so that Dr. Eddington could talk to him, and then we headed west, as instructed, toward the harbor.

So you were not with the party that discovered Dr. Harvey's body?

No. My party did not find Kazue, either, although I understand she has now been located. That was the end of my involvement, for when I returned from our search around the harbor, Dr. Eddington informed me that Mr. Pickford had been taken back to Tokyo. Later that morning, I was sent back to SCAP headquarters.

At no point did Mr. Pickford speak to you about his involvement in what had occurred?

No. The only other information I have has been told to me in the course of these investigations. When I found Mr. Pickford in the water, he was not speaking coherently. He told me nothing of substance.

13

NOTHING COHERENT, nothing of substance.

A bilious forty-eight hours went by in the trapped air of my hotel room. It was too hot to breathe. The curtains were drawn and the lights were off and the radiators were surely on overdrive. I didn't move from my bed. Since reading the report I'd been sunk in this darkroom full of murky imaginings, the surface hardly stirring. The more pills I took, the more blood I saw on Satoshi's hands, and then my mother's hands, hands falling onto a concrete floor, heavy as guns.

When conscious, I tried to focus on the television screen floating in the corner. It wasn't tuned properly, but it offered some tempered light. At least there wasn't total darkness. In total darkness I would have woken every five minutes, wondering if I'd just been born. I couldn't have coped with that, with going back and living life all over again.

I took so many pills and they fuelled so many sick dreams. I took them whenever I found the energy to move an arm, washing them down with warm Pocari Sweat. I befriended the bellboy, Takeshi, the one who had brought me Chiyoko's fax. He seemed genuinely concerned for my welfare. I had it in my head that Takeshi and Watanabe were the same person; whatever happened, whatever would happen, he was a solid presence. He crossed the carpet to bring me drinks, and biscuits, and sleeping pills. Pills to mix with my pills. Each time he visited, I extended a timid fistful of money into the dry beyond, watching his shadow flood the sad blue walls. The rest of the time I lay in bed, banknotes nested under the soggy duvet, their edges scratching at my arms and legs.

The television really did have terrible reception. I kept staring at it, trying to make out what the programme was about, but all I saw was myself. Not me as a forty-one-year-old. Me at various moments in my life, glimpses of nebulous situations I had found myself in.

I still remember my past in fragments, as though viewed on a half-tuned television. Images bunch together, rolling and catching themselves in knots. There is no sequence, no narrative, just a succession of fragments.

In one fragment, I see myself as a child in my father's old office in the Square Mile. He is behind his finely finished desk, rummaging through a pile of papers, sheets flying out like a flock of white doves. His pinstriped arms struggle, comically, to cradle the pages in mid-air. His secretary, the one he eventually ran off with, is perched on the edge of the desk, slim nylon legs dangling down, breasts dangling down too, gravity winning as she leans in to assist with the paper-chase. The child version of me sits in an enormous antique chair on the other side of the room. The wood is scarred but my skin is blemish-free. Outside a storm is blowing; perhaps school is closed for the day, perhaps it is the day that a giant oak tree crushed the gates of St Joseph's Primary with thrilling aplomb.

Sketchy clusters of white pills fill the screen. My father stays but his face is changed. There is a new messiness in the skin around his eyes and nose. He is wearing the same suit but a different shirt, the collar softer than the previous one, button-down, and he is leaning on another stretch of polished wood. His desk is a dinner table now. Me, him, Chloe. He is buying us dinner at a place with spotless knives and forks and shimmering wine glasses the size of vases. We are toasting something but before our glasses clink my father fades away into a blur of chalky tablets and it's just the happy couple in the frame. We are sat at a table in our Guilford Street flat and my fingers are on the tawny skin of her arms. She is jigging a foot to and fro and her sandal is slapping the sole. There are glasses here too, a pair of them standing side by side, one containing champagne, the other brimming with carbonated water, and somehow the way the fizzy fluids hang suggests a world suspended partway between liquid and solid, the bubbles swimming up from nowhere, bringing extraordinary brightness. Chloe is stroking her stomach and laughing. Behind us is an open window, and some sheep, and children who seem to float in the green gleam of cut grass as summer slowly rolls across the city.

I blink the water from my eyes, then see a darker scene.

Chloe and I are in Greece, on holiday, a sticky August evening in 2005. Two tiny quivering figures in a packed nightclub, a mass of jigging bodies pressed together, like one machine with five hundred moving parts. And a band is playing on the stage. My skin is a mottled monochrome and I have empty rings under my eyes. I am in a sullen mood. Chloe has been moaning all night – she wanted to come, was insistent on coming, but now she's here she thinks it might not be a good place for someone in her condition, eighteen weeks pregnant, stomach fat with life. But I say she should live a little. My camera hangs around my neck, ready to document bald guys in black T-shirts running fat fingers over fretboards. I say what she always says to me, that we should live a little, and I cup a protective hand across my lens as a riff charges through the heaving room. Pyrotechnics go off behind the bassist, cylindrical things spitting out a controlled spray of sparks. And at first this seems to be the most entertaining part of the evening, until the lead guitarist's mouth droops as the sparks hit soundproofing foam in the drummer's alcove, until some fool turns to me and says, 'Yeah, awesome, this is awesome, catch it on camera,' tugging at the SLR strap, and I think, no, it's not awesome, this can't be part of the act. And I see Chloe's face crinkling and reddening with slow-burning fear. It tenses up and flares until it is unrecognisable, someone else's face entirely.

Only as the fire bursts across the ceiling and the grey smoke consumes the band do people start to panic. A minute, maybe less, and the whole room is glowing a hazy orange. The singer tumbles off the stage, engulfed in flames, flailing helplessly on a deck of sizzling amplifiers and crackling electrics. Fuck, not a stunt, not an awesome stunt. The rest of the band scuttle for the west exit but I take Chloe's hand and we run in the same direction as the mob. Here, come, outside. Everything grey, everything grey, coughing, running, holding on, and then her skin slips from my skin, it slips away.

Where is she, where, now, there. Reduced to a child's

half-phrases, a foreigner's shy stutter. Lost, lost. No way of seeing through the ghostly swaying mass. Someone on my arm, not her, a fragile woman falling slowly sideways, her voice and others, one the echo of the next, some confused fugue, hymn voices rising up to my ears. Can't find her, too many shapes glued together by debris and smoke and ash and people on the edges looking like banknotes in a breeze. Can't find her. A shoe flying up, a wallet drifting down. Can't find her. Can't find her in the smoked dead light, can't find myself, too drunk on the stink of burning beer, too tightly wrapped in the molten hum.

But I find the west exit, coughing up muck, I find it and I think that might be hers, that tiny black rucksack up ahead, ridden up on the back of a neck, blocking hair, blocking face. See that rucksack yards away going down the narrow steep stairwell with the slither of unburnt light at the bottom. Everyone tripping down there, heading for the gap in the doors, squeezed gouged pinched, black smoke billowing out of ears and mouths and eye sockets. The doors open outward but they are chained shut. Everyone is scrabbling to exit, everyone is a contortionist, but they are chained shut. And it happens so quickly – they pile up, one on top of the other, the falling on the already fallen, the awful smoked agony of boots and arms and muffled cries, and the rucksack gone from view, gone, I have lost it, I have lost her, lost, lost. I punch someone's head to make them easier to climb on. Lost, lost. A sharp object, a car key maybe, an intact shard of the everyday, gets thrust into my cheek. Lost and lost and lost. The bodies in front of me are liquefied now, dark blood spurting from my cheek in dying arcs, and everyone crumples, everyone loses, everyone on top of everyone. My camera lens digging into the small of a back and my lips mouthing 'Pregnant, no, she's pregnant, no' and my limbs becoming a grey strand in an unthinkable knot of darkness, a dark wriggling human knot, not a single ribbon of light between us.

And later, much later, gulping air that tastes of water, I am told she is gone and I am alive. The idea is too abstract to take hold.

The screen pulses darker, then darker again.

All kinds of images flicker, blended together in fast-forward. Too many to describe or identify, yet each of them in some way familiar. All these things in the mirrored surface of the television, all these images going back and forth. The familiar, faded reflections of familiar, faded lives, racing like leggy flames across the embellished glass.

'Mr Fossick, you need to get out of the bed today. The world is an oyster!'

It was a voice so near that it might have been coming from my own head. Perhaps it was Takeshi's. Perhaps he was throwing the curtains open. The wafer skin of my eyelids seemed to be soaking through with the yellow of the sun, the turquoise of the sky.

A window clicked open and I shivered in the light.

14

'I BET you reckon you're kinda enigmatic,' Chiyoko said, defrosting me in the warmth of her stare. 'Just turning up like this, without a word about where you've been these last two days.'

Something about the foyer of the Hotel Villa Dolly suggested an abandoned discotheque, circa 1985. She was standing under a trembling glitter ball in which the pink of her hair fragmented into a tropical palette, each shade ordered and clarified by the next.

'I'm not trying to be enigmatic,' I said. 'I'll tell you all about it if you like, but it might obfuscate things even more.'

'I don't even know what that word means.'

'There you go then, obfuscation in a nutshell.'

'Whatever. I thought you were a goner, Fossy.'

'I've been detoxing.'

'Detoxing?'

'Sort of, yes.'

'Looks like you've been sort of detoxing with some soy sauce.'

I followed her gaze to the strip of white T-Shirt flanked by my coat lapels. A trail of soy sauce ran from the neckline to the waist. I had spent pretty much all afternoon putting away platters of cooked fish, bowls of rice and strips of beef. A forty-eight-hour diet of custard creams and carbonated drinks had left my body insistent on sustenance.

'I guess you're right,' I conceded. 'There does seem to have been some soy sauce involved.'

She said, 'Fair enough, Mr Foss. Did you get my fax?'

'I did, thanks. It appears George did meet a grizzly end, as you predicted.'

'Yeah. I mean, I didn't read the report, obviously. It's none of my business what went on with your guy Satoshi. It just came up when I searched for George Harvey, so I thought I'd send it to you.'

A pool of early-evening light spread at my feet, soaking the suitcase to my left and the satchel to my right. Further into the foyer, sparse overhead strip lighting lent the mirrored walls a low-wattage glow.

She said, 'I see you're taking me up on that offer of a place to stay.'

'If the offer's still there I'd be grateful. Seems like an intriguing place you have here.'

'Kinda unusual, I guess. For you. But the love ho is a Japanese tradition.'

'The love what?'

'Love hotel. For people to get their rocks off. By the hour if they like. Not a whorehouse, you understand. Just a hotel with extra features. Vibrating beds and all that.'

'Vibrating beds?'

'Uh-huh. Plus karaoke machines, disposable dildos, indoor jacksies.'

'Jacksies?'

'Of course. People like to wash before jumping in the sack. Hygiene first, pleasure later.'

I cleared my throat. 'Do you mean jacuzzis?'

'Exactly. As I said, jacksies.'

I found it strangely comforting that there were some dark corners of the English language still outside her jurisdiction.

'So,' I said, 'you work here?'

'Sure do, Fossy.'

Chiyoko explained that the hotel was open day and night, but that she only did night shifts. She claimed this didn't render her exhausted at university. 'Basically I just sit behind that counter over there,' she said, 'mostly snoozing.' The counter she pointed to would have been at home in a high street bank, except that the glass screen between the customer and the employee was frosted.

She said, 'I don't even have to ask the customer what room they want.'

A mood-lit panel on a wall dealt with that. It had buttons bearing pictures of various rooms, each with their prices beneath – one price for a 'break', another for 'overnight'.

'We get frustrated salarymen having an affair, or going at it with some Chinese working girl. There's very rarely any trouble from guests. Love hos have been around for ages, since after the Second World War. Japanese families who ran simple lodgings would rent out their spare rooms to the occupation forces.'

I thought about Reginald Pickford for a second, about how he came to be in the water with bloodied hands.

'If there's any trouble,' Chiyoko continued, 'I just call for

138

Daisuke. He's the owner. A retired sumo wrestler who lives out back.'

'9 to 5' grated out of an exotic-looking Sony ghetto blaster, and — humming along to Dolly Parton's lyrics — Daisuke and Chiyoko danced around the dining area at the back of the hotel.

The difference in their respective sizes was comical. She was a tiny, waif-like thing. Daisuke, a heaving mound of thick limbs and turgid features, completely dwarfed her. Sitting in an easy chair, grinning between sips of green tea and drags of cigarette, I rolled my eyes across the contours of his flesh. It was the same texture as the long-weathered timber beams supporting the walls and ceiling. His hands were criss-crossed by dark veins that looked like dirt tracks, and everything about his appearance spoke of earthiness, hardness, endurance. He creaked across the blue-tiled floor like a giant ship making its way through choppy waters, and I watched from the mainland, included yet distanced, tapping my feet to a slightly different rhythm.

'Daisuke just *loves* Dorry Parton,' Daisuke beamed, delving a meaty hand into a bowl of peanuts on the windowsill. He turned the volume up a notch and exited the room backwards, deftly avoiding the ironing board standing by the door. Maybe it was just a peculiarity of his English accent, but he sounded incredibly camp. It was hard to reconcile the voice with the body. I whispered as much in Chiyoko's ear as she pulled up a plastic chair.

'Oh yeah,' she said loudly, 'he's gay as a window, old Daisuke.'

My spluttered laugh sent a fine spray of green tea across

my T-shirt. I stubbed my cigarette out in a Coca-Cola ashtray, put my mug down and inspected the damage. Its life as a white T-shirt was officially over.

'Gay as a what?'

Chiyoko smiled and said, 'It's an expression.'

'I see. Isn't it a bit unusual for a sumo wrestler to be homosexual?'

'Why do you think he gave it up? It's pretty homophobic, the sumo world. Once you're out, you're *out*. There was an incident, with another wrestler . . . he doesn't like to talk about it. He got a job managing this place, left his wrestling days behind him. Eventually bought it out and changed its name to Hotel Villa Dolly, on account of his being a super-big fan of Dolly Parton. In reality, he never wanted to wrestle. But he's from a long line of wrestlers, his family passed on the burden. He felt it was a thing he had to do.'

Daisuke returned to the room clutching a can of Diet Coke. He was flanked by two yelping dachshunds. They were as chubby as a baby's arms, their torsos seemingly tied tight at each end with invisible string. They went straight to Chiyoko, who scooped them up and stood there clutching them to her breasts.

'You like sausage dogs?' she asked.

I indicated that, overall, I was fairly neutral on sausage dogs.

'They're Daisuke's. This one,' she said, lifting one blank-looking dachshund into the air, 'is Fire, and this one on my left is Ice. Ice has silkier ears, see?'

I saw no discernible difference between the two dogs, but I nodded.

'Daisuke loves dogs,' said Daisuke.

Without warning, Chiyoko thrust the dachshunds into my arms. I held them for a minute or so, their tough paws fastened to my torso, before she took them back again.

'I'm surprised they're not both called "Dolly",' I said.

Daisuke frowned, setting off a domino effect that saw thick crease lines ripple downward from his brow, through his mouth, before finally settling in the folds of his chins. Clearly I'd said the wrong thing, but I was too busy looking for a resemblance between the dogs and their owner to worry too much about how I was perceived. The dachshunds didn't share Daisuke's creased skin and worn nose, but they had a similar way of wobbling across the floor.

'Daisuke's just bitter,' Chiyoko said. 'We tossed a coin and I got to name the dogs. Fire and Ice: it's the title of a poem by Robert Frost. Good poem. I'm a super-big Robert Frost fan, see.'

'Why such a big fan?'

'I love Tokyo, the possibilities of a huge city. But when I read, I kinda want to get away from the congestion. I want some privacy. I want to be in the countryside with a bunch of snowy trees.'

In the hotel office, a man with a speckled face was staring into an empty coffee cup. 'The early evening shift guy,' Chiyoko said, barely acknowledging him as he picked up his cup, bowed and walked past us. A few seconds later, through frosted glass, we saw his smudged form exiting the building.

I took a seat and we talked for hours, her night shift slowly unravelling into morning. The office was little more than a fair-sized cupboard behind the reception counter. There was one L-shaped pine desk. It propped up a luminous laptop wired to two security cameras out in the lobby. Besides the desk, the wooden floor bore my leather armchair and Chiyoko's wheeled office chair. The walls boasted a calendar bearing pictures of dogs in various states of excitement: pouncing, rolling, hanging. There was also a framed picture of Dolly Parton and a network of small wooden boxes housing room keys.

The first couple arrived at just gone two in the morning, teenagers arm in arm. We watched them cross the lobby on the laptop screen. He was dressed conservatively in jeans and a short-sleeved shirt. She wore thick lashings of bright white and black make-up around her eyes and mouth. Her wild, bleach-blonde locks were swept back with a thick headband that looked like it had been purchased in Disneyland. '*Yamanba*,' whispered Chiyoko. 'Bet they go for the karaoke room on the first floor.' The girl pressed an illuminated button on the wall-mounted panel and two high-pitched beeps emanated from the laptop.

'Told you – first floor written all over them.'

'Yamanba?'

'Yeah, it means . . . kinda like . . . a mountain hag? The girl has a particular style that makes her a mountain hag.'

'Mountain hag?'

'Yeah, that's English, right?'

'Technically, yes.'

We fell silent for a long while. The sound of a mountain hag yodelling into a microphone came dripping through the ceiling, then petered out. The only other noise was a background whirr from the streets outside, the inflated music of the night hissing into the early hours.

'So,' Chiyoko said, 'any more thoughts on how to find your man Satoshi? I assume you're still looking to deliver that mysterious parcel of yours?'

'Have you got anything to drink?'

'Um, sure.'

She opened a drawer and took out a small, flat bottle of whisky and two plastic cups. As she poured, the clock on the laptop screen behind her blinked its digital reading: 03:38. She handed me a cup and I breathed in the aroma, vanilla pods and crisp toast. The eventual taste on my tongue, a mordant fizz, was a disappointment.

'I've given it a bit of thought,' I said. 'I have his real name now, largely thanks to you. Reginald Pickford. I might try a few veterans' organisations, see if they can help me track him down.'

'Well,' Chiyoko said, wincing as she tipped some whisky into her mouth, 'I really hope it works out. I can see it means something to you, doing this for your mother.'

'Odd, isn't it? You spend your childhood trying to please your parents. Then, from puberty onwards, you just humour them and please yourself. But when they die . . .'

'Their views suddenly matter again?'

'Exactly. Full circle. But I guess you're still in the please-yourself phase.'

'Oh, I don't know about that, Fossy.'

'But they're alive, right?'

'Never knew my father. I mean, don't even know who he is. Mama's still alive. But it makes me sad talking about my parents, so let's change the subject.'

'You're going all bare minimum on me. That's my role. What does your mother do?'

'What does she do? What kind of question is that?'

'A pretty normal one. Career, occupation, job.'

'Mama used to work here. Now she's kinda retired.'

With that, Chiyoko swivelled round in her chair and started flicking nimble black fingernails across the laptop's keyboard. Realising the conversation was over, I retrieved *Psychologies of Defeat* from my suitcase. I'd need something to talk about, if I eventually met Satoshi.

It was another hour or so before we started talking again, this time about how Chiyoko was paying her way through her master's degree by working at the love hotel. She said the literature stuff was just for fun; she didn't want a career in writing or teaching. She planned to try and get a managerial position somewhere like the Shibuya Grand after graduating. 'But the thing is,' she said, 'I'm not sure I look right for the job. They're very superficial, those places.' I told her she was as pretty as any of the receptionists at the Shibuya Grand. 'I know that,' she said quickly, 'but the girls who work in those places have a specific look.' She wasn't sure that pink hair and black nail varnish would fit in. 'It's all about whitened teeth, Gucci handbags and manicured fingernails. You have to conform to the crowd.' I was about to agree that they had beautiful nails, but thought better of it.

Just then, a huge shadow washed over us. It was Daisuke's. He stood in the doorway to the office, a vigorous smile revising his face. He said something to Chiyoko in Japanese, then turned to me.

'Bedtime!' he announced, his face wobbling with a vibrato giggle.

'But it's not five thirty yet,' Chiyoko said. The fact she

addressed him in English made my eyes moist; I can't explain why.

'Daisuke can't sleep,' Daisuke said. 'So he might as well be here.'

Chiyoko stood up and said, '*Arigato gozaimasu.*'

He pounded across the floor and lowered himself into the chair she had sat in. He did so slowly, with extreme caution, like a circus elephant backing onto an absurdly undersized stool.

'Chiyoko show you the room,' he said.

After an uncomfortable thirty seconds in the hotel lift, which carried a maximum of three persons and played muzak Beethoven out of speakers nested in the metal ceiling, we arrived on the thirteenth floor. Chiyoko flung open the door to my new room, then stood in the middle of the carpet twirling the key card in her hand. I parked my suitcase and satchel.

Given I'd imagined a seedy cellar full of whips and leather swings, the reality of the love hotel room wasn't so bad. The bed didn't look like it vibrated, but it was of a size commensurate with its importance in such an establishment. It filled most of the room, and looked absurd next to a tiny window affording a postage-stamp view of the city. Besides the enormous bed, the only feature distinguishing this room from one in your average kitsch hotel was a rather sad-looking cabinet of sex toys bolted to a wall. The glazed contents looked like oversized penny sweets.

'How do you like it?'

'It's perfect. The toys are a nice touch, too.'

'Never know when they might come in handy,' she said,

sitting down on the bed and placing the palms of her hands on the tops of her thighs. Her denim jeans were wrinkle-free. She held that position for a few seconds but then, as if suddenly remembering something long forgotten, got up and wandered over to the window. She stood there, with her back to me, looking out at Tokyo.

Without breaking her gaze she said, 'Guess you're planning to spend tomorrow looking for Reginald. But how about we try and catch an early dinner together?'

'Dinner?'

'Yeah,' she said, pressing a forefinger against the pane of glass. The putty around the edges was broken and the enamel of the frame was furrowed. She inspected her fingertip, perhaps for signs of dust or condensation. 'I know a nice sushi place, in Omotesandō. Super simple. Only if you feel like it.'

'That . . . sounds good.'

'Good.'

'Good.'

I found myself sorting through the next few things I'd say, organising them into a sensible order, lining up small comments and asides.

She leaned into the window and said, 'Come check out the city. This is my favourite time of day, everything waking up.'

Slowly I moved up behind her, until the gap between my ruined T-shirt and the back of her sweater was as thin as an envelope. Her spine arched a little, but her hands lost vigour, the palms doing a soft swing backwards until the thumbs came to rest on my thighs. Some drowsy comment about the view from the window began to roll off my tongue and, by the time it had, one of her hands was relocating to the back of my neck. Her fingers drew my face forward, my eyebrow skimming a twist of pink hair, all the way down until my nose was millimetres from a turquoise earring. I closed my eyes and longed for a comforting smell. The smell of roast beef on a cold Sunday, the scent of fresh laundry on a rainy Monday, the uncut pages of a new book, the chemical tang of bathing photographs. But all I inhaled was unfamiliar perfume. She let her head drop back against my chest. Her backside pressed against the thickset strip of denim over my zip. I could hear the meter of her breathing, even and confident, and nothing else.

I waited for my penis to harden, but nothing happened.

I took a step back and looked over her shoulder, out of the window. Cars heaved across the tarmac ribbons that twist through Shibuya, reverberating amid the urban roar that lies on the other side of silence. A runny sun prepared its ascent over the city, wrapping the horizon in a thin band of liquid yellow. Jam-packed crowds merged together in the cramped corners of morning. They looked like so many identical insects, faceless, trudging, surviving.

Surely it would harden.

'I'm tired,' she said. 'Are you tired? I'd better head upstairs.'

I thought, That's the pills for you, they make everything numb.

I said, 'Won't you be going home?'

'Upstairs is my home,' she said, walking towards the door. 'I live here.'

15

I TOOK a bath because it was there. It was nearly eight, eight in the morning.

I lay bowed in the tub, hearing a shackle of car alarms ringing out into rush hour, unleashing their electric screams one by one. Alarms and false alarms, a million hunks of solid metal hard-wired for panic. It was strange to be lying so still, but feeling a sense of movement as the sirens pulsed through my bones. I ran some more hot water. Yesterday's courage, the worldly confidence required to get myself out of the Shibuya Grand and into this strange hotel, had evaporated. I was left with a terrible hollowness in my chest. The temperature in the bath approached perfection, on the verge of scalding hot. Beads of sweat burst on my face as I sunk in deeper. I started to think about the cordless phone in the next room. I should ring Freddie, see if she had remembered anything else about Satoshi that might help the search. At least tell her I'd made it to Tokyo, that I was trying my best. All around the room, droplets hung like jewels from low-slung chains of condensation. The heat was overpowering. I should ring Freddie. I grabbed a towel. It was the same shade of pink as Chiyoko's hair. I stepped out and went to the bathroom mirror, using the cotton to clear the glass, to see myself.

Sitting on a corner of the non-vibrating bed, staring alternately at the phone on the dressing table and the cabinet of sex toys hanging above it, my ears started to ring. I plugged them with my fingertips but the ringing continued to penetrate. It couldn't be a car alarm; the alarm was surely coming from inside me. Perhaps the heat had set off some new illness, a type of tinnitus. Either way, I was tensing up.

The tinnitus proved to be the soundtrack to which other, better-worn diseases played out: familiar nausea, similar fever, snarling my stomach and melting my top lip.

I needed pills.

I pulled on creased clothes and thought about my mother. She used to say that every person lives by their own sound-track, their own music, a unique rhythm and tone that defines them as a person. Yet my mother had kept her own music hidden; she had invented ways of muffling the sound. Not when the dementia drowned her out, but long before that, the slippery years in the family home. Even then, every-thing was locked away behind lists and rituals and piles of old mementos. She was quick, she was chatty, she was witty, but she never once told me anything about herself that mattered. I had the feeling that there was something constantly unsaid, an important absence, a shadow falling between us. Satoshi was just a grey edge of that sloping shadow; he gave a shape to all the things I didn't know, but the dark space was bigger than just him.

Where were my pills?

I was back in the bathroom, feeling dizzy, running my

hand across the top of a glass cabinet, barely looking any more but touching, hoping to touch plastic. I groped my way through a disconsolate mound of toiletries. Facecloths unfurled. Toilet rolls began to tumble into the sink, into the toilet, onto the floor. My chest gulped down steamy, bubble-bathed air. I tried to think of the familiar. *Cromer – Harrison – Sidmouth – Hampton – Heathcote –Wren – Calthorpe* – And then I remembered. I remembered to look in my suitcase. I hadn't unpacked the pills. I found them between balled socks, unscrewed a few lids with shaking hands, snapped tablets in two and threw halves into my mouth. There they went, foaming bitterly on my tongue, the drugs doing their righteous work. I gulped down a mouthful of bile-flavoured froth. I examined all the labels on all the bottles, taking comfort in the selection process, then eased the second half of two tablets in through the thin slot between my lips. I flinched with illicit pleasure as the anaesthetic fizz fouled my mouth. No more anxiety, very soon.

I took a piece of battered notepaper from my coat pocket and stared at Freddie's phone number. I lay on the bed, waiting. Waiting for images of my flat to come back to me, and the street names all around it. Waiting for everything to settle into a neat, still picture: familiar things, frozen and framed and at rest.

Covering the distance between the bed and the dressing table, past my satchel holding the package and the letters and the obituary and the Watanabe transcript, I felt a sunnier disposition taking hold. I picked up the phone and dialled Freddie's number.

'Oh, hang on, hello?'

She sounded groggy, her voice curdled by thick sleep, and I realised it was late in Longcross.

'Freddie, it's Foss. It's Rob.'

'Good Lord. I see. It's night-time, Robert. At this sort of hour I'm not quite with it. I don't expect to hear from people.'

'I'm sorry, I didn't think about the time difference.'

'The time difference?'

'I'm in Tokyo, Freddie.'

It took her a while, but then she said, 'That's splendid! Terrific news! With Mr Satoshi?'

I explained the developments to date and she made enthusiastic noises at appropriate junctures. When I referred to Satoshi's surname being Pickford, a carbonated laugh bubbled up the line. 'Pickford!' she said. 'Of course! Pickford! This would have been a lot easier if I could have remembered that blasted surname. I'm sure I shed memories every day, just like all this dead skin on my elbows. Why's it always elbows that dry up like that? I barely use mine. But anyway, wonderful to have his surname under your belt. A key clue.'

'Thing is, Freddie, I was hoping you might have some other . . . clues. Or perhaps know of a military organisation that can help me track him down.'

'Clues, clues . . . No, nothing I can think of. And veterans' organisations aren't really my cup of tea. But, as I say, I'm not at my best at this time of night. I'm all adrift.'

'I'm sorry about that, I didn't think. Perhaps I can give you the phone number for the hotel I'm staying at? In case you think of anything after you've had some rest.'

I read the telephone number from a sticker on the handset and, for good measure, the digits for the fax number too.

Although she was evidently groggy, struggling to find pen and paper and energy, I eventually heard Freddie scratch these details down. I confirmed three times that the hotel was indeed called Villa Dolly.

'Oh,' she said, 'I almost forgot. The woman from Oxfam called by the other day.'

'What woman from Oxfam?'

'Oh, the charity shop. The one that took your mother's old clothes and things. You know that red jacket of hers? The rather nice one. Made of linen. Yes. Embroidered with silver thread and gilt spangles. You must remember it. Fastens with bows of salmon-pink ribbon. She was wearing it the night before . . . Well, anyway, they found a letter in the pocket.'

'A letter?'

'Yes. Haven't read it of course. But it looks old. The pages are a bit grey yellow, a sort of foot-corn colour.'

I took an enormous lungful of air, about to leap into heavy water.

'Freddie,' I said, 'is there a fax machine in Finegold Mews?'

'A fax machine you say. A fax machine . . .'

After a minute or two she decided that there was a fax machine in the warden's office, and agreed to send me a copy of the letter.

'I suppose it'll have to wait until the morning.'

'Oh no,' she said, 'there's a warden working all hours. Might as well put my slippers on and bother her now. The night-shift warden doesn't have much to keep her busy. Boring job really, quite dull for the poor old dear. But I suppose everyone has to work, nine to five or not.'

Suddenly, as she said that last sentence, my ears popped. I found myself turning to look out of the room's one window. It was as if I had been in a car, in a tunnel deep underground, and now, after a slow, rattling ascent, that car was bursting out into wide sunshine. I thought back to the receptionist at Roppongi World Plaza. He said Satoshi went to work at 9 a.m. every day. And the obituary, Dr Harvey's obituary. It read like a catalogue of academic institutions and publications. Universities, books, articles. I had overlooked these lines of enquiry, these avenues, and yet they weren't so much avenues as fat motorways, autobahns marked by the painted light of a stuttering white line. How had I not thought to follow that line?

'Freddie, that would be great. If you could fax the letter the Oxfam woman found, that would be great.'

I said goodbye, put the phone down and sat on the edge of the bed. Then I stood up, looked out the window and sat on a different edge of the bed. I needed to tell someone about this latest development in the Satoshi search.

My first idea was to go down to the hotel office and sit with Daisuke, but once inside the lift I found myself staring at the button for floor 14, the only floor above my own. Before I knew it, the elevator was screeching upwards at my instruction.

There were two doors on the fourteenth floor, and one of them had a picture of Dolly Parton tacked to it. I knocked on the blank door. No answer. I was about to give up when it opened a crack, just wide enough to reveal a thin slither of Chiyoko's face. She rubbed her one visible eye and then, seeing that it was me standing there, let out a breathless shriek as if she'd been struck. In one fluid movement she slipped sideways through the opening and pulled the door shut behind her.

'I thought you were Daisuke,' she whispered, clutching shut her silken dressing gown, a silver pendant dancing in the shallow dip between her breasts. She was close enough that I could feel the quick tickle of her breath on my throat.

'Sorry, you were asleep.'

'No, no, I wasn't asleep.'

A noise came from inside the room. A sleepy groan. We both heard it. The skin around my eyes and nose became hot.

'I'm sorry, I'm interrupting.'

'No,' she said, 'really, it's fine.'

She muttered something else, but by now I was halfway back to the lift, finger diving for the button.

Downstairs in the hotel office, Daisuke was wedged in the leather armchair. In his dark clothes he seemed to have merged with the seat, to have succumbed to its immovability. I stood in the doorway, watching as he read a book from back to front. A blue coffee cup was embedded in his hand. It looked tiny there, swamped by the thick folds and pouches of his fingers. Music was coming from the laptop's speakers, the sole of his right shoe pounding the floor to the rhythm of 'Islands in the Stream'.

'Bee Gees classic,' I said.

As Daisuke glanced up from his book and grinned, I tensed and blinked and tried to stop thinking about Chiyoko having sex upstairs. Electric images of her with a boyfriend or husband or customer were bleaching every other detail around me. It was like driving straight into the sun, your windscreen half ablaze.

'Parton version better,' he said, provoking the obligatory nod and murmur from me. 'You need different room?'

'No. The room's great. I was just wondering if I could use your laptop.'

'Be your guest.'

I took a seat in the swivel chair and behind the laptop I saw, for the first time, a thin grey fax machine. I opened a window onto the Internet and tapped various words into a search engine ('reginald pickford anthropologist', 'reginald pickford academic', 'university japan pickford', 'japan anthropology pickford'). None of the results looked promising. Still, I could do a proper trawl of the university websites later. And through academic publications. Simple really, even for someone like me, an incompetent amateur detective soaked in grief and medicine.

Reflected in the laptop screen, I saw Daisuke put a bookmark in his paperback and place the book on his knee. I turned to face him.

'You like to read, Daisuke?'

'Yes. Daisuke likes reading.'

'I think I'd like to go to a library this morning. Know any big libraries?'

'Yes, know big libraries.'

'Daisuke, I just knocked on Chiyoko's bedroom door and . . . realised she had someone in there.'

'Oh,' Daisuke said, sucking the last dregs of coffee from his cup. 'I don't think Chiyoko-san was going to say about this yet.'

'No reason why she should. I just feel a bit embarrassed. I hope she didn't think . . .'

My voice tailed off, my thoughts found nowhere to go, and into the vacuum came the insistent beep and flash of the fax machine.

Frog Cottage,
7b Cotham Brow Road
Cotham
Bristol

10 September 1946

Flat 56, Rashleigh House
Thanet Street
London

Dear Alice,

It has been a long while since I saw you last and I hope my letter finds you well.

Sitting down to write this, I must admit that I still picture you as a young girl playing draughts with Reggie after school, not as the fine young woman you're now becoming. I have just paid a visit to your mother in Clifton. She tells me that you are staying with a friend at the above address now, that you have secured work at an agricultural college. How wonderful it must be to have the chance to soak up London and build an adult life there. How war has made us all grow older in so little time.

My dear, I have some news about Reggie to report. I received a knock at the door Monday last, and when I saw it was a telegram boy my heart broke. In an instant the clock wound back and I was preparing to receive the same words they gave me for Harry – killed in action, letter to follow. So I had a cry when the boy opened his mouth, when I realised that this time it was such better news.

The message said Reggie was returning home and, true to that promise, he has now arrived back in England. Ordinarily I would not interfere in his affairs. He is his own man now, after all. But I felt that you should know that he is safe and physically in good shape. I am sure he will write himself soon enough. He is recovering from difficulties, otherwise there is no doubt in my mind he would have written to you already.

I have just returned from visiting him. He is staying at a place called the Woodland Sanctuary on Belle Isle, Bowness-on-Windermere, in the Lake District. He is suffering from severe shock, they say. It is obvious that he has seen the Japs do terrible things and that these things have put a strain on his state of mind. Although he did not speak about it, I feel that it must have a lot to do with the death of his Uncle George. I assume you have heard about my brother. George was murdered. It seems likely some local savages killed him in an act of rebellion against the occupation forces, a brutal night-time attack on a quiet, unarmed man. It is quite horrific and a huge strain on us all – particularly Reggie, who it seems witnessed much of what happened. First his father, now George. It is a lot for a young man to come to terms with. We have lost so many good people in the war.

Reggie's superiors in Japan have sent him back on the condition that he spend at least two or three months in the Woodland Sanctuary, recuperating. The Sanctuary needed me to sign some consent forms for a course of insulin treatment, which apparently can work wonders. They are hopeful that he will recover fully and get his old self back. After the treatment I am certain that the two of you will be together. I know in my heart it is what Reggie still wants, and I cannot wait for the day when I welcome you into the family. In the meantime, no doubt a letter from you would do him the world of good.

Take care, my dear. I hope to see you very soon.

Yours sincerely,

Margaret Pickford

16

So he came back. That was the thought clogging my head as I stepped out of Daisuke's yellow Toyota Yaris, a car that looked like a well-sucked sherbet lemon. Something happened, and Satoshi, Reggie, whoever, came back to England. But had he come back to my mother?

Like a doting parent on the first day of a school term, Daisuke walked me up to the gates and pointed me in the right direction. There were energetic lines across his forehead and in the corners of his eyes, as if the Tokyo Metropolitan Library wasn't a safe place for a foreigner to visit.

He said, 'Chiyoko collects you for dinner at six.' Then he delivered a friendly shoulder slap that sent the SLR swinging round my neck in a wild fit. At some point I'd have to start using it, keep Perry smiling.

I joined a queue for the front desk and took in the surroundings. My eyes settled on a man descending a zigzag staircase on the north side of the room, a kind of indoor fire escape that offered no escape at all. He was the only moving image in a place of massive stillness. I watched him take each step carefully, cradling two fat pink hardbacks in his arms, hugging them to his chest like newborn babes.

Harsh panelled light from the high ceilings sent his shadow tripping downward ahead of him, and on the floor it met the cross-hatched imprint of the staircase, a diagonal dance of angles.

Expansive buildings often fill me with dread, but I have always felt at home in libraries. There was a small reference room at my secondary school, and I would while away my lunchtimes between the rows of books. The librarian was a woman called Shirley, memorable for keeping three small dogs secreted under her desk. 'Shirley and the shih-tzus': that's how she was universally known. If the stewardship of the school library came up in playground conversation, which admittedly it rarely did, librarian and dogs were treated as one unit. And yet Shirley laboured under the illusion that the dogs (Bonnie with the pink bow in the topknot of scalp fur, Bertie with the blue bow, Brian with no bow at all) were a secret that only she and I shared. Early on, I witnessed Bertie escaping from his cardboard basket. He began to eat *Far from the Madding Crowd*. A deal was struck: I would ignore the dogs, and she would ignore the fact that, against library protocol, I ate my packed lunch in the History aisle every day of the week.

When I got old enough to ride my bike around town – a beautiful Raleigh 3-speed with a hockey-stick chainguard – I used to visit public libraries. Weekends, week nights, school holidays: a library was generally where I could be found. Mum was nervous about this pastime. She had a colourful paranoid streak when I was small and it took time to fade. One minute she would be warning of the dangers posed by other library goers: 'Paedophiles are highly literate, you only have to read *Lolita* to realise that.' The next minute she was opining on library-related acts of God, quoting specious statistics to back up her claims: 'Every few seconds someone is killed by a falling book, Foss, every few seconds.' But in all the time I was holed up in reading rooms, no accident befell me. I dived into children's stories at first. But then biographies, histories, novels, photo books. I discovered Henri Cartier-Bresson and Walker Evans in libraries. You could just sit there and look at whatever you wanted.

'O-hi-o-goz-i-mus.'

It took me a second to switch from past to present, to realise I was at the front of the queue. A woman with avid veins in the bridge of her nose sat behind a counter. I half expected to hear muffled barks as her chair creaked forward to accommodate a seated bow.

'Good morning,' I replied.

'May I enquire,' she said, making the transition between languages without so much as a blink, 'as to whether this is your first time in the library?'

Her English was as impressive as Chiyoko's, but the accent, cut glass and antique, an entirely different idiom.

'It's my first time in this library, yes.'

A thin stack of reference cards suspended between her long fingers, she examined me with cautious warmth, thought puckering the skin between her eyes. The small plastic name tag pinned to her breast pocket told me, in raised lettering, that her name was Yasuko.

Yasuko gave me a detailed introduction to the services available at the library. She explained that a 'special feature' of the building was its four subject rooms: the General Reference Room on the first floor, the Social Science Room on the second, the Humanities Room on the third, and the

Natural Science Room on the fourth. There was a fifth floor which housed the 'Tokyo Room', a section comprising more than forty-three thousand volumes of local historical materials on Tokyo. Her voice seemed to wobble with pride as she pointed out that the Tokyo Room held the city's history right back to the year 1603, when the Tokugawa shogunate government was founded in Edo. Looking at the camera hanging around my neck, she made a point of emphasising that no flash photography was allowed.

She said, 'I suppose you will primarily be interested in the English-language titles?'

'How did you guess?'

'Oh,' she said quickly, 'I did not mean to imply that your Japanese linguistics were in any way lacking, or that the scope of your studies would be limited to –'

'Not at all. I speak no Japanese, so it's the English-language titles I will be looking at. The social science periodicals, in particular.'

She lifted her chin. '*Excellent*,' she said. 'I am of mixed Anglo-Japanese parentage, by the by. My father owns some land in West Sussex.'

Someone in the queue behind me cleared his throat, and I climbed the steps to the second floor without further ado, clutching at the handrail like a climber roped to a rock face.

I wandered between the vaulting stacks. Occasionally I picked out a Japanese hardback and fanned the pages, shafts of white space and puzzling data flickering out at me. An English book was tattooed with painstaking sketches of muscles, tendons and sinews. My mind jumped back again to those early schooldays, flicking through photo books and illustrated health manuals on the human form, stealing guilty glimpses of naked bodies, the prelude to adolescent torch-lit readings of Cleland and the dirtier chapters of Lawrence. A shelf ten yards away held a picket fence built from lanky English-language encyclopedias. Sections on the south wall sagged with economics, education, linguistics, modern history, ancient history, geography, psychology. I brought some of these books to my face and breathed in their air. Each released a different smell, the scent of a particular time or place, a dusty perfume that endured in the library's unique weather. Like good photographs, books can preserve something of the fleeting and unrepeatable moment in which they were created.

It was twenty-four hours since I had last slept, but every time the impulse to yawn creaked through my jaw I found a new corner of the library to engage with. I pressed the camera to my diaphragm, barely able to resist the temptation to photograph the slick multicoloured spines, flirt with unusual textures, trap meaningful aromas. I felt like I was rediscovering the intuitive tourism of childhood. I thought about stories I had read, stories that I wanted to read, stories that I had to possess, but also about Satoshi.

Something had happened. His narrative had gone off the rails, he had ended up in some kind of asylum. I wondered, not for the first time, about his involvement with George Harvey's death. Perhaps a local really had attacked Uncle George in that fishing village outside Tokyo, perhaps Satoshi had merely witnessed the murder, but somehow that explanation felt too bland, too neat, to be true. And then there was the fact of his bloodied knuckles. How could the mere act of bearing witness leave his hands in that state? I was consumed by an impulse to know the worst. The worst of his secrets, and the worst of my mother's too. Were they ever reunited, or did she spend the rest of her life, married years and subsequent decades alone, waiting? Waiting naively for his epic return, clearing the patio of weeds. He was on her mind, that October afternoon. His face may have been the last recognisable image she saw. His story drew her in, and now it pulled at me.

Squatting in the section devoted to English anthropology books, glancing at the hands of my watch, I realised that morning had already spun into afternoon. I scanned the spines for the name 'Pickford'. I also kept half an eye out for 'Satoshi', although that hardly seemed likely to herald anything.

'May I assist you in any way?'

The voice put period-drama emphasis on the vowels: eny wey. It was Yasuko, peering down at me as if through a microscope. I made an ungainly mess of creaking to my feet, the diminutive organism fidgeting under her magnified gaze.

I told her I was looking for any materials by an English academic named Pickford. First name Reggie, or Reg, or Reginald.

'May I ask if you know the title of any of his works?'

'Unfortunately I don't.'

'The academic institution that he works for?'

'No.'

'His publisher?'

'No.'

'Perhaps the date of publication?'

'Also no, I'm afraid.'

She scratched her chin, so I scratched mine.

Yasuko said, 'It is probably best practice for us to commence by utilising one of the computers over there, to search for any materials in Mr Pickford's name.'

She was full of good ideas. We started by searching for books. Two dozen results popped up if we put the name 'Pickford' in the 'author' field, but none appeared to have anything to do with anthropology. Still, to the extent that the titles sounded vaguely related to social science, I noted them down on abandoned printer paper. 'Reginald Pickford', 'Reg Pickford' and 'Reggie Pickford' yielded no results. There was a Roland Pickford, who had written a 726-page tome on the origins of social work back in the eighties (now in its fifth edition), but we disregarded him.

Then things improved drastically. We searched for periodicals rather than books, and a single result flashed up on our screen:

Crossing Cultural Borders: The Anthropology of War and Liberation, ed. by Dr P. Jenkins and Mr R. <u>Pickford</u>, *Japan Studies Series (no. 24), 2004.*

'That one!' I said.

Yasuko looked shocked by my outburst. She knew I had momentarily forgotten myself, that ordinarily I belonged in that category of person whose speech never warranted an exclamation mark. She printed out the entry and clicked through a couple more screens. 'Interestingly,' she said, 'Mr Pickford – according to our records – only edited this one edition of the periodical, back in 2004. It is a monthly periodical, but he only edited this single edition.'

'Can I look at it?'

'Well, one would hope so, let me see. Right . . . here we are. The only issues of the periodical which we keep on the premises were published after January 2005. So we would have to order Mr Pickford's edition from one of the other libraries in our network. But you will certainly be able to view it, following delivery.'

'Delivery? How long will that take?'

'No more than five working days.'

Working days. The concept was entirely lost on me. I was aware of the slinking shape of weeks and months, but I'd lost touch with the ways people like to cut and paint them.

I asked her if there was any way of speeding the process up.

'Well, that is not something that I . . . Let me think.'

A conspiratorial tremor edged across Yasuko's upper lip. Her features were vaguely defined, her hair perfumed with some mystical essential oil, but the veins in her nose looked more prominent than before.

'Perhaps less,' she said quietly, glancing side to side, 'given that it seems to be of such importance to you.' She looked down at the camera. It seemed that, in her eyes, it was a kind of badge of honour, a thing that made me deserving of flexible librarianship.

She asked if I wanted to take a look through the more recent monthly editions of *Crossing Cultural Borders*. 'Mr Pickford may have been a contributor to many,' she said, 'even if he only edited one.' Apparently authorship of individual articles didn't show up on the library search systems. I told her yes, I'd like to see them all, and she headed for the staircase, the straightness of her back emphasised by the curves and diagonals of the steps she descended.

Within two minutes she had re-emerged juggling four card-board boxes. 'Well,' she said, perhaps noticing me wincing at the sight of the stacked cardboard, 'you did ask for all of them, and there are two more back in the storage room.' She put the boxes down in a small reading room bookended on one side by a heavy red curtain and on the other by a display of newspapers, a patchwork of isolated headlines and pictures. As she disappeared to recover the remaining two boxes, I started digging through the periodicals.

The rest of the afternoon passed like this, with me foraging through paper, voraciously at first, then with creeping lethargy. Occasionally I wandered over to the computers and ran Internet searches. None of the universities' websites mentioned a Reginald Pickford, but then most of them only listed professors, not the full complement of staff.

Before I knew it, the minute hand of my watch had swung east, past the symmetry of six o'clock. I went down the stairs and out into a shifting crowd, a tapestry of boots, eyes, shirts, bags, glances. In the still centre, seeming to have a permanence that the drift of bodies around her could not claim, was Chiyoko – open-mouthed in the cold, tapping the digits strapped to her wrist. She said nothing as she took my hand and hailed a taxi. We ducked into the back and I soaked up the high-rise chaos towering over us, the muddle of six, eight, ten storeys, the insect antennas, the hunched street lamps, the buzzing signs, squat chimneys, converted lofts and neon shocks.

Why did I feel less terrified than before?

17

THE SUSHI restaurant was thin, smelt of warm wood and was presided over by an oxlike man in an apron. He shouted a full-tilt greeting as we entered, holding a knife theatrically high over an ice bed of tuna, salmon, eel, squid and other recently killed things. It was his scrutiny of us, rather than the weapon-wielding, that made me nervous.

'Daisuke loves knives. Has he showed you his collection yet? He's got knives from all over Japan. He uses them, he's a really good cook and stuff, but it's still a kinda weird thing to be obsessed with. I mean, a knife's just a bit of cutlery, right?'

'And Dolly is just a singer,' I said, taking a seat opposite her. 'And a dachshund is just a dog . . .'

'Fire and Ice are supercool. There's nothing weird about being obsessed with those guys. Anyway, on the subject of obsessions . . . are you making progress at the library?'

'I think so,' I said. 'I think I'm slowly closing in on him.'

'Uh-huh. And you reckon this article will point you in the right direction?'

'Hopefully. I have a name now, plus his letters. And soon I'll have a copy of his published work too.'

'And when you've found him, you'll go home.'

'When I've found him, I'll get to go home.'

We both started to speak at the same time, stopped, laughed, and sat looking at our surroundings. The restaurant wasn't busy and the exit wasn't far away, but I took the precaution of scanning each occupied table, each face with its figured frown or slack yawn, and making it all still and flat and fixed. If only I could do the same with my mother's past, I thought. Make it stop sliding around in my head.

'Listen,' I said. 'About knocking on your door.'

'Forget it.'

'Your boyfriend must think —'

'I don't have a boyfriend, Fossy. There are boys, of course there are. You think boys aren't going to fall for a girl like me? I'm a catch and a half. Some poor guys spend half their lives knocking on my door.'

She sat there smiling. I told her that nothing much seemed to faze her, and she asked me what it meant to be fazed. Then she asked how my Japanese was coming on.

'Not bad,' I said, unhooking the camera strap from my neck and picking up a red-tipped bottle of soy sauce. 'Here I have some *shōyu*.'

'Hmm . . . not quite.'

'What? The Bible said soy sauce was called *shōyu*. It definitely said that.'

'It's kinda right, but kinda wrong too.'

'I even used that word when I was eating in the Grand. The waiter didn't tell me it was wrong, and he was a waiter, a professional.'

'The same waiter who didn't tell you that you had *shōyu* all over your T-shirt?'

169

I mulled this over. 'The very same.'

'Well, to be fair, it *is* called *shōyu*. It's just that in little sushi places like this they call it a different name: *murasaki*. *Murasaki* ordinarily means "purple".'

'Purple?'

'Yeah, purple.'

I shrugged. At least in my flat I knew what everything was called: sofa; table; anglepoise; laptop; pills.

She said, 'What hope does a *gaijin* like you have, right? It's just there's a weird code for stuff in sushi restaurants.'

Chiyoko paused as the waitress placed two cups and two laminated menus on our table, then filled the cups with green tea.

'They have their own language, these places. For example, in here an egg is called *gyoku*, which actually means "jewel", and rice is called *shari*, which translates as "Buddha's bones". The code words change depending on the location of the restaurant. Take *shako*, for example. It's the name for a type of shrimp, but sometimes when people order it they just ask for *gareji* – garage – because *shako* also means a joint where you park your car.'

'All crystal clear.'

When the waitress returned, Chiyoko stared longingly at the menu and ordered an extensive selection of mysterious things. The waitress's face reconfigured with each item ordered, constantly lending itself to new adjectives.

'This place is a pretty decent sushi restaurant. It's cheap as you like, but they don't sacrifice quality. You like sushi?'

'Never had it.'

'What?'

'Nothing against it. I've just never eaten sushi before.'

'You're joking, right?'

'I'm not joking.'

'Sashimi?'

'No. None of that stuff. In the restaurant at the Shibuya Grand I just went for cooked fish, cooked meat. Seemed safer. And I don't eat out a great deal back home.'

'Wow,' Chiyoko muttered, 'never eaten sushi.'

It took her a while to compose herself before continuing.

'As I was saying, this place is good. But some of the conveyor-belt places, they mislabel stuff to make more money. Take tuna, for instance. There are two basic types: *maguro*, your sushi staple, and *toro*, the more expensive kind. There's been loads of scandal recently. Some sushi restaurants have been mixing red *maguro* with a special type of oil. The oil is a pale yellow colour, like margarine, and it turns the red *maguro* pink, so it looks like *toro*. All the oil kinda sinks into the middle of a piece of fake stuff like that, so the trick is to take a taste of the middle section before you gobble down all the evidence. There are whole books written about the science of fake sushi.'

'Do you read them?'

'More into reading my Bobby Frost, to be honest. Supposed to be writing a paper about him at the moment. Bet you're a closet poetry fan, huh? There's definitely some deep stuff going on behind those piercing eyes of yours.'

'My wife,' I said, wrong-footed by the mention of piercing eyes, tricked into a flustered response, 'she was into poetry.'

'So you were married once. Interesting. Now we're getting somewhere.'

Our food arrived on a wooden board. Chiyoko measured out soy sauce into a little white porcelain dish. She used the thicker ends of her chopsticks to transfer some sashimi onto a lacquered plate, then reversed them to eat. I did the same, clamping the tapered ends around a fat wedge of salmon and carefully lifting it. When it was just millimetres from my face the furled fish dropped into my soy dish, sputtering dark liquid everywhere.

'Watch that T-shirt,' she said, without looking up.

'Thanks, I will.'

I set about the business of wiping down my camera with a napkin.

'So. Tell me about your wife.'

So. Mum had liked to shift conversations the same way. We would be talking about rainfall, about weedkiller, about vitamin D, and then she would drop that word 'so'. A day-glo word bringing dazzlement to comfortable, shadowy conversations. So: are you thinking about finding a permanent contract with a publication?; are you sure she's happy with you going on shoots?; did you send your father a birthday card? As if the questions had a logical connection to what went before them.

'What do you want to know?'

'Something that's a bit more than nothing.'

'Is that another quote?'

'No, that's just me.'

'She liked poetry.'

A sense of out-of-placeness, of lostness, dragged at my tongue.

'OK, yep. Told me that already. What kind of poetry?'

'Romantic poetry. Did a PhD in Romantic poetry, in fact.'

'A girl after my own heart! That's cool. I like Romantic poetry. Wordsworth. Daffodils are my favourite flowers. And?'

'And she quite liked Frost. Though he doesn't count as a Romantic poet, I suppose.'

'Uh-huh. At least that's what I think. Some people would say he's a Romantic, but I reckon he's more of a realist. My lecturer says Frost captures the fears and miscommunications that keep people apart. There are photographers who can do that too, right?'

'The good ones can, the great ones. Take that empty chair over there. An average photographer would see a lifeless thing, a piece of dead furniture that signifies nothing. But a great photographer might photograph empty chairs all day. They might capture the ways in which chairs move here and there, crowd together and disperse, congregate in all sorts of ways, reconfiguring themselves according to the needs of their sitters. They could photograph a chair outside this restaurant, then photograph it again as it travels inside for the night, then again as it rests upturned on this table. And those images could tell you a lot about the life of chairs, but also about the people and places they adapt themselves to.'

'You see the potential of the chair, Fossy. So I reckon you must be a great photographer.'

'My photos have been dead for years. Fireless things that don't capture anything. With me, a chair's a chair. I've lost the knack of appreciating this person or that person, this place or that place. It's a hard skill to recover once it's gone.'

'You keep the camera with you, though. In case you get the urge.'

'In the hope I get the urge.'

Chiyoko crammed a large piece of soy-soaked tuna into her mouth. I picked a matching piece. It tasted warmer and softer than I had expected. *Toro* or *maguro*, I couldn't be sure.

She said, 'Did you photograph your wife a lot?'

'Yes.'

'How did it end, between you and her?'

'Badly. How else do these things end?'

'You forget that I'm only twenty-four. What do I know about endings?'

'Don't pretend,' I said, successfully depositing a chunk of sea-bleached fish onto my tongue, feeling it dissolve artlessly, 'that you're not more world-wise than your years.'

'Well, a girl can pretend every now and then. It's half the fun. Did one of you have an affair? Or did you just *grow apart*?'

A woman appeared in glistening rainwear, bringing news that the weather outside had turned. I saw green-tea steam rouge Chiyoko's face. I said, 'She died. She was pregnant, and we were on holiday in Greece. There was an accident, a pile-up of people.'

Chiyoko put a hand over her mouth and spoke through her fingers. 'I'm so sorry.'

'No need to be.'

'God.'

'It's fine.'

'Is that . . . Is that when you got that scar on your cheek, in the accident?'

'I'm not bothered by it.'

'Of course. It's only a super-small scar. I just wondered. Scars add character to a guy's face, anyway. Some celebs have fake ones put on.'

She carried on talking about scars. I was listening to her, but only at the edges. I could hear the helpless, twisted rush of the crowd squirming deep in my memory. I could see them too, the victims becoming one, a Chinese whisper of movements. Then the human shape dissolved into an expanse of still water, leaving only one solid figure: Satoshi, kneeling in the middle, his hands pressing down on the moonlit surface.

'And . . . you haven't had kids since? I mean, you don't have kids with anyone else?'

'No. No kids, no girlfriend. It's been a while since I've gone out and met any new people.'

'You're meeting new people now.'

'Strange but true.'

She said, 'I'm sorry about bringing up your wife. I have a habit of putting my feet in my mouth sometimes. It's just . . . why are you laughing?'

'Nothing. And if you've got any other questions, feel free to ask.'

'Well . . . your father. You haven't talked about your father much. But only if you want to talk about him, of course.'

'There's not much to say about Dad. He spent a few years screwing his secretary and then Mum found out. The standard blueprint for a middle-class affair. It got round the entire neighbourhood, and much to their consternation Mum forgave him. So he did it again, then moved to the States with the new love of his life. After his money, of course. Nice enough, as it happens, but her skin breathes avarice. She's Uruguayan. Desiree, Dauphinoise, some potatoish name like that. Half his age. The two of them send me the odd postcard.'

'Well, at least that's kinda nice? And as for the age thing –'

'He's a weak man, my dad. The worst kind of weak, because he won't tolerate weakness in anyone else. After I married Chloe, he and I became a bit closer again. He even stayed with us a couple of times. But then the accident happened. He gave me about a fortnight's breathing space afterwards. Then, I'll tell you what he said, he said: "Robert, extended mourning is just a category of self-pity.""

'Wow. But . . . well, he's still your dad, right? I mean, I don't think a person can turn their back on their parents, whatever they've done. That's one of the things that struck me about you that first day . . . you were prepared to put everything on hold to do this thing for your mother.'

'Everything was pretty much on hold anyway. Let's have some more green tea.'

We had some more green tea and Chiyoko ordered extra sushi. 'Just ten or twelve pieces,' she said. I sat back and watched her dispose of them with quick graceful flicks of finger and wood. After she had chewed the last piece, the movement of her jaw substituting for speech, she signalled for the bill.

As our taxi pressed us towards the Villa Dolly in time for Chiyoko's shift to start, a sluggish melancholy thickened in my veins. I looked out at the choked neon of the street, the grey rain falling in sheets across the city. I thought about the Gray's Inn Road. My point of departure felt so distant that I wondered if I would ever find my way back to it. I closed my eyes and saw Satoshi's hands. No gesture, no sign, just the anonymous backs of his hands. If the palms were facing me they might have been telling me to stop; if they were curved towards him they might have been beckoning me forward. As it was, they were just hands. They might as well have belonged to a dead man.

* * *

With morbid images still juddering behind my eyes we entered the hotel. One of Daisuke's booming greetings sounded out from behind the reception desk. Chiyoko headed upstairs to take a shower, and I went to join him in the hotel office.

He sat in the swivel chair, sharpening a large knife with a chrome contraption, listening to Dolly Parton, one of the sleepy sausage dogs nuzzling a limp lace from his shoe. His face wore that artless half-smile people have when they are fully happy. The sight of a smile like that was so arresting to me that, for a second, I didn't notice the gaunt figure sitting in the armchair next to him.

She was squinting at the pages of a magazine. Her back was supported by a thick pillow and her knees were covered by a red blanket, its deep colour emphasising the yellow-grey of her slack skin. I guessed from her hair, dry and thin but free of silver strands, that she was in her forties or fifties. But other aspects of her appearance, particularly the deflated face and trembling hands, suggested a much older woman.

'Her name is Kagami,' Daisuke said, producing a fold-down chair for me. 'Kagami-san, this is a friend of Chiyoko-san. His name is Fuss.'

Kagami looked up from her magazine and gave me an exhausted smile. She adjusted her position slightly and the glossy paper slipped from her wasted fingers, causing Fire (or was it Ice?) to jolt awkwardly onto all four paws. She looked down at the dog with such a studied sadness, as if causing this disturbance was too much to bear.

'Her English not so good,' Daisuke said.

'Is Kagami a relative of yours?'

'No,' he said. 'She sits with me sometimes.'

When the Dolly Parton album ended, Daisuke produced a box of chocolates from a drawer and we sat there eating them. He made Kagami's choices for her, carefully matching individual shapes and patterns to the card in the box. She sucked on the soft-centred ones, and as she did so her eyes seemed to become too big for their sockets. Her facial expressions, shuffling between fear and joy and surprise, made it seem like she had never eaten anything before this moment. But the sound she made when eating was the same as the sound we made. The tiny saliva slurp. The small deep gulp.

In the lift up to the thirteenth floor, my ears were full of these sounds. I have a vivid memory of them even now, the noises we made eating chocolates in that room.

Give or take a few minor details, each of the three days that followed was a rehearsal for the next.

On those three days, I woke at around eleven, a few hours of fitful sleep behind me. Morning slowly soaked through the love hotel's economy curtains, turning the vast, rumpled bed sheets into a crinkly mess of light and shade. My first conscious act was to prop myself up on a pillow and read one of Satoshi's letters, or the one from his mother, or the Watanabe transcript, or Harvey's obituary. I found myself smoothing the paper with my palms, as if trying to erase all evidence of previous readings. Before getting out of bed, I generally had a go at masturbating, with limited success. Sometimes I thought of Chiyoko. Mostly I focused on some imagined picture of amateurish erotica. Then I popped half a pill, showered and joined Daisuke for a breakfast of eggs and ham. I was increasingly happy in the love hotel's chrome kitchen, yawning and smelling coffee, watching Fire and Ice wobble around, my hunger growing as I began to take fewer drugs. Chiyoko packed her handbag in a panic and ran past the breakfast table, playing out a routine that involved grabbing a slice of toast from my plate. Once she had left for lectures, Daisuke drove me to the library in the yellow Yaris. I spent hours there, flicking painstakingly through old editions of *Crossing Cultural Borders*, hoping that one of the academic pieces would be by a Mr R. Pickford. I ploughed on without success, taking breaks only to use the toilet or visit the 7–Eleven across the road. Other highlights of my daylight routine? An occasional visit to the fifth floor, to take in the scent of the rare books there. I liked to breathe in the Kaga Collection and the Morohashi Collection. I had one or two attacks, mostly when I remembered old attacks. Generally, though, the panic stayed suspended in the air around me, closing in less often that it had used to.

In the evenings, I ate with Chiyoko and then joined her in the office. We stayed up together, talking and watching customers in various states of embarrassment and lust. We laughed at the baby voices these strangers exchanged when they thought no one could hear. It was Chiyoko's favourite thing to speculate on their secret lives, and when I tried to ask about people she might know better, like Daisuke's emaciated friend Kagami, it was mostly without success. She would say something short and toneless – 'Kagami likes chocolates and has cancer' – and before I could think about how sad those two facts were, sitting side by side in the same sentence, she would begin describing how that businessman with the designer tie was into whips and chains.

When all this talk became too much, I went to my room and smoked and bathed and pestered Freddie with phone calls, urging her to try and remember more about Satoshi. 'I'm afraid I can't tell you what you need to know,' she said. I used the hotel laptop to send a couple of encouraging emails to Perry, not mentioning that I was trying to bring another project to a close before starting on his. Occasionally I also used the laptop to check BBC news. Mostly, though, I stayed ignorant of whatever predictions and alerts freighted the airwaves.

At around five in the morning, just before Chiyoko's shift finished and Daisuke took over, I called it a night. It seemed sensible to retire just before she did. I brushed my teeth, I took a look at the package, I wondered whether it would ever be delivered, and I turned out the lights.

Three days and nights like this. Each an echo, an elaboration, a repetition of the last.

Then, on the afternoon of the fourth day, the journal edited by Satoshi arrived. With that, everything changed.

18

IT IS a beautiful thing, window-gazing. Strange how I'd forgotten that.

'Looks arctic out there,' I said to Chiyoko. But she had already fallen back to sleep, leaving me to stare out at the endless expanse of snow beyond the train's rattling glass. So much of it: a gratuitous surplus, more than any place needs. It was strangely liberating being in the carriage, restricted by both the route and the window. Unable to veer off course, I watched the island of Hokkaidō unfold in a single self-contained frame. Soon Sapporo, its grit-covered capital, would reveal itself. But for now urban life belonged to a different world entirely.

I felt relaxed, except in my legs. They seemed to have seized up with lactic acid, as if I'd been running all night. Yet we were being delivered to Satoshi with minimal effort: a taxi had taken us from Villa Dolly to the train station, and now the Hokutosei sleeper train was slinking us through the padded forests and white mountain-tilts of Japan's seismic north. Us and our belongings: the suitcases in the luggage hold, Chiyoko's shoulder bag and garment bag and laptop bag, and the satchel pinched between my feet. A snowball sun illuminated all of these things, except for the satchel. The satchel took shelter in Chiyoko's cool shadow. The contents included the package, which had started to smell faintly of baby wipes, and the wad of other documents uncovered to date. All these valuables were wrapped up in my unsalvageable, soy-stained T-shirt. And there was one new addition which I had yet to wrap up with them: on the little fold-out table in front of me, weighed down by a bottle of Pocari Sweat, was a dark photocopy of an article by Mr R. Pickford and Dr P. Jenkins.

The article. As well as co-editing the journal, they had written one of the articles together. It was, as I had discovered in the library the previous day, a fairly bland thought piece on how the Second World War created a series of new 'spaces' – discursive, geographical, ideological – in which anthropologists could study fundamental elements of human nature. The meatiest paragraph contained a set of questions which the authors said they hoped to explore in a series of future articles: what were the connections between war and anthropology in the nineteenth and twentieth centuries?; how did wartime contexts affect the nature of anthropological study and its institutional development?; how did work in occupied territories or prison camps progress anthropology as an academic discipline? If Satoshi and his co-author ever answered these questions, it wasn't in a future edition of Crossing Cultural Borders.

No matter. The exciting bit was nested in the italicised text underneath the main body of the article.

Dr Patrick Jenkins is a Visiting Professor of Anthropology at the University of Hokkaidō, Japan, and past-Chair of the African Studies Program at the University of British Columbia.

He has held academic appointments at Harvard, the University of Toronto, and Rutgers, and a research position at the Center for Advanced Studies in the Behavioral Sciences, Stanford. He has lectured at over twenty universities in North America, Europe, Africa, Japan and Australia.

So far, so good. Congratulations to Dr Jenkins on his illustrious career. But then a few words which, when I first read them over Yasuko's shoulder, brought a wide marvelling smile to my face.

Mr Reginald Pickford is a British-born academic who has lived in Japan for most of his life. After the Second World War, he worked in Tokyo for the Civil Information and Education arm of the Supreme Commander Allied Powers. During this time he carried out customised anthropological research for occupation forces and Japanese government agencies. He now lectures at the University of Hokkaidō.

For a long while I stared at these words, ignoring Yasuko completely, not moving an inch. Only through silence and stillness could I keep from disturbing the dramatic air that the discovery had brought to the reading room.

Even if he had left the University of Hokkaidō in the five years since the article was published, someone in the city of Sapporo would know where he was living.

Perhaps phoning ahead would have made sense, but the impulse to jump on the first train up north had been irresistible. No sleeper compartments left, just these stiff seats, but it didn't matter. Sometimes spontaneous travel was the only answer, or so Chiyoko said. It made sense that Chiyoko —

outgoing, energetic and curious about the world – would hold this view. But I was still surprised when she said she wanted to join me on my trip. It seemed that Daisuke sealed her decision. He kept saying that she needed a break, that it had been two years since her last holiday, and she looked at him with huge earnest eyes as he promised to take care of everything at Villa Dolly. He told Early Evening Shift Guy to cover her slots in the office, and Early Evening Shift Guy – on hearing this news – looked no more crushed than usual. It occurred to me that this depressed-looking twenty-something might have been the person in Chiyoko's room that first night, but he was one of those people who seem to lack the energy to blink, let alone conduct a fling with a beautiful girl.

When we arrived at Sapporo station, swapping the gentle sway of the train carriage for the thick twitch of bodies on the platform, I had a brief setback. The usual narrative of syrupy phlegm, dizzy spells, abridged heartbeats, jostling teeth. It took half an hour of solitary confinement in the station toilets – taking deep stale breaths, staring at the cubicle walls, going through the streets that flank the Gray's Inn Road – before the panic thinned and cooled. When I re-emerged, the first thing I saw was Chiyoko's face, pink with impatience.

'What's up with you, huh? Leaving a girl hanging like this is not cool.'

'Sorry,' I said. 'It's been a sixteen-hour journey, though. What's another thirty minutes?'

'I was bored of the landscape. Then I got bored of sleeping. Now I'm bored of standing outside this toilet.'

We spent a tense half-hour walking the streets in silence. Somehow I ended up wheeling her suitcase as well as mine.

I assumed she had a destination in mind, a hotel district or a tourist information office, but I didn't ask and I didn't particularly care. My panic quota for the day had already been exhausted, and I felt a fuzzy contentment. It was like this when an attack slipped from the present into the past. Something enabling happened; I was free of one less worry. Not that there weren't other concerns. I was troubled by my lack of warm clothing, for a start. I wasn't prepared for the weather to be so savage in comparison with Tokyo. The freezing air groaned unrelentingly through my bones and the misty sun, a symbolist blur of yellows and oranges, seemed to radiate no heat. We walked north but my eyes were drawn west, towards a road heading out of town. The line of the kerb was punctuated, every five yards or so, by mounds of dirty ice. Blasts of powdered air let out shrill sounds as they tore between the peaks. After the crowds of Tokyo, it was odd to see roads like this disappearing into the horizon, mystically fogged.

Fifteen minutes into our hike, we stopped in the middle of the blanched pavement so that I could delve into my satchel. I removed the stained T-shirt, leaving the papers and the package naked against the rough leather, ripped it down the middle and wrapped the limp cotton around my neck. Chiyoko watched with smug detachment as I performed the operation. She wore a series of scarves, earmuffs, jumpers, hats and gloves.

'I'm snug as a bag in a rug,' she said.

'It's a bug,' I said frostily. 'Snug as a *bug*.'

We dipped our heads down low and walked into the carping wind.

*   *   *

'I didn't know you'd booked somewhere.'

'Well, I did,' Chiyoko said. 'Sorted it all back at Dolly. A friend of Daisuke's knows the manager, so we get a discount.'

I had hoped for something on the outskirts, in the countryside, but she had found the busiest street in Sapporo. I stared up at the gleaming tower of tinted glass, its dark grey windows floating like monoliths above us. 'How big a discount?'

'How am I supposed to know? Stop worrying, Fossy Wossy.'

I shot her a look.

She looked back at me and said, 'It'll be nice to stay somewhere special. Before you know it, you'll have given that Satoshi guy his package, taken a pic or two, and be back in that bachelor pad in London. What are you going to use your cash for there, huh?'

'Fine,' I said. 'Let's see what my meagre savings are good for.'

We walked through the revolving door and entered the foyer. It was already decorated for Christmas, a teeming palette of reds, whites and greens. There was a hideous soft pile rug on the floor. A small child in a fur hat with lowered flaps was sitting on it. His arms were crossed and his bottom lip was out. He looked like he was engaged in some form of anti-chair protest.

'Don't you just dream of being able to stay in places like this the whole time?'

I told her my dreams were hazy things, but I supposed an upmarket hotel might have a place in some of them.

We were quickly accosted by a member of staff who repeatedly sucked in her cheeks. Shrewdly, she turned her attention to Chiyoko. Words were exchanged. With assistance from a tight-jacketed bellboy, we took a glass lift up to the twenty-second floor. One of the transparent panels faced straight out onto Sapporo, framing frightening chunks of text and girders that seemed to have floated free of the city. Not as many synthetic signs as Tokyo, but still flickers of Sony, Suntory, Canon, Kirin, Honda. Shreds of primitive language adrift in a foreign sky. I felt like I was adrift too, in some space capsule high above the curves and grades of the earth.

The doors opened. Chiyoko and the bellboy charged down the corridor, wheeling suitcases behind them at double speed. I followed at a slower pace, bogged down in money-related thoughts. I wondered if I should take some pictures of Hokkaidō's street signs for Perry. I could shoot random adverts and warnings from different angles, obsessively duplicating them as Evans had done in the seventies. He'd started by pointing his Polaroid at anything that looked meaningless. Surely I could manage that.

It wasn't a bad room. But, whichever way you looked at it, there was only one bed. A double, granted. But only one.

'Maybe we should call after that bellboy,' I suggested. 'Or ring reception.'

I parked my suitcase on the stocky carpet, the carpet that was costing me the earth.

'What's that, Fossy?'

'You know, tell them there's been a mistake with the room. Mention about the bed.'

'There's only this room available,' she said, hanging various skirts in the wardrobe.

* * *

I was anxious to get to the university before dark, but Chiyoko insisted on conducting a tour of Sapporo first. As we wandered, I searched for street names. I found more than in Tokyo, and the area struck me as easier to navigate. It was laid out in a grid pattern, and Chiyoko explained that blocks were labelled north, south, east and west around the central point of the city's compass, the Television Tower, a red and white construction built in the mode of the Eiffel Tower. Unlike its Parisian relative there was a four-sided digital clock halfway up the structure. It hung there, flashing hours and minutes in all directions. Underneath, on concrete patterned by shadow-girders, people in thick clothes sold souvenir statuettes to sharp-elbowed tourists.

To my relief, we walked west, away from the sightseeing throng, until we came across a second-hand shop that sold me a scarf, a hat and some gloves. Since the only colour available for all three was a psychedelic lavender, I found myself momentarily see-sawing between vanity and necessity. Eventually I came down on the side of the latter, but with the heavy reluctance of a self-conscious teenager. It wasn't that I minded being seen as a fool, it was just that my preference was not to be seen at all. There are some clothes under which you can forget who you are and quietly connect yourself to the next man and the man after that. Funeral clothes, for instance. At Mum's, Longcross Church had been crammed with individuals connected by blackness, one ending where the other began. I knew that wouldn't work with lavender.

Outside the shop, I put on the hat and gloves, then started packing the scarf into the neck of my jumper.

Chiyoko said, 'At least they all match, huh?'

'This is true.'

I pulled a loose thread hanging from one of my gloves. A disconcerting length of wool made a coiled dive for the pavement.

'You know what, Fossy? I want to go to a bar and get super drunk.'

I said, 'We need to go to the university first.'

'Everything will be closed by the time we get there. You know these professors. Fresh start tomorrow, huh? Then we'll be efficient.'

'I want to find Satoshi, get it over with. Then I can get some proper photography done. So far I've got a shot of my suitcase, that's it.'

'He can wait. So can the pictures.'

'Normally I'd agree. I'm a great advocate of waiting. But today's an exception.'

'Come *on*, Foss Doss. It's getting dark. There's no point us going now, running around campus like headless dicks.'

'Headless what?'

'Headless dicks. It's an expression, right? A dick's a type of chicken.'

'You're thinking of a "cock",' I said, looking for some wobble of embarrassment in her pupils. There was none.

'Whatever. In the meantime, I know this great bar. It does these drinks with little flakes of gold in them.'

'Will there be hordes of people there?'

'Sure. That's the idea, right? The Japanese dream. Urban living. That's what I love about big cities – completely different people brought together in a small space, all getting stupidly drunk.'

*   *   *

189

Despite my protests, we hit the bar.

Chiyoko began by lining up shots of clear liqueur flecked with gold flotsam. It didn't come cheap. After a few gritty mouthfuls we graduated to beer and tequila and whisky. We started talking about Satoshi and my mother. I ended up telling her more than I intended to. It was probably a combination of factors: the skill with which she drew me out, the warmth of the alcohol on my tongue, and the heady pleasure that comes with broadcasting your feelings after years stuck on mute.

To start with, the tables around us were living things, hunched and throbbing. They were swamped with liquid groups of salarymen chugging lager and laughing like helium-pumped children's entertainers. But one by one, in surreal fashion, they fell asleep at their tables, rippling into stillness. Eventually the whole bar became a low-lit morgue of bodies slumped among brown glass bottles. As Chiyoko and I ordered some plum wine, a few of them crept, zombie-like, into the beckoning darkness of the street. By midnight it was just us, a few other stragglers, and the entertainment – a dinner-suited Japanese man who continued to play a Casio keyboard in the corner. After bashing out a number of memorable versions of 'the hits of Eric Crapton', he went through the Derek and the Dominos back catalogue, mangling the words to 'Layla'.

Chiyoko looked straight at me and said something. The expression on her face suggested it was a meaningful comment, but the words themselves were drowned out by distant, brawling vocals: 'Layla, you garrotte me on my nose. Layla . . .'

At some point, everything goes out of focus.

19

I TOOK a sip of Pocari Sweat and readjusted my pillow, trying to outmanoeuvre the pain in my jaw.

'Seriously,' Chiyoko said, rolling onto her side. 'I just came out, and you were there on the floor. It was *so* funny.'

'It doesn't sound like me, though. That's the thing.'

'It was definitely you, Fossy. I practically carried you out of there.'

'I'm on some medication at the moment. Probably something to do with that.'

'And the drinking.'

'And the drinking.'

It must have been close to 6 a.m., in the double bed I couldn't afford. I was wearing socks and a watch. A giggling Chiyoko wrapped a smooth thigh around my waist, and I could feel her pubic hair bristling against the stretch of taut skin over my hip bone. Under the surface, a thousand nerve endings were tingling.

She said, 'You were, honest you were, just laid out flat, with this stacked Chinese dude standing over you.'

It hurt to move. I pressed my fingers against the swollen skin between my ear lobe and jawline. At some stage, in the bar, I had incurred this injury. According to Chiyoko, she came out of the toilet, nose freshly powdered, and saw me lying in the middle of the floor, face down in a pool of Sapporo's famous brew. It scared me that I had no memory of the incident. I was lucky to be alive. The dangers of being blind drunk in a perilous world were immense.

'He was Chinese?'

'Yeah, think so. One of those guys on the table by the keyboard player, with the white girl. Big for a Chinese, though.'

'So,' I said, recapping for clarity's sake, 'I'm lying in a puddle of lager, and this Chinese man with heavy fists is standing over me?'

'Uh-huh. He looked annoyed.'

From what I could piece together, relying on my limited knowledge of bar-brawl etiquette and certain recurring themes in Chiyoko's account, it had started with me spotting a Western girl on the other side of the bar. She was sobbing into her mobile phone. Shaking off my own problems, feeling an unexpected pang of drunken sympathy, I went to see if she was all right. My mistake was not leaving when her thickset Chinese boyfriend arrived.

'He looked like a basketball player,' Chiyoko confirmed, 'only more muscular, like a wrestler. But with those football shoulder pads.'

I imagined myself staggering into walls, falling down manholes, choking on my own vomit. I remembered snippets of things I had told Chiyoko about my mother and my wife and my life.

A dulled moment passed. I sipped my Pocari Sweat. Chiyoko stared at the blank television screen in the corner.

'It's nothing to do with you,' I said eventually.

'I know *that*,' she said, her hand moving across my stomach. 'Which begs the question, do you get it up at all?'

'That's . . . a fairly direct question.'

'Yep.'

'Look, I'm sorry.'

'Didn't anyone ever tell you that you shouldn't say "sorry" in the bedroom? It's a turn-off for a girl.'

'To be fair, I thought you were already turned off.'

'You know,' she said definitively, 'you should try stamps.'

'Stamps?'

'Yeah, you know, postage stamps.'

I stared at her blankly.

'You know, little adhesive rectangles you stick in the corner of envelopes. Evidence that you've paid for —'

'I am familiar with the concept. Just not what they have to do with this.'

She moved her hand down across my pelvic bone and stroked my crestfallen penis with a fine-spun finger.

'OK. So. You take a sheet of stamps, right? One of those ones where all the individual stamps are connected by those little things, the little outer edges where you can rip them away from other stamps.'

'Perforations.'

'I'm not sure that's the word.'

'That is the word. Trust me.'

'Well, OK. So you tear away a little column of stamps, a vertical strip of say four or five.' She lifted the duvet with one hand and glanced at her other hand, or my penis, or maybe both. 'Actually, three ought to do it. And you take your little column of three stamps, still all held together, and you stick them on the underside of your thing. Just here,' she said, tapping a polished fingernail for the avoidance of doubt.

I flinched impotently.

'Chill,' she said, 'I'm not going to hit an artery or anything. You need to loosen up, Foss Bros. Anyway, you stick this strip of stamps under there before you go to sleep. Obviously you have to lick them first, or whatever, so they stick in place.'

She yawned. Her cleavage was just visible over the top of the duvet. Her breasts were a creamy colour, lighter than the rest of her skin but darker than the duvet cover.

'And? You stick them in place, go to sleep. Then what?'

'Oh,' she said, 'well, the rest is pretty straightforward really. You stick them on, go to bed, and see whether the stamps are still connected to each other the next morning. If they are, you've got a physical problem. Whereas if they've separated out – you know, along the perve-forated edges – your issue is a mental one.'

'You're kidding, right?'

'No, I'm super serious. I read about it somewhere. If they separate out, you know you've had a hard-on in the night, and that the barrier you need to overcome is purely psychological.'

She yawned again, pulled the duvet high around her neck, and went to sleep.

The day started again at noon. We showered, had a quick breakfast of toast and painkillers, then headed in the direction of Hokkaidō University. We didn't talk about the alcohol and the aborted sex. I felt a niggling need to ask her who she had shared a room with at the Villa Dolly, but it seemed exactly the wrong moment to ask.

My hangover was wrapped all around me like a fuzzy force field, but the crisp air cutting through the university grounds gradually brought me back to life. Searching for the main visitors' entrance, we found ourselves strolling through avenues lined with snow-jewelled poplars, elms and oaks. We came across a campus museum. Chiyoko wanted to go inside but, for once, was too tired or half-hearted to press the issue. A few minutes later, we chanced upon a bust of William S. Clark, an American academic who, according to the plaque, was a former vice president of the agricultural college that had once stood in the grounds. I remembered, from one of the lectures Chloe used to give me, that he is speculated to have been the mysterious 'master' in Emily Dickinson's poems. Chiyoko wasn't interested in this information. 'She was a reclusive weirdo. What kind of writer only dresses in white?'

We stopped twice to ask passing students for directions. They gave Chiyoko uncomprehending, blank-eyed looks. You'd think she was speaking a language they could not identify, let alone understand. I received a volley of curious half-smiles, the way you might stare at an oddly marked dog crossing your path at a safe distance. There was a thin layer of snow on the ground and I spent a lot of time gazing at other people's footprints.

Eventually we chanced upon a student who seemed more relaxed in our company. His hair was long and greasy and he kept sweeping it back behind his ears. I wondered if he hadn't had a chance to buy shampoo for a few days, or if he didn't like the way his hair went fluffy when it was washed, or if there was some other deciding factor that hadn't even occurred to me. Either way, he was happy to take us to the anthropology department. We walked along with him at his pace, which was painfully slow. He seemed the type for whom everything is slow. I pressed the satchel to my hip.

Greasy Hair introduced us to a secretary and receded, sloth-like, into a dark corner of the building. The secretary frowned as Chiyoko explained who we were looking for, all kinds of layered troubles sculpted on her brow, but soon she was jabbering away with terrific speed, pausing for thought only when her own long vowel sounds permitted her space to do so. '*Ah sooooo.*' She disappeared down a corridor. Chiyoko turned to me.

'She seems to know who Reginald Pickford is, but she won't say more than that until she's spoken to one of her bosses.'

Suddenly I felt scared. Satoshi could walk out of any number of doors at any number of moments. What would he look like, remember, say? The thumping of my heart became delirious, panic-driven, but also somehow rich. I tried to steady it by observing the imperfections in the walls. Waist-high marks and dents, probably from the armoured edges of lever arch files or the zips of passing bags.

When the woman returned, she brought a carefully tanned Westerner with her. I noticed that he carried a scar not dissimilar to mine. It was the one flaw on his face: a thin pink line, two or three inches long, running from under his right eye to the crevice between nostril and cheek. He was too young to be Satoshi, and his features bore no resemblance to my mental image. He wore corduroy trousers, a tweed jacket and leather slip-ons – the sturdy fabrics of English academia. But, as he approached, I could smell a distinctively un-English, throat-catching cologne.

'Patrick Jenkins,' he said, squeezing my hand and already leading us somewhere. The name instantly jarred in my head. Dr P. Jenkins, co-author of the article in my satchel. 'Please come in, take a seat, make yourselves at home.' American, not English. His nationality was in his voice and his bright white teeth. Something about him suggested multiple gym memberships.

He said, 'Fine day to walk through the grounds, isn't it? Glorious day. Full of fresh snow.'

Chiyoko and I sat side by side, mumbling our agreement, waiting for Patrick Jenkins to settle into his chair. His office was an advert for mahogany. Everywhere you looked there was dark wood: two free-standing cupboards, a drinks cabinet, a footstool, a hatstand, and the chairs we were sitting on. Most impressive of all was the grandiose, implausibly clean desk that stretched between him and us, straight grain and pocket-free. Its beautiful, reddish sheen made me think of the desk in Dad's study at number 17. He had spent every weekend at that desk, within the study's sacrosanct borders. The room contained him.

Jenkins finally sat, leaning forward, arms stretched, fingers meshed together in an elegant lattice. My jaw hurt.

He said, 'How can I help you, my friends?'

I started talking. I heard myself spitting out 'ums' and 'ahs' at a disconcerting rate. Jenkins had a quality of intense directness, fixing me with an absolute gaze, an unflinching scrutiny, which put my tongue off balance. He was one of those people who can erect transparent walls and invite you inside, dimming and muffling everything that isn't about you and them, making you feel scared and privileged at the same time.

'So anyway,' I said, still too somnolent to cut through my own babble, 'I was in the library in Tokyo for a while, trying to find out which university Mr Pickford had worked at, and it emerged that he worked here, or had some links here, or lectured here.'

Jenkins blinked his honeycomb lids as he spoke. He told me that Satoshi had indeed worked at the university once, a few years back. I was thrown a few scraps of information about the areas in which he had specialised: wartime anthropology, concepts of occupation, the mentality of defeat. I spent some time studying that pink scar, and eventually got to the point.

'So. I appreciate you might not remember a specific date, but what year did Mr Pickford move on from here?'

'Well, let me think. Tough one. Reg left the university back in 2006, I would say.'

'In 2006?'

'Yes, around then, I'd say so.'

'And do you know which university he moved to?'

'Which university? I seem to recall that he didn't move on to another university. I'd say he didn't take another university position.'

'So . . . he retired?'

'That's more accurate, yes. He was no spring chicken, after all!'

He gave me another flash of white teeth, then tilted his head a fraction to give Chiyoko the same.

'Does he still live in Hokkaidō?'

'Wow! Tough questions. I have no idea, actually. I'm afraid I just don't know.'

'You don't keep a record of forwarding addresses? For departing staff?'

He shook his head.

'Isn't there a need to redirect mail, tie up loose ends?'

'All excellent questions,' he said, scratching a nut-brown knuckle. 'I can tell you're a man of the world. And the answer is, we do try our best. But you know how admin can be, my friend . . . what did you say your name was?'

'Mr Fossick.'

'You know the score, Mr Fossick. Sometimes busy people like us are simply not as good at the admin side of things as we should be. You know how it is.'

'The thing is, I really must get hold of Reginald Pickford. It is very, very important that I find him.'

I gave Jenkins a frown, and within seconds his quicksilver face had rearranged itself to mirror mine.

'I do appreciate that, Mr Fossick, I really do. I say this to you as one humble professional to another. May I ask, is he a relative of yours?'

'No, he isn't a relative.'

'I see.' He repeated it again: 'I see, I see.'

His voice was hypnotic. Blood ran sluggishly through my veins. The room was suddenly stifling, melting my resolve and bloating my tongue. Hot tides of turpentine seemed to swim up from the surface of the desk. They washed me in odours of gentility, flavours of respectable, sanitised things.

I said, 'Someone must know where he is. It's an emergency, otherwise I wouldn't be here.'

'I hear exactly what you're saying, Mr Fossick. And if I

felt there was any more I could say, please be assured that I would say it. Reg Pickford was in many ways a brilliant man. A worthy addition to this institution and a skilled, sensitive analyst of what we in the trade call the *human condition*.'

'Did you ever work with him, Mr Jenkins? Is it Mr Jenkins, or Dr Jenkins?'

'Just Patrick, please . . . I can't recall us generating a combined work product as such.'

A scenario played itself out in my head. In that scenario, I reached into the satchel at my feet, pulled out my photo-copy of the *Crossing Cultural Borders* article, and laid it on the desk in front of him. But in reality my hands stayed flat, a few inches from his.

'Is there anyone else we can speak to? Anyone who might have a better idea of where we can find Mr Pickford?'

He struck a thinking pose, but it seemed to me he was simply waiting for an adequate interval to pass.

'I fear not,' he said, glancing at his watch. 'I really wish I could help more, of course, but apart from anything I have a class full of unruly freshmen waiting for me!'

He stood up, grinning that painfully bright grin. My inten-tion was to keep sitting, but I found myself standing, shaking his hand, watching the slight bow he gave Chiyoko, a fitting end to what I sensed had been a kind of performance. He showed us back to the secretarial bay, squeezing my shoulder and speaking in a tone of fatherly amusement.

'If I could be so rude as to ask that you two see your-selves out?'

We wandered back through lifeless corridors, past a cluster of bruised payphones bolted to the wall. Age-black buttons and pocked handsets, heavy with the melancholic aftermath of crackly conversations. Underneath the phones, on the linoleum floor, lay a stocky book. Chiyoko identified it as a telephone directory. She crouched down and fanned the pages, searching for Reginald Pickfords. I pictured her for a moment on my sofa, looking through prints, picking the ones she liked. After a minute or two she put the book down, stood up and shook her head. Then, squinting into the distance, she said something in Japanese.

It was Greasy Hair. He returned Chiyoko's greeting and in slow careful stages came to a stop in front of us, tilting minutely forward on the balls of his feet.

'I heard you tell the secretary you want to find Pickford-sensei,' he said. He pronounced each syllable painstakingly in a voice that hovered between weary detachment and incipient curiosity.

'That's right,' we said, both at the same time, surprised to hear the words in stereo.

'I did not know him but when I started here . . . people talked about him.'

We took a half-step forward. We encouraged him to tell us everything he'd heard.

'I don't want to get in any trouble,' he said.

Speak freely, we told him. Tell us, tell us everything. And as other students started filing past, he exhaled heavily and began to whisper.

Reginald Pickford had left the university of Hokkaidō the year before Greasy Hair arrived. He was spoken of fondly by some of the anthropology students then graduating. A teacher who encouraged methodical thinking but was wary of definite conclusions, could at times be less mild than he looked, but always seemed fair and engaged and interested, belted up in a big-skirted coat, often carrying a punctured can of cold coffee, spending morning tutorials breathing the fragrance through the hole. Sometimes his face seemed full of wry English humour, sometimes there seemed to be a sadness. He left the university suddenly, overnight, who knows where. His exit followed an argument with another lecturer, the speculators said, maybe even a scuffle. Better-informed acquaintances said it would not be proper to say, the university might get annoyed, they didn't want to gossip, and anyway it was all second-hand, they weren't there, they couldn't be sure. This is all Greasy Hair knew, these were the colliding points of half a dozen stories, impressions, asides. Nothing about Satoshi's former life, his marital status, his home or his hobbies or his hates. Nothing about his secrets.

Except for one thing, just a rumour, coaxed out of others, now coaxed out by Chiyoko's calm insistence, my desperate need to know. There was a story that Satoshi, decades before joining the university, might have attacked a man.

'Attacked?'

'Yes. Just a rumour. Understand I do not want to say anything bad about your friend. I do not know what the truth is.'

'But you heard,' I said, 'you heard he had attacked a man?' He nodded.

'Injured the man?'

With an air of gentle resignation he nodded again.

'Killed the man?'

No nod, but a blink, a complex blink, dark eyelashes

clumped in twos and threes that seemed to come down from various elevations and perspectives.

He began to turn and said, 'I have to leave now, sorry, sorry.'

I reached out to pull him back by the hood of his sweater, but Chiyoko darted between us and delicately took him by the hand. She produced a biro from somewhere and, with the lid between her teeth, wrote on Greasy Hair's outstretched palm. He bit his lip and fed himself into a slow student line full of pads and pens.

'What was that all about?' I said.

'I gave him my number. In case he remembers anything.'

'He'll probably think you want to sleep with him.'

'So what? He's kinda cute, in a scarecrow sort of way.'

We walked on. Staged sunlight danced over the scarred paint of the passageways, mellowing the surfaces with its slowly shifting glow.

Chiyoko said, 'Do you think it's true, the rumour, that he actually killed somebody?'

'I don't know,' I said, and as I said it I knew we were both thinking of George Harvey, knew that this mute thought would come and go, would work its way into my days and nights, my changing dreams, until the time came to deliver my mother's gift.

Outside there was a light breeze, nothing like the previous day's squealing wind. We crossed a gravel drive flanked by the frozen stems of dead flowers. They rustled in mock applause as the cold air caught them.

We ended up in a bakery, sitting on wrought-iron chairs, hunched over a table warped by coffee rings. My fingernails nudged at a tower of one-yen coins fresh from the baker's till as Chiyoko methodically made her way through a third, then a fourth doughnut from a plate decorated with skylarks.

'Hangover food,' she said, her words muffled by the weight of deep-fried dough on her tongue.

The last few hours had given me more of a sense of the man Satoshi had become, but I still had no finished image of him, no settled features on which to focus my bleary obsession. He was still a blank, hands without a face, an absence rather than a presence. I thought of my mother, and of Chloe, and somehow it felt like they were part of some unseen audience, watching my present failures unfold. I looked at Chiyoko, lifting a fifth doughnut. Why had I dragged this young girl halfway across her country? What did people think, looking at a middle-aged man like me sitting with a young girl like this? Question marks billowed in my mind, yet the answers meant nothing to me. I should probably have felt shame. Or fear. Or at least that familiar friend, anxiety. But I just felt hollow.

'You should eat something,' she said.

A pill, I thought. Maybe I should eat a pill, let it skid across my tongue down into my stomach, flooding my bloodstream with benevolent polymers. I picked up a coin between thumb and forefinger and spun it in the centre of the table. It made a sound like a dentist's drill and gave off a faint spiral glow. As it slowed, it veered towards my hot chocolate and came to a rattling halt by my elbow. A penny for the old guy.

'A doughnut. Or a hot roll. Something, huh? You have to eat. It's good to eat. I'll get you a hot roll.'

'I'm not a hot roll kind of guy.'

She ignored me and went up to the counter, returning with a portion of focaccia cut into a wedge. As she laid the plate on the table, her tongue flitted across her top lip, absorbing stray doughnut crumbs.

'They didn't have any rolls left,' she said, trying to meet my eyes. 'What kind of bakery runs out of rolls, huh? But this stuff is good – it's Italian-style. It has bits of olives and tomato in it.'

It was a while before I relented, but she was right, it felt good to eat. My face still hurt from the altercation with the basketball thug, but a brief feel of the hollow valley between my jawline and ear lobe suggested that the swelling had gone down.

'Why don't we put an advertisement in the papers?' she said. 'Could be worth a try, huh? You know the kinda thing: "If you know the whereabouts of Reginald Pickford". We can put my cell number at the bottom.'

'Probably a waste of time,' I said. 'More words, more sentences.'

'Oh come on, Fossy, you need to get out there and struggle for what you want!'

'I am struggling.'

'You show no signs of it.'

'The signs are inward.'

The table next to us became vacant and the baker, a man with rolled shirtsleeves and thinning hair, started rearranging its chairs in barely perceptible ways.

'All I'm saying is, feel free to cheer up once in a while. It makes a journey less painful.'

I told her it wasn't a question of cheering up. She shrugged and asked if I was finished with the foccacia. There's a traffic-free motorway between Chiyoko's stomach and her heart.

'We should make a list,' I said. 'Of all the universities in the country that have anthropology departments. Then we should ring them all. I should ring them all.'

'Uh-huh, good idea. That's exactly the attitude we want. We'll start tonight. And the advert?'

'I suppose we've got nothing to lose,' I said. Even if it ended up being another dead end, it was something more than nothing.

I grabbed a napkin and Chiyoko produced the biro she'd used on Greasy Hair's hand. I wrote down what I wanted in the advert:

Attention: Reginald Pickford/Satoshi
Please get in touch urgently.

'Then we'll stick your mobile number at the bottom, if you're happy to do that. I guess we should put the ad in both English and Japanese papers. If he's still in the area, it might be a Japanese person who ends up reading the newspaper and pointing us in the right direction. Someone from the university, a neighbour, maybe a Japanese wife.'

'Sure thing,' Chiyoko said. 'There's three or four local newspapers worth trying. I can ring them when we get back to the hotel, get the advertisement placed in the morning editions.'

'If it doesn't work, I think it's time for me to head home.'

'What about the photographs?'

'I think I'm suffering some kind of artistic dementia. I

look at things too hard to actually see them. My pictures have no memories.'

She said, 'Maybe that's why they're interesting to look at, huh? You'll see Satoshi soon enough. We're close, I can feel it.'

'You might be close, but I'm nowhere near.'

I looked around and was briefly startled by the number of people eating the same foods, everyone's jaws moving to the same rhythm, carried on the soft roar of their own chewing. The memory of eating chocolates in the Villa Dolly came to mind again. Me, Daisuke and Kagami — that gaunt woman with the eyes too big for their sockets. The three of us making tiny slurping sounds as we ate.

20

NOT PATRICIDE, not matricide, not infanticide. Is there a word for killing uncles?

I went to sleep pondering the possible causes of Dr Harvey's death and I woke from boggling dreams of Mr Satoshi. He had been standing on a shoreline in the moonlight, but before I could get a proper look at him he collapsed, vertical to horizontal in a heavy split second. No warning. Lips blue. Skin white. A tiny tremor of life on the eyelid. Then stillness. Out of nowhere, frogs started falling from the sky, all protruding eyes and parachute webbing, tumbling down on him like alien hailstones. I felt smothered and sweaty. Chiyoko brought me a cool facecloth. She pressed it to my forehead, stroked my ear, drew me into her chest.

Her mobile phone rang twice before breakfast.

She picked up the first call, but when a shrieky female voice addressed her in English she handed the handset over to me.

The voice said, 'Why has this guy got two separate names, Reginald and Satoshi? What does it mean? How can anyone have two names, one English and one Japanese? It doesn't make any sense.'

I thought I could make out an Australian accent, or maybe

Kiwi. Whatever her nationality, she sounded like she was foaming at the mouth. I ended the call without saying a word, but barely a minute later the phone in my hand rang again.

To my surprise, it wasn't the foaming Antipodian but a crackly voiced Japanese lady. Her English was poor, all vowels and no consonants. I looked at Chiyoko, standing in front of me in her nightie, and handed her the phone.

'She used to have her hair done by a man named Satoshi,' Chiyoko said, covering the mouthpiece with her hand. 'He was a super-nice hairdresser. She wonders if it's the same man you're looking for.'

'Ask her if he was Japanese or Western,' I said. Odd if he went from anthropology into the hairdressing business, but both required a certain way with people. Chiyoko questioned the woman. The questions were punctuated by significant pauses. During these silences Chiyoko seemed to be examining my face for the secret meaning of the words she was hearing.

'Uh-huh,' she said. 'Uh-huh.'

Maybe three whole minutes passed. It could even have been four. By which time Chiyoko was talking excitedly into the phone, pumping out syllables at record speed. Eventually she ended the call.

'Well?'

'She says her Satoshi was Japanese, and that he died thirty years ago.'

'That was all she said?' I asked, exasperated.

'Yup. She sounded like a really nice old lady, though. Made me think of my mother for some reason.'

'Have you spoken to her recently, your mother?'

'Of course. We speak all the time.'

She stripped off. I watched her turn away from me, lift the nightie over her head, wrap a towel around her body, pull her knickers down past her ankles. Before she kicked the knickers away my eyes fell on a crease that ran along the inside of the crotch. She tiptoed into the bathroom. I took the package out of my satchel and held it in my hands. It had started to feel warm of late. I put it back, re-read the letters and the other documents, and tried to remember why I was in Japan.

What a farcical crusade. Our third day in Hokkaidō ran uneventfully into the fourth, and the fourth into the fifth. Each morning we woke up in each other's arms, tangled up in this strange sexless relationship of ours. We got breakfast in the hotel restaurant. Chiyoko made me swap my cornflakes and toast for more traditional Japanese fare, and I ended up in a routine of rice and miso soup. I started to quite enjoy it. We went out onto the streets. We talked about splitting up so that we could cover more ground, but it never happened. Often we stopped somewhere for a sushi or noodle lunch, then returned to the hotel to carry out amateur detective work via the phone and Internet. On the Internet I glanced surreptitiously at my online bank balance. My savings looked limp. A budget hotel, even a mid-range hotel, would have made sense. But we were used to our lodgings, and part of me wanted a finite end to things, a bankrupt point at which I would have to turn back, regardless of the result. Besides, I'd get round to taking some saleable photographs sooner or later.

In the afternoons, Chiyoko called Daisuke. She often put her mobile phone on speaker so the three of us could talk. She'd ask him how everyone at the hotel was doing, and she sounded so concerned in her questioning that I again started to wonder about Early Evening Shift Guy. Was he a jilted lover who had been placed on suicide watch? We had a cheap dinner, a few drinks in one of the nearby bars, and sat up in bed chatting. Occasionally she read me poems from the little Robert Frost collection she had brought with her from Tokyo: 'Desert Spaces', 'Out, Out', 'Birches'. Being read to – it was like the old days with Chloe. I wondered if, even back then, there was some small part of me that had yearned nostalgically for the future, for a time when those sticky nights looking out on the sheep would be a fading memory.

At some point, either during day four or day five, I ran out of pills. At first, this sent me into a fizzing, hour-long panic. In the midst of it I believed, with absolute conviction, that I was experiencing a heart attack, a real one. Only after the pain had settled into exhaustion did I admit to myself that my senses were not dimming over in death, just contracting in the brightness of my own fear. How had I not realised that I was running so low, that I didn't have another bottle? How would I get hold of my doctor back home? I decided to check out what was available at the local pharmacy, but time passed and I didn't get round to it. Perhaps a few drug-free days were achievable. So what if the medicines were all swallowed up and absorbed? Maybe it was just what I needed, to walk the streets naked, free of the old chemical fug. Find Satoshi, deliver the package, take honest pictures, return home.

Based on information from the Ministry of Education, various websites and the local library, Chiyoko and I built up a list of every university in Japan that had an anthropology department. Between us, we called all of them, but none had heard of a Mr Pickford. One social science faculty boasted a Mr Pickering, but the lecturer's embarrassed assistant described him as being 'not much more than sixty years, and very younger-looking for his age'. We also regularly returned to Hokkaidō University, trawling the grounds for students or staff members who might remember him. We didn't see Greasy Hair and I felt foolish for not getting his name. On one occasion I was sure I saw Dr Jenkins spying on us from a lit window high above a crooked tree but, before I could say anything to Chiyoko, he disappeared behind a pigeon-pale curtain. The most exhilarating afternoon saw us talk our way into the student common room. But most of the students sprawled out on mismatched sofas had only been at the university for a year or two, and soon enough a security guard asked us to leave.

As the sixth and seventh days came and went without any leads, I started to struggle to get out of bed in the mornings. Every day held the same routine. Habit is a great deadener. I tried to keep searching, studying, uncovering, but everything in the Sapporo winter seemed lifeless. Even the streets became dead to me: dead straight, dead wide, dead and buried in snow. The only intrigue was the brown-paper package. I weighed it my hands, thought about the three eggshell-white envelopes inside, and wondered what secrets they contained.

But then the eighth day.

Our eighth day in Sapporo was different, out of the ordinary. About an hour before our usual dinner time, Chiyoko announced that she had an errand to run. I was reading her book of Robert Frost poems at the time. I found myself in that thin space between sleep and wakefulness, lacking the energy to query what errand could be required in Hokkaidō's early evening snow. When she came back, it was 10 p.m.

'Don't be annoyed,' she said.

Up until that moment I was confused, even a little worried, but it hadn't occurred to me to be annoyed.

She said, 'I met that guy from the university, the one with the hair.'

'Greasy Hair? You had dinner with Greasy Hair?'

'A drink. A couple of drinks. He called this afternoon when you were out having a cigarette, said he'd found out a bit of information about Satoshi. Wanted to meet and kinda . . . talk it over.'

'And you didn't think to invite me along?'

'I thought it would be better if I did it alone. You know, flirt a bit, make him feel warm and fuzzy. Harmless stuff.'

'Harmless stuff,' I said, feeling inexplicably angry. 'Harmless handjob, harmless blow job?'

'What's wrong with you? Not that it's any of your business, but we had a couple of drinks and I left. Maybe I should have told you he'd called. In which case I'm sorry, OK?'

It wasn't OK. I was no longer choosing the words that came out of my mouth. I felt the prickly heat of betrayal stinging my skin, radiating through my body gently yet fiercely.

'So, what did the greasy little bastard tell you?'

She turned away, then swivelled back round, twists of pink hair flapping like a school of fish on a fire. 'He said he could get an address for Satoshi.'

'An address?' I said.

'Yes. One of the older students, a postgrad, told Greasy Hair he has Satoshi's address written down somewhere.'

'And?'

'And this guy is going to dig out the address, give it to Greasy Hair, and Greasy Hair's going to text it to me tomorrow.'

'You're joking, right? How naive are you? He said he was going to text you tomorrow. He gave you no information other than that in the course of – what was it – four hours?'

She said nothing. Her skin was drained of colour, empty of meaning, and the back of my neck was on fire.

'If I'd been there, I would have shaken it out of him, made him go back to the university and take me to the other guy. Whereas now, either he slept with you or he didn't sleep with you, apparently it's no business of mine either way, but one thing is certain: we're never going to hear from him again.'

She gave me this sharp look I'd never seen before, a Stanley-knife stare.

'I'm angry,' I said.

'Yes,' she said, 'I can see that. Super angry. Good for you, makes a change.'

'What does that mean?'

'Whatever.'

'What are you getting at?'

'What do you care, Fossy?'

Rage galloped through my veins like a hoofed animal and I could see, to my satisfaction, that she was angry too.

She said, 'You don't give a shit about anything but your own well-being. Isn't that the truth? Take a pill from your pocket, that travelling drugstore of yours, and think I won't notice, huh? Read some pathetic letter in secret. Lock yourself away in the bathroom. You help yourself out now and then, of course you do. But what have you done for me? What have you done for anyone else, huh? What have you ever done? Nothing.'

'Nothing? *Nothing,* is it? Stick to what you know, Chiyoko. Drinking and fucking and having a good time.'

'You,' she shrieked, 'you don't give a fuck about anyone! You think you're some kind of suffering recluse, the only one with a past, and that makes it OK to be permanently *not here*. And it doesn't, Robert. Try joining the real world. You think I don't have problems? Well, I do. Maybe I'll tell you about them one day, one day when you've woken up, joined the human race, stopped wallowing. That thing your father said to you after Greece. Did it occur to you that now, years on, there's a small shred of truth in it? *Self-pity*. When are you going to stop pitying yourself?'

'You silly little slut.'

Slut. The word was a plate crashing through a television screen, the cue for her to do anything, to say anything, to smash the whole place up. But, instead, she grabbed a towel that had been drying on a radiator and pulled the bathroom door shut behind her. It seemed to take an age to close, and something about the sight of it was shaky, had a quality of delirium.

After a minute or two, as my neck and ears started to cool, I heard the shower go on. Showering. Always showering. I sat by the window in an ant-like wooden chair, thinking about things I should have said. It took me a moment to realise that I was gazing into another window, the floor-to-ceiling glass of a room in a hotel across the street. There was nowhere else to look. A willowy young woman in a white shirt and a black cotton skirt had her back pressed up against the windowpane. A man in a grey suit was kissing her neck. A slice of his face was visible over the back of her shoulder. The only other part of him I could see was the faint outline of his right hand; it cupped and caressed the woman's buttocks under the thin black veil of the skirt. She leaned back into it, the cotton trapped between his knuckles and the glass. He freed his hand and hitched her skirt up. She wore hold-ups. His fingernails flitted around one of the elastic rims and down across the stretch of shiny nylon. Now his other hand was coming into play, lifting the skirt further, right up around her waist. The motion revealed her white knickers. As he pushed her harder against the glass, she wriggled, and he used his tucked thumbs to peel the knickers down inch by inch, until they formed a taut bridge between her thighs. I squeezed my eyes, tired by the intensity of my own prying.

Chiyoko was out of the shower, searching for something in a bedside drawer, wrapped in the giant white towel. I gave her no warning. I moved up behind her and took the towel in my hand. It dropped to the carpet. It unwound there like a giant swirl of melting ice cream. I pulled my T-shirt off, kissed her neck, unbuttoned my jeans. She stayed completely still. It was only once I had pushed her flat onto the bed that she moved. She fidgeted beneath me. Her hands started to caress and pull on my balls. I pinned her wrists to the bed sheets, somewhere high above her head, thinking how I could fit three of these wrists in each of my hands. I bit her shoulder gently as her nipples hardened against my chest. 'No,' was the word I chose to whisper into the whorl of her ear. I moved across her gently at first, then harder. I started to forget who I was. She didn't say a word, not a joke about how long it had taken to get here, not even an encouraging little comment on the pleasure or the pain, and I welcomed the silence, I was grateful for it.

'Better?' she said, when it was over. And I struggled to read her, to hear her. I was about to say something neutral, to roll onto my side, but she started laughing.

'What?' I said, stroking her neck with a forefinger.

'You know what, Fossy? I think I've learned something about you. That you're not a person who gets lonely, particularly, but you're not a person who wants to be alone either. Am I in the right ballpark?'

'Maybe.' I propped myself up on a pillow and stared at my clothes, twisted together in a heap at the end of the bed, looking like refuse in a snowy field. 'Is there any difference at the end of the day, between loneliness and aloneness?'

'I don't know. But if you ever call me a slut again I'll chop your balls off and no one will ever want you. And, for the record, I haven't done anything with anyone for over two years. So if you're going to call me names, how about frigid bitch or something along those lines?'

'But what about –'

'Stop talking,' she said. 'Go back to the bare minimum, I kinda liked you that way.'

We fell into quiet bliss, pleasure thinning my skin.

And then came mammoth delicate dreams, punctured by a steady drilling sound. Darkness had filled the room. It took me a moment to realise Chiyoko's phone was vibrating on the bedside table.

She slunk onto the edge of the bed and picked it up.

'Don't get excited,' she whispered, moving the phone away from her ear. 'It's just Daisuke letting me know how things are going.'

So went our eighth day in Sapporo.

21

'I JUST think, after him being so good about giving me time off, I owe him a little present. It's just a nice thing to do, and he's already got all the Dolly Parton albums, loads of dog toys . . . Are you even listening?'

'What?'

'This is serious, Fossy. You need to help me pick one he'll like.'

'I know,' I said, trying to shake off thoughts about Satoshi, about what might hover in the scant light of his dreams, about whether he was all that different to me. 'It's just . . . a knife's a knife, right?'

'To you or me, maybe. But Daisuke really likes knives, so it's the perfect thank-you gift. He's doing me a real favour by taking care of everything at the hotel. So just play along and let me know whether that one feels good, OK?'

Here we were, in a knife shop in a Sapporo back alley, my ears ringing with the sound of steel. I was crouched over a plastic tub containing whetstones and foggy water. The chosen knife was in my hand, and the old Japanese man crouched next to me, apparently the owner of the shop, was going to show me how to sharpen it. With his dark green robe, unshorn hair and wispy white beard, he fitted my mental image of a samurai warrior from some bygone age.

I said, 'Chiyoko, I know nothing about knives. Shouldn't *you* learn how to sharpen it, test it out?'

She said, 'I'd rather capture you doing it.'

She was a few metres away from the knife man and me, half perched on a small card table covered with newspaper and rolls of black cloth. Her mobile phone had a camera and she aimed it in our direction. I wondered how many others were doing the same thing at this precise moment, viewing the world at arm's length through a digital screen.

'The thing is,' I said, 'how do we know he doesn't already have this one in his collection?'

'He collects them from different places he's been. He won't have a Sapporo knife. He's never been here.'

Her hand angled the camera phone, choosing a viewpoint from which to trap me in stillness and gloss.

'But will he really want one this big?'

I looked down at the knife. It really was big, and heavy. Simply holding it above the plastic tub made my forearm convulse.

'Yes,' the knife man said, his first English words since we arrived. 'Big. Sharp. Santoku knife is big and sharp.' He laughed.

'*Chi-i-z-u!*' Chiyoko exclaimed, and in the unexpectedly brutal flash I found myself blinking when I should have been smiling.

'Big,' the knife man said, looking admiringly at his own work, 'and *sharp*.'

And heavy, I thought. Don't forget heavy.

'The Santoku is a general-purpose kitchen knife,' Chiyoko explained.

'Fish, meat, veggie table,' the old man added.

All three of us stared at it for a moment. The unshouldered blade. The eight-inch leaf of glinting metal. The atom-splitting edge.

Chiyoko said, 'The word "*santoku*" means "three good things". Let me see, there's . . .'

She tailed off and studied the ceiling, struggling to express the three good things in English. Against all odds, it was the knife man who chimed in with the necessary vocabulary. 'Sricing, dicing and mincing,' he shouted, before dissolving into more laughter. 'Three good thing!'

He jabbed an elbow into my ribcage. It very nearly knocked me off balance. In the required crouching position, my legs were tired before the lesson had even begun. Whereas the knife man, who must have been a good thirty years older than me, looked like he'd be happy rocking back and forth on the balls of his feet forever.

He tilted his weight forward and took a whetstone from the water, shook off some of the excess, and laid it across the top of the tub. Then he took my right hand and repositioned my grip on the knife's handle. He manoeuvred my right thumb so that it lay stretched across the heel of the blade, and extended my right index finger along the spine. My left hand found a supporting position underneath the right. He rocked backwards and leaned his elbows on his knees, a look of intense concentration on his face. It was as if he was waiting for the knife to tell him what his next move should be, and as he waited the morning sun kept leaking through the large grubby window at the front of the shop.

The interior walls were covered with hundreds of different blades in glass cabinets, all of them glittering brilliantly as they caught the light, shivery with reflections. Meat cleavers, paring knives, vegetable peelers, sushi slicers. Strangely beautiful things.

'You must hold,' the knife man said, 'and try to sharpen.'

I gripped the handle tight. He placed a coarse hand over my hand, the surface of his palm peaked with little teeth of hardened skin that grated against my knuckles. He guided me, bringing the Santoku across the whetstone. After a few minutes like this, he turned our joined hands and we laid the knife across the whetstone at a four o'clock position. 'This stroke better than short stroke,' he instructed, repeating the words several times as we pressed hard and pushed the blade up with long, fluid movements. We reduced the pressure as we glided back down. It was an odd feeling, the knife man's hand on top of mine, honing this segment of hard metal.

'Good,' he said eventually. A single word, said quietly and evenly, which filled me with an inexplicable warmth.

I kept repeating the backwards and forwards motion, adjusting my finger position after each set of strokes in the way he showed me. When the whole front side of the blade had been sharpened, we flipped it over and set to work on the back using a reverse stroke. His hands still riding mine, we sharpened the tip with a smooth, arc-shaped flourish. There was something hypnotic about the whole process, something unfamiliar yet perfect.

'I'm no expert,' I told Chiyoko, 'but if you're going to buy a knife, I think you should buy this one.'

'Fish, meat, veggie table,' the knife man said. He walked

over to the card table. Chiyoko stood next to it with her purse in her hand, the teeth of the zip unlocked. He wiped the knife on a sheet of newspaper and wrapped it in thick black cloth. When the transaction was over, Chiyoko put the purse in a tiny sequinned handbag and held it up for us to see.

'It's safer with you than me,' she said.

I put the knife in my satchel with a smile.

We navigated the city's icy grid in silence. Not a ponderous, oppressive silence. Not the bloated silence that hangs around a terminally ill patient, full of the presentiment of loss. Just a light, vacant absence, like a pleasantly empty stomach, the promise of nourishment round the corner.

'I'm super starving,' Chiyoko said. 'How about we stuff ourselves at the fish market?'

She seemed, of late, to have an uncanny purchase on my thoughts.

It was still morning, somewhere between eleven and half past, and last night's snow began running through down-spouts, riding kerbs, slinking into hooded drains. As we reached the outskirts of the market, thin wet sounds thick-ened into the lazy buzz of vending machines on pavements, each machine freighted with bright cans, tubbed ice cream, vacuum-packed underwear. Then came the faint neon hum from restaurant windows, windows displaying burnished plastic counterfeits of food, one remove from the real thing. I had avoided marketplaces for years, but I was hungry and oddly calm.

The deep centre of the market itself was a throbbing, living thing. Pale fish hung in nets like washing tablets, tossed in clanking drums and rolled around. Other glossy corpses were being stacked onto small carts and wheeled between tightly packed restaurant shacks. Old men in azure overalls and rubber boots carried out elaborate surgery on a huge headless tuna, making smooth incisions with metre-long knives. Younger staff made less elegant work of a frozen swordfish, attacking it with a large bandsaw, sweating into their sleeves.

We slipped through estuaries of people into quieter streams flanked by blue plastic boxes. The boxes contained water and half-alive fish. Pipes led in and out of them, charging the liquid with rich air. Sounds of bursting bubbles and splashing tails mingled with the rumbling in my gut. Eels thrashed; snapper writhed; cod beat; plaice flapped. Halibut, one on top of another, rippled serenely. Their anonymous neighbours, the ones that looked like animated aliens, protested in similar style: the red, spiky thing with the underbite and the ridged head; the ten-inch snake-like coil with the feeble teeth. Each gasping for air, scuffling for space. All fighting to break outside, all soon to be sushi.

A long time since I'd noticed so many things about one place, since I'd felt a scene come alive like this. I didn't have my SLR. There was something liberating about carrying nothing around my neck, being free of the burdensome weight, collecting impressions without preserving them. I found myself commentating on every last thing, describing colours and textures, shapes and lines, asking Chiyoko about names and rituals and tastes. I could not stop.

We passed stalls stacked three-deep with melons.

'Have I got my exchange rate right? Some of those melons are nine thousand yen. That's over forty pounds.'

'So?'

'For one melon?'

'You think about money a lot, huh? Some of the bluefin tuna are thirty thousand dollars. How about that for a hit on your wallet?'

She grabbed my hand and dragged me towards a row of wooden huts behind the melon stalls, each doorway full of sawdust footprints. We ducked into one of them and took seats at a low bar lined with pudgy bottles.

'What are these?'

'*Shōchū* bottles,' Chiyoko said.

'*Shōchū*?'

'Uh-huh. Alcohol made from sweet potato, barley or rice.'

She ordered a bottle and I took a sip. It tasted thick and earthy.

'This one is a rice *shōchū*.'

As she told me about the composition of the drink, two salarymen looked up from their meals, translucent slithers of barely dead prawn poised between their chopsticks. They seemed amused by my lesson, so I gave them a look and they turned back to their crustaceans.

We took our time with the food. Chiyoko had a second helping of sea urchin, grated radish and bright white rice. I had some extra salmon with the last of the *shōchū*. When our bowls and boards were cleared away, we ordered an enormous bottle of Sapporo beer and decanted it into two tiny, frosted glasses, her pouring for me, me pouring for her. We sat talking as other customers took their places at the bar. Their eyes shone hugely with hunger. A Beatles song, 'Strawberry Fields', filtered down through speakers cut into the ceiling.

'You know,' I said, 'I feel good.'

'Good?' she said, crinkling her nose.

'Good, happy. Without being too sentimental about it. For the first time in a while.'

'You didn't feel so good last night, when you had me pinned to the bed?'

As I began to smile, her phone let out two muffled beeps from her handbag. She found it, pressed some buttons, then swapped the phone for a packet of cigarettes, casually offering me one.

'I didn't know you smoked,' I said.

'You didn't?'

'No, I haven't seen you smoke once.'

She withdrew her offer with a shrug and put a cigarette between her lips. Then she struck a match and seemed to forget about it. She sat there smiling. I watched as the corners of her mouth lived their own life. They turned upward and downward and dimpled and creased. Her eyes were dark brown, but I saw now that they were painted with the faintest fleck of incandescent blue. This small detail excited me, romanticised my perceptions. An overblown thought came to mind: if I could stop the clock on my life, I would do it here, I would do it now.

Just before the match burned down to her fingers, she ducked her head so that the cigarette caught the flame.

She said, 'So you think you're cut out for happiness after all, Fossy?'

'I don't know,' I said. 'Is it like that, you're either cut out for it or you're not?'

She dropped her match into the dead beer bottle.

'I kinda think long-term happiness isn't what it's all about anyway. I think of my mother, and feel a bit down every now and then. She's . . . I see her getting old. It upsets me just to think or talk about it. About how there must be all these things she hasn't done and might not get a chance to do. But I guess if you assess an old person from the point of view of a young person, it's always going to seem like something's been lost or missed.'

I thought about Chiyoko's words. And then I felt a trickle of nausea through my bones.

I said, 'Kagami, the lady Daisuke introduced me too. The one who likes chocolates . . .'

'Yes,' she said, threading a finger through a curl of pink hair. 'Did you finally guess? She's my mother. Not many boys get to meet Mama, so you're privileged, you're a lucky boy indeed. Riddled with cancer. Bad, huh? Healthy two years ago. It's really bad now. And when she was younger she was . . . a prostitute. A proper slut, huh? Oh God, I'm sorry, I just . . . She's my mother and she was a good mother and she brought me up in the hotel, looked after me in a room on the fourteenth floor. And now that's where I look after her. Funny, if you think about it. Full circle. And I try not to . . . I don't like to dwell on this kinda stuff too much. Because if I dwell on it I just want to . . . walk out into a snowy field and lie down, you know? All of which is to say that, when you walked into Starbucks that day, I kinda . . . I knew what was going on. It was the first time in a little while that I'd seen someone else who was ready to walk out into the snow. Maybe that sounds weird, who knows.'

She let me hold her hand but wouldn't meet my eye. We just sat there breathing, each breath a kind of sigh.

I said, 'This will probably sound trite. But I'm sure she's

had a lot of happy moments, especially with you. And those moments will mean more than you think. They'll mean everything.'

Eventually Chiyoko said, 'Yeah. Maybe. Moments. Moments of grace. Like when you look up and see a field of daffodils dancing around in the wind. There's this place called Fukui City where you get winter daffodils, and at Christmas they're all snuggled up against each other, swaying, as if they're keeping warm together. Not to be soppy, but . . . you could have had the most shitty day, yet you see them, the flowers, and it gives you a special feeling.'

I leaned forward and kissed her.

She said, 'I'll take you to see them sometime, the winter daffodils in Fukui City.' And, as she said this, something in her eyes changed. The blue light in the pupils jostled and shimmered, flickered and waned.

I felt sure my wife's eyes had a similar thing, a blue fleck that could change like that.

But perhaps there was no blue at all. Perhaps I have laid that detail over my old memories, like cling film on a bowl of leftovers. An attempt to keep her face fresh, to better preserve it.

When I woke up the next morning, Chiyoko was gone.

22

WHAT TIME was it?

Light filtered through the asparagus-coloured curtains and turned the interior a murky green. She was not beside me in the five-star bed. She was not padding across the rich carpet. I listened carefully, waiting for the sound of a toilet flushing or a tap running. But the few sounds I heard were from other rooms and the city beyond them: coughing, crying, car alarms. The sounds of crises, real or imagined. My eyes scanned the room and turned their bland gaze towards the bathroom door. I expected to see it shut and framed in thin yellow light. But the door was open and the bathroom was dark. I switched on the bedside lamp.

She was gone. No make-up on the dressing table. No handbag on the floor. Her knickers and tights were no longer drying on the radiator. And her suitcase, that had gone too.

The tight-tucked bed sheet kept me trapped for a second and in frustration I knocked a pillow to the floor. Then I got up and walked around. The *Hokkaidō Times* hung in splayed sheets from a chair. The only possessions she had left behind were in the bathroom: a bottle of pink hair dye and a tube of cotton-wool pads. My things looked unfamiliar because they were no longer tangled up with hers. But they were all there, roughly where I'd left them. A swirl of lemon and mint drifted out from behind the shower curtain.

Perhaps she's arranged for us to move rooms. Perhaps all her stuff is in the new room. Perhaps she tried to wake me for breakfast, but I was knotted in sleep. Yes, that was it, she'd be at breakfast.

I pulled on some clothes and found the room key. An Olympic procession of metal rings connected it to a wooden brick, tough to carry and hard to lose. One ring was caught up with the zip of my camera case, obstinately unresponsive to my yanks and twists. I slung the polyester strap around my neck, key dangling at waist height, and got the lift down to the ground floor.

As I approached the hotel restaurant I found myself breaking into a shambling jog, my brows swelling with instant sweat. I wiped my face with my sleeve to stop the salt itch. The restaurant was lifeless: no lights, no food, no customers. The chairs were upturned on the tables. Why wasn't she here, with her breakfast?

A Japanese man wearing an apron emerged from nowhere and asked me if he could help.

I said, 'Breakfast over?'

He looked at me blankly. His eyes not sizing me up, not betraying disdain, not boring right through me, just blank.

'No breakfast today?' I said, struggling to regulate the flow of oxygen through my lungs, the smell of mop water rising around us.

'No breakfast, sir. Breakfast starts at seven, sir.'

Was he telling me that breakfast was over? That she'd already had breakfast?

'What time is it?'

He looked at his watch, then at the key hanging from my camera bag. He opened his mouth carefully, as if he knew that whatever answer he delivered would be the wrong one. 'Six fifteen o'clock,' he said.

'Six fifteen?'

'Six fifteen, sir.'

'How can it only be six fifteen?'

He didn't have an answer so I took my business elsewhere. I moved into the foyer. I crossed its gaudy rug.

'May I help you, sir?'

It was the receptionist's turn to look at me without emotion. I caught my reflection in the mirror behind her. Wisps of sleep-crazed hair burgeoned in every direction.

'I'm in room two-two-four. Fossick. I was wondering . . . I can't find my friend, anywhere. Thin, pretty girl, pink-haired, Japanese. Small build. Around your age. Perhaps she left a message for me?'

'Just a minute, sir. I will check our computer for you.'

Fingernails, perfectly filed, shaped, polished, hovered over one key at a time. Nude pink, pearly-tipped, beautiful and useless.

'Which room did you say you were in, sir?'

'Two. Two. Four.'

'Yes, sir. Here we are. Mr Fossick. The room is in your name, sir. We do not have any record of anyone checking out.'

'Well, of course you don't. No one has checked out. There's no talk of anyone checking out.'

'We have a ten per cent deposit, sir. It was paid over the telephone when the booking was made. The payment card was in the name of Chiyoko Kobayashi. Is that your friend, sir?'

'It is.'

'Well, sir, we have no record of her checking out, and the rest of the room cost is . . . awaiting final payment.'

'No messages then.'

'Sorry, sir? Do you wish to settle the room balance?'

'Useless.'

'Pardon, sir?'

'Useless place,' I said, swivelling round and heading straight for the glass exit. I tripped on the edge of the rug, crashed to my knees.

'And this rug doesn't work!' I shouted, spraying spit on its ugly surface.

No coat, no scarf, no plan, no idea. Iced wind tearing through my ears and bouncing the camera against my chest. A sub-zero smell in the air, the frozen cabinets aisle of a supermarket.

I found myself scuttling in the direction of the fish market, scanning the streets, dim-lit by long lines of lamp posts and the first signs of dawn. Men with left-swerving hair crowded around pallets of tuna, big and smooth and bruise-blue, beheaded. Torches waved around the circumference of the sawed neckline, illuminating the huge, yawning interior. A space big enough for Chiyoko to have climbed inside. A bell clattered and a man standing on a blue box started shouting. Other men shouted in response. Another bell. A cart arrived. Five men hoisted a fish on board. She wasn't inside. Another bell, more shouting, another fish. No sign of Chiyoko.

I ran around the city, following the lines of a senseless

spider diagram, confounding established methods of search and rescue. I doubled back on myself, dodged bustling hordes of early risers here and there, got lost in side roads that led back to covered ground. The streets were full of grey glass and sepia snow, fire stairs and mobile phones. Is that her phone ringing? From a pocket, from a gutter?

I can't explain why I was in such a panic, but I was. She had cried herself to sleep. She had been a different girl to the one I knew. She could have done something stupid. She could have wandered out into the snow in the middle of the night.

I found myself in an alleyway filled with homeless people, zippered limbs rippling gauzy bedding. What if they've taken her, what if she's zippered too? Some sniffed at me, some spoke to me from the shadows, and it was a shock to feel their eyes on my back, a relief to know that I could turn away from them, but what did it mean, what did it mean that she wasn't here? I gave a shirtless man with a spaniel a banknote and he said something in Japanese, pointed to the dog, pointed to the sky, gesticulated wildly. I found the clock tower, walked under the Television Tower, raced through the grounds of Hokkaidō University and the Hokudai Shoku-something botanical garden, past the Winter Sports Museum and the Salmon Museum and the Literature Museum and the Modern Art Museum. Is that her in the ticket queue?

Please let it be her.

No, no, keep moving. I passed a line of shops selling only soy sauce. Endless varieties: some yellow, some tan, some as black as oil. The window of a bakery, a breakfast place, a knife shop. I saw her between loaves of bread, bowls of miso soup, glittering blades. And the great, great crowd, the endless current of people quaking and gleaming and throbbing and moving, slowly, slowly, foot by foot, some-where.

There – a pink blur.

No – just a sequinned hat, more red than pink.

Doorways full of sunny dust made it difficult to see inside, brought memories of whirling spokes of smoke, opaque yellow-grey smoke, the vestigial light of a distant fire.

Children hopped past on a pavement chalk-marked for games; Coca-Cola ciphers blinked into life; the sun climbed high over the city. New light, cool and bright, made build-ings glow. And Chiyoko was nowhere.

And then I started taking photos. Bizarre yet logical that it should be so, that the next step in the search should be to investigate each corner of Sapporo through a lens. She could be under that bench, among the grey swirls of gravel; or in that jewellery-shop window, among glinting things beyond most means; or inside that television lying in the street, the screen caved in, off air, sculpted glass teeth like shards of light. Maybe she was hiding behind the sizzling neon signs of life, the kanji characters, the hieroglyphics, the synthetic SONY, SUNTORY, SAMSUNG. Or beyond glass office walls, smudged with reflections of other glass office walls, so blurred as to appear not as real things but as memo-ries.

At first it was abstract shots like these – bits of things, one thing and another, things singly, things in combination. But then without thought I started to picture other people, for the first time in years, as if suddenly I knew that I could only find what I was looking for through other people, that other people could bring me closer to Chiyoko, or myself, or whatever it was I needed in my life. I pointed my camera at lean nervous bodies, pressing the shutter button uncontrollably. It didn't feel like me pressing it, the images were making themselves, the shutter was wired to my brain, the mechanics of the camera no different to the mechanics of my arm or my eye. Point and shoot, point and shoot. Old bottle-hard women got caught in my glare, looked at me angrily, so I brought the camera down to waist height and randomly shot from the hip, haphazard clicks at skewed angles. Outside a baseball ground I saw interlinked metal barriers bearing one English sign saying 'CROWD CONTROL'. I did not photograph it. I looked for people, found some pressed up against the empty ticket booths, more homeless. Some in clusters but some on their own, outcasts from the group. It's the outcasts that crowd in on you, like Satoshi's little girl with the white box. The unspoken testimony in their eyes jostles your thoughts, petitions your senses. I pointed my camera at these loners without asking, winking into the viewfinder as though down the sights of a rifle. Point and shoot, point and shoot. I felt a sense of other people. Whole lives – accidents, jokes, loves, betrayals, illnesses, murders, memories, secrets – passed through my camera, disappearing into a single moment of absolute stillness.

People disappear. That's what I thought as I cut slower and slower shapes through the city, my imagination conjuring a nauseating catalogue of possible horrors and misfortunes. And that is what I was still thinking when, eventually, at eleven minutes past midday, I pulled up outside a police station and went in.

They found me a policeman who spoke decent English.

'My friend has disappeared,' I told him. 'Your friend will return,' he said. It happens all the time. People go off for the day and forget to tell anyone. Maybe she couldn't sleep and decided to head to the fish market, to see the tuna being prepared. 'I've been to the fish market,' I said. Maybe she got a call from a friend in the night. 'She took her luggage with her. She took all her things.' Well then, she probably returned to Tokyo. An argument of some sort? Not many suicidal people care to pack their suitcase and take it with them. 'But . . .' But what? Come back tomorrow, all will be better tomorrow.

On the way to the hotel I stopped at a payphone and called the Villa Dolly. Daisuke hadn't heard from her, but he didn't sound concerned either – even when I told him about how upset she had been the night before. 'Daisuke thinks Chiyoko-san does things like this. She is a funny girl.' An unpredictable girl. He thought she'd be in a bar some-where, or on the train to Tokyo. She wasn't a nine-to-five person. She did funny things. And he doubted she'd wait long before calling to check on her mother. 'She calls me three times every day,' Daisuke said. 'First time she's had holiday from caring for her mother. First holiday and she calls three times a day.'

Daisuke's words offered little clarity or comfort. That didn't come until I had re-entered the hotel, sheepishly avoided eye contact with the receptionist, and flopped down on my bed. Only then did I notice the envelope. It was lying on the floor by the bedside table, an upended pillow half shielding it from view.

23

I TUCKED my thumb into an unadhered corner of the sealing flap and ripped along the length. The handwriting was small and the letters weren't joined up.

Dear Fossy,

I'm sorry. I feel bad sneaking off like this.

Last night, when we were in the sushi place, greasy hair texted. Not to gloat, but I knew he would. A couple of shots of that gold-flaked stuff and people start to open up. I wanted to tell you last night, I really did. But I guess I was enjoying our time here so much. I wanted things to stay the same for another night. Just wanted to sit and talk to you, I guess. And then I managed to get all upset.

By the time you read this, I will probably be on the train back to Tokyo. The Shinkansen — couldn't face that boring sleeper train again. I've got my mother waiting, and Daisuke is amazing with her but it's not fair on him any more. Plus I have to study. Plus early evening shift guy is probably going to have some kind of heart failure if he keeps doing my shifts as well as his (do you think the poor guy's in love with me, just a little bit?). And anyway I'm no good at goodbyes or arguments. I half expected you to wake up as I was packing my things, but you sleep better these days.

This Satoshi thing, it's something you have to do by yourself. You told me that back in Tokyo and I probably should have listened. I thought I was a good listener until I met you, and now I feel like the only thing I'm good at is talking.

You need to go to this address: S2E5 Chūō-ku.

Greasy hair says it's a big old building not far from the fish market. He says you need to ask for a woman called Wendy. When you're done, you know where I am – in that little office, waiting for someone interesting to come through the door.

Please don't be angry with me.

You mean a lot.

Love,

C

Besides this one-page note, written on a piece of hotel paper, the envelope contained a stack of 10,000-yen notes. Crisp and new like a deck of cards. I didn't bother counting them. I tossed the letter and the money onto her side of the bed. The taut bed sheet bore the faint imprint of her presence. Cruder traces too: a lipstick stain, a pubic hair.

When Chiyoko's words had found traction in my mind, I headed to the hotel bar. I took a window seat. I laid out Satoshi's letters on the table in front of me, along with his mother's letter, the obituary and the transcript of the Watanabe interview. The more I read them, the less I had to read. Remembered phrases, whole passages, turned into music, replaying on an endless loop in my head. I looked away from the words and I could still hear them, their chimings and interchimings, the way they echoed. I sensed the full spectrum of chords, light and heavy, that made up Satoshi's life. The documents weren't the only things with me: under the table, in my satchel, there was the package. The package containing the Jiffy bag. The Jiffy bag containing three eggshell envelopes, probably full of more pages. The nested layers of a paper onion, paper on paper on paper. Did I even want to know what was in the middle? Most of all I was tired of carrying the package around, looking at it every day.

A yawning waiter brought me peanuts and another whisky. I drank and ate. Then I ordered a butterscotch schnapps, because it was a drink they had, and some more snacks. Perhaps there were a few loose pills in the bottom of my satchel. I rummaged around, nails scratching at the leather, but all my hand found was heavy cloth.

The knife. She had forgotten the knife.

24

BEFORE HEADING to the address on Chiyoko's note, I allowed myself one final distraction. I walked to a post office and waited while a man with a wiry body and a pinched face weighed my cardboard box and stuck a label on it. It contained two film canisters. My images of Hokkaidō. Air-sealed, ready for a chemical bath. Benches, shops, signs, broken televisions – but also people. I felt that some of the less abstract pictures might be worthwhile. I imagined Perry's face, the box landing on his desk. He would creak forward in his leather chair, give his ponytail a satisfied tug. *Thank God, you old fucker. Thank God you've remembered how to see.*

At first, I couldn't find it.

'Not far from the fish market,' according to Chiyoko. Yet, as night closed in, no one in or around the fish market could tell me where to go. People holding canvas bags and Thermos flasks looked at me askance. They all seemed huge, padded out in winter coats and hats and furs. I pointed at Chiyoko's note and they receded with nervous laughs and speedy bows. One man, vacuum-packed in a puffa jacket, pointed a gloved finger east, up a misty hill. But there were no buildings visible in that direction, only a surplus of white trees.

Snow fell fast on the city of Sapporo. It built a blank layer between earth and sky, blemished only by the stubble of frozen plants. A lilac dusk blurred with the lavender wool of my scarf, consuming me with its colour. I didn't know what I'd done with the gloves and hat. My fingers and ears were numb with cold. The wind sighed, and the air it exhaled was thinner, much thinner than that which sheathes the Gray's Inn Road. Funny how I didn't find myself missing that corner of London any more. I was somewhere else entirely, where the half-light strained my eyes in new and imaginative ways. However much I squinted, the surroundings refused to tidy themselves into distinct shapes and fixed distances.

Another man, so ruddy-faced as to seem on the verge of cardiac arrest, backed away from me with a bow. I was not going to get any more clues. The plot had been exhausted. I was simply going to have to press east, up that misty hill. I took Chiyoko's note and my alcohol breath and crunched through the tilted snow.

Glancing back periodically, eyes following footprint embroidery, I saw the market getting smaller. The blue plastic tubs that once contained fish were upturned now, transformed into urban snow-barriers. The characters with dark overcoats were no more than silhouettes. Up ahead, there were no footprints at all. The landscape, so muffled and blank, contained me.

I came upon a slippery path flanked by skeletal trees. The effort required to keep upright exhausted me, but I followed it, let it wind me up a steep incline. It wasn't clear where that path ended; it looked at first as if it simply took off into the skies. Only as I clambered further did a picture start to compose itself. A Gothic spire rose up in the distance like a lethally sharp weapon. Slowly, a whole building was revealed: the spire sat atop a clock tower; the clock tower sprouted from a snow-coated roof; the roof lay on a vast box of bricks. I dipped my head, hair heavy with tree-filtered slush, and carried on climbing.

The path ended on flat ground, twenty or thirty metres from the isolated building. The snow had settled into plough lines in the earth, forming a crowd of swirling routes that led nowhere. I walked towards an illuminated arch directly beneath the clock tower. It burned yellow with the perfect symmetry of a candle flame. A dark masculine form stood where the wick should have been. I expected him to make some small movement as I drew closer, but he stayed motionless.

'*Konbanwa*,' I said, coming to a halt in front of him.

'*Konbanwa*,' he said, with a small bow. From his lips, it sounded like a different word altogether.

His face looked like it had been thrown together at random. In isolation, his features were conventional. Each could have found a happy home on pretty much any face. Yet they didn't quite fit together. His ears were girlishly delicate but his nose belonged to a boxer. His cheekbones were high and pale and well defined, yet further down his face they sank into cocoa-coloured jowls. The body was simpler to behold: it had an honest adult bulkiness to it.

'Good evening,' I said.

He frowned. 'English no good.'

'My Japanese isn't so good either.'

He frowned some more as I handed him Chiyoko's note. I pointed at the address with a livid, fat finger.

'Here?' I asked. 'Correct? Here?'

He nodded. 'There someone English,' he said, beckoning me to follow him.

We came to an electronic security scanner. What possible need could there be for it here? Perhaps this was a famous monument. Maybe it was an old museum. He took my satchel and glanced under the flap, then abandoned it on a shadow-streaked table. He wasn't a great security guard: no questions about the package, for a start, nor the knife. He invited me through the scanner with a thick flourish of his hand. When a beeping sound pierced the silence, he pointed to my pockets. He stared at my fistfuls of coins, then found a little plastic airport tray to hold them.

As I walked through for a second time, on this occasion without alarm, he said, 'Collect when check out.'

'Check out?'

He nodded.

'I at least need my satchel back. I'm only here to see a woman called Wendy.'

His eyebrows did an inebriated jig when he heard the name. He gave me the satchel and guided me down the corridor. It was dim-lit, cold and somehow forlorn. I started to feel nausea swelling in the pit of my stomach and it occurred to me that, since running out of pills, I'd been almost symptom-free.

The corridor opened out onto a warmer space and feeling started to return to my fingers. White walls, heavy carpet and lots of light. The ceiling was high and framed with swirl-shaped mouldings. The windows were bordered by thick curtains, tied back with sashes, and there was a small television in the far corner of the room. Four people were sat in a row watching it, their hair visible over the back of a cerise sofa. As the muddle-faced security man led me towards them, they bobbed up from behind the sofa in unison, like a mob of swivelling meerkats, and stared at me. They were a mixed bunch – different ages, sexes, sizes – but all of them pale and thin, their cheeks stripped of flesh.

A little glass-walled office was tucked in an enclave off to the right. We stopped outside it, inches from the glass, looking in. There were two lamps in the room, but neither of them was switched on. There was no need: spokes of light streamed in from the television area. A Western woman sat inside, hefty and tousle-mopped, and we seemed to be waiting for her to notice us. She was at a desk, scribbling on paper. Her face had a greenish aspect to it. Her eyes, lost in the loose folds of her face, looked like two spots of mould on a cabbage. A cabbage ripening in a greenhouse.

Security guy tapped on the glass.

'Ya!' shouted the cabbage. 'Come in, will you!'

As we stepped inside, her little black eyes darted from my face, to my waist, to my shoes, before settling on my nose.

'Wendy,' she said, extending her hand but staying in her chair, 'Poplar.' She spoke with a nasal, staccato South African accent. I walked over and shook her hand, told her my name.

'Bounce,' she said to the security guy, following this with a phlegmy chain of quick-fire Japanese words. He nodded and turned, clicking the door shut behind him.

'His name's Bounce?'

'Ya. It's just a nickname, obviously. It makes things easier if each of the residents has a Western nickname.'

Although uninvited, I took a seat in the single wooden chair facing her. It was considerably lower than her chair. I looked up at her; she looked down at me.

'Residents?' I said.

She coughed, phlegm wobbling in her throat. 'Y-a-a-a-a,' she said, the drawn-out sound seeming accusatory, as if it was the necessary counterbalance to a deficiency in my mental faculties. 'Residents.'

'Let me explain, Wendy. I may be in completely the wrong place, of course, but I think you are the person I need to speak to. A friend of mine, a girl named Chiyoko Kobayashi, she told me to come here. She was told by a guy called . . . he has greasy hair. And he found out from this postgrad who . . . Well, to give you the short version, I was told I needed to speak to you.'

'To *me*, hey? So you're not looking to check in?'

'To check in? No. I don't think so. I just want to talk to you for a few minutes. I am here to try and see . . . a resident, I suppose. Or an employee. I'm not sure which. His name is Pickford, although he may also go by the name of Satoshi.'

Her eyes widened for a second, although not wide enough for me to make out any white padding around the pupils.

'Chiyoko, hey?'

'Yes.'

'Pretty name, hey? If you like that sort of thing.'

'I suppose so, yes.'

'How is it you've come here to see Satoshi? You're from the university, are you?'

'Satoshi is here, then?'

'Oh yes,' she said, 'he's always here.'

25

THIS WAS it. I was aware that my search had come to an end. I looked at my hands, saw how they trembled silently. My shirt cuffs embarrassed small hairs on my wrists.

Wendy Poplar said, 'And you say you're from the university?'

'No. You mean Hokkaidō University?'

'Hmm, ya, of course. It's been a few years, but to start with a couple of people from the university visited him.'

'Satoshi?'

'Satoshi.'

'I see. Well, I'm not from the university.'

'So where *are* you from? You've got to be from somewhere, hey? You can't just walk in and have a poke around. It's not a bloody zoo.'

'Of course not. He's my . . . uncle.'

'Huh,' she snorted. 'Family, hey? Family's a rare thing with this sorry lot. They drive me mad, I tell you.'

She lifted a hand and waved it around aimlessly, then pointed a finger at the television area. The residents were studying the screen with single-minded devotion. It looked like a documentary about deep-sea creatures. A squid was swimming up from the sea floor, and a nearby fish with an enormous pouch-like lower jaw looked set to unleash violence upon it.

'Excuse me for asking the obvious,' I said, 'but what *is* this place?'

'You mean you don't know?'

'No.'

The squid squirted out a cloud of black ink, a desperate attempt to avoid being eaten.

'Ya,' she said, following my eyes. 'Antisocial mollusc, the squid.'

As with anyone who revels in maintaining a position of authority over others, it took a while to get any basic facts out of her. People like Wendy Poplar realise that information is power, and they hang on to it at all costs. She had the highly strung arrogance of someone too preoccupied with her own importance to know or care how she was perceived.

It transpired that the place was called Fernhall House, Fernhall being the name of the American First World War veteran who had set it up. From what I could gather it was a care home or asylum, servicing expats and locals who needed twenty-four-hour access to help. Wendy was keen to emphasise that residency was voluntary ('No one sectioned round here, hey?') and that Fernhall House was the only place of its kind in Hokkaidō. It was clear from the manner in which they were slumped in front of the television, etherised and vacant, that the residents were not well. They didn't just look bored, they looked withdrawn. They looked sunk. Like my mother, like Chiyoko's mother.

'So this is really a kind of . . . mental facility?'

'Mental, hey?'

Her skin flared from green to red. She flexed a round hand and grabbed a large black book from her desk. For a moment I thought she was going to hurl it across the room at me, but instead she slammed it down flat on the oak. *Bang*. The impact reverberated around the whole room. 'Mental,' she muttered bitterly.

'I'm sorry if I've caused offence.'

'*Mental* is not a word we use round here, sonny. These people deserve to be treated with dignity, hey?'

As the shock of her outburst subsided into silence, I struggled to restrain a smirk. The prospect of her treating anyone with dignity was comically remote.

'This is a long-term care facility. Ya. A care *facility*. Understand? No mental people here.'

She fell silent again.

'Ya! No one mental, hey? What we have here is people suffering from some *issues*.'

There was an extended silence.

'Many of them fought in wars, you know? Some just have a spot of dementia, nothing more. The brain equivalent of a sore throat.'

She seemed immensely pleased with the analogy.

I said, 'Dementia, I see. Alzheimer's and so on.'

'Huh,' she scoffed. 'Everyone always goes for that one. Alzheimer's, ya. Alzheimer's we have. We've got Alzheimer's in spades. Bucketloads of Alzies. But also multi-infarct, vascular blockies, that kind of thing.'

She went on talking for a long time. She told me that there were over sixty diseases that could cause dementia. I didn't bother telling her that I already knew all of this, that

I'd read every book on the subject. I knew that in some cases dementia was just part of a whole host of problems and symptoms. I knew that in most cases it could not be reversed. I knew that new surroundings and new people could trigger panic in the sufferer. I knew that it could change a personality, make a person irritable, moody, angry, until they recognised nobody, least of all themselves, and relatives couldn't bear to visit, and when the sufferer died you had to pretend to grieve, when in fact all you felt was empty relief. Yes: empty relief. Thank God, you thought, because you'd already used up all the grief, you'd been mourning them for years. I already knew all of this, and much more, but it didn't stop Wendy Poplar talking.

'Anyway, dementia only affects a few of the people here, hey? A few of the Impaireds. Bounce has a very mild sort. The Chronics, the ones you see watching television over there, they're a different ball game. They have all kinds of problems. Schizophrenia, dissociated identity, tic disorders, panic disorders, anxiety disorders. Ya. You name it, the Chronics have got it.'

'What about Satoshi?'

'He's an Impaired. But he'll be a Chronic soon enough. They only go one way when they get to his age.'

'What's the nature of his . . . ?'

'Problem? Don't you know, him being your uncle and all?'

'No. I've never met him. Mother's brother. Estranged. My mother died and left a parcel for him, that's why I'm here.'

I opened my satchel and showed her the package.

'I come into contact with a lot of family feuds in my line of work,' she said, giving me a knowing smile, as if I should now understand what kind of woman I was dealing with. 'With Satoshi, the docs think it's PTSD. Post-traumatic stress disorder. In all likelihood, it's down to things that happened to him in the post-war period. You know he worked in Tokyo during the occupation? Difficult time. Mostly PTSD sets in within three months of the traumatic event. Ya. But in some cases, it's years – decades – before the symptoms emerge. Satoshi doesn't talk about it, whatever the trauma was, and won't see a counsellor. So it's hard to know exactly what's going on in his head. But a main symptom of PTSD is reliving the ordeal. Through thoughts. Ya. Thoughts and memories of the trauma. Flashbacks, hallucinations, nightmares. They try to forget but they can't. Opposite problem to the demented ones. But he gets by OK. We have him on drugs that help.'

'Drugs?'

'To calm him. There was one occasion, one July, when he got very agitated. Made a pile of old photos and papers in his room, tried to set fire to them. We started him on drugs. He's been better since.'

'Can I see him?'

'You'll need to sign the register first. He'll be in the games room. But if he's playing chess, you'll have to leave him until he's finished. He's usually playing chess, if he's not in his room going through his things – books, photos and so on. We can stand and watch, hey? They won't mind that.'

She picked up the black book from her desk. On a page with red ruled borders I wrote my name.

'Follow me, Mr Fossick.'

I swallowed hard as the walls of the corridor closed in on me, the boundaries narrowing all the time.

26

I WAS the outsider in Fernhall House, but they were all outsiders really. Outside society. Outside time. You hear people say that those in asylums and care facilities are out of their minds. But in truth their minds are often the one thing they are *not* out of. Their whole being is sheltering behind walls of muscle and bone. Everything they are – and are not – exists within their sacrosanct headspace.

The games room was the Impaireds' territory, and for a second, as we arrived in the doorway, they froze. All in unison, one being, my presence momentarily disrupting a collective thought. I scanned the human mass, twenty or thirty thick, and wondered if one of them was Satoshi. The residents were clustered in little cliques, hunched over green card tables, playing all manner of games. Scrabble, gin rummy, draughts. A few of them talked to each other, or at least exchanged monologues which could pass for conversation, but in most corners there was hollow silence. Every face was ashen and soft, as if long submerged in cold water.

'Where is Satoshi?'

'Hmm. Can't see him, hey? Must be in the toilet. Give him a minute. He'll be here soon enough.'

It was a universe like any other. I could already see that there were command structures and hierarchies in place. Some games were the exclusive preserve of certain women: they hissed like effervescent pills at anyone outside the bridge clique who wanted to have a go. There were particular armchairs – the coveted ones by the fire or the window – that were the private domain of particular men. Special constituencies evolved around the poker table, the snakes and ladders table, the snap table. Cigarettes and boiled sweets were distributed by certain people in a certain way; you needed to know who to ask and how to ask. Loners wore meditative looks; their minds may have been a battleground for competing memories and truths, but their bodies spoke only of defeat. It was like any business, or family, or society. Amid the innumerable shades of kindness and cruelty that make up the pattern of everyday life, each individual knows his place.

I watched, but at a remove, the bystander's distance from a messy scene. Wendy picked out some of the key characters for me. There was Jennings, who looked much younger than the rest. He was an Impaired with 'early onset' dementia. His favourite thing was to dance his long fingers along the keys of an imaginary piano. Most of the time he stayed in his room listening to Chopin records. He was notionally present in a game of gin rummy with a spindly bipolar man called, counter-intuitively, the Fat Controller. Apparently the name was on account of his nightly refusal to relinquish command of the television remote control, even when he wasn't in the television area. I saw that he had it now, protruding from the breast pocket of his shirt, the red 'on' button facing outward like a badge of honour.

Wendy continued to give me her inside track on everyone. She was enjoying herself, breathing through her mouth and rolling her black eyes ecstatically. Playing Scrabble in the corner we had a heavily made-up woman desperately clinging to her late forties or early fifties, her wrinkled cleavage sinking into a low neckline, and a handsome, tanned man who could have been anywhere between sixty and eighty.

'Who are they, playing Scrabble?'

'That's Sadie. Nicknamed Sadie the Saddle.'

'Why's that?'

Wendy looked me up and down before answering. 'Ha ha. Ya. You'll work it out if you stay long enough, hey?'

'And the tanned guy?'

'Him? If you'll excuse my French, he's known as The Shit.'

Sadie and The Shit sat in front of a door. It was closed, but some yellow light seeped under it. The pool of light extended to the table next to theirs, where a bald man with an excessively shiny head sat staring at a chessboard littered with pieces. There was an empty chair opposite him.

'Why's The Shit called The Shit?'

She gave me a long answer to this question. I tuned out halfway through, but gathered that he liked to offend others through incessant swearing.

'What about the bald man?'

'Can't quite recall without consulting my records. I call him Bald Man. Friend of Satoshi's.'

A toilet flushed. The door behind Sadie and The Shit creaked open, its shadow slowly lengthening across the carpet. An old man emerged.

'That,' Wendy said, 'is your Uncle Satoshi.'

* * *

Did I have, all along, a specific picture of him in my head? I suppose I must have done, because I was overwhelmed by a sense that he didn't look as he should look. I felt he should have one of those useful faces that appear striking one minute and perfectly ordinary the next. He should have white teeth and honest eyes shining amid a network of dignified bones. He should have a stately crinkle at the corners of the eyes. But the real Mr Satoshi had none of these things.

He walked doggedly towards the bald man's card table, rolling the sleeves of a thick jumper up to his elbows, staring at the chessboard as he lowered himself stage by stage into the empty seat. They recommenced their game in silence. Both of them leaned forward heavily from the hips, their forearms resting on the green tabletop and their heads almost touching. Satoshi's arms had that brownish tone that buildings get as cities slowly stain them. Apart from the arms and the chess set, the only thing on the table was a spiral-bound notebook with a red crayon tunnelled through the rings.

'Can't interrupt now, hey?'

I didn't respond. All I could do was wait. I kept thinking that at any moment he would look up and fix me with a stare, that he would see in me some flicker of my mother. I kept the jangling nerves at bay through my fervour in assessing him. I scanned his features over and over, but I couldn't familiarise myself with them. It seemed a shadow had fallen between us, leaving his characteristics veiled, unlit. He sat in silence. I couldn't even hear him breathe. I attributed to him a deep, smooth voice, but I supposed it was just as likely to be thin and rasping.

'He doesn't seem to say much,' I whispered.

'Not much, hey? An understatement, I have to tell you. Satoshi doesn't say anything at all. Ya. Nothing.'

I turned to face her. 'What do you mean?'

'He arrived here about three years ago, hey? Well, for the last two years, he hasn't said a word. I mean, nothing.'

'Nothing at all?'

'Nothing. Not because of any physical disability. He's what they call a voluntary mute. He says nothing.'

Much as I loathed her, there was an authority to her words: *he says nothing*.

'Is it a symptom of his PTSD?'

'Nah. The doc says it's by choice. Ya. Weird but true. Satoshi has just decided not to speak any more.'

She pressed her chin into her neck and it all became one big fleshy mess.

'How does he express himself? How does he get by?'

'He has that little pad and crayon,' she said, nodding in the direction of the card table. 'If it's important, he writes it down in there and shows it to you.'

'Why a crayon? Why not a pen?'

'Ha, you really have to ask, hey? In a place like this, the pen's a tool of torture, of self-harm.'

Just then, one of the residents let loose a joyous, child-like giggle. It was The Shit. Sadie sat back with her arms crossed, staring at the Scrabble board with a look of rueful resignation on her face. The Shit leaned forward in his chair. Tiny movements of his forefinger inched a line of Scrabble tiles back and forth. He muttered arithmetic under his breath. Then he stood up, pointing down at Sadie.

'Double letter score on the "K" – ten – plus the

others, and triple word score on the "G". Total? Sixty-six! *Woo-hooo*.'

The Shit beat his chest and dug for new letters in a green felt pouch. The rest of the residents turned to look. On the board beneath him the tiles were lined up for us to see: 'FVCKING'.

'That's not allowed!' Sadie protested. 'It's a swear word, and you've used a "V" instead of a "U".'

'Fuck you!' The Shit yelled back.

It was not the right time to approach Satoshi. He was still staring at the chessboard as though his small life depended on it.

Wendy Poplar seemed to be warming to me, and I tried to encourage it. I needed her on my side. She held information, secrets. I was prepared to be servile and toadying if it kept her from shutting me out of the picture, from dropping casually devastating remarks about the severity of Satoshi's condition without going on to explain everything, the full diagnosis, the context and the colour. She said she would take me to Satoshi's room when he headed to bed. He was one of six residents in Sector 1D on the ground floor. He had his own bedroom, but shared simple cooking facilities and a communal area with his 'sector-mates', all Impaireds.

'Will you answer some of my questions about him?' I said, following her through the corridors. It was unpleasant, watching her baggy-trousered, short-legged waddle.

She said, 'Ya, why not.' She paused and did some kind of back-stretching exercise. 'Luckily I'm not rushed off my feet this evening, hey? We can use my office.'

We sat down, I asked my questions, and Wendy answered

them with annoying little flourishes. She had a habit of glancing down at Satoshi's resident file, which lay fanned on her desk, and saying things like: 'Well, of course, I have confidentiality issues to consider, but between you and me . . .'

Physically, he had no fewer ailments than you might expect for a man of his age. The medics said he seemed to make light of his problems, shooing them away when they tried to examine him. But there were issues that occasionally required attention. He suffered from muscular contracture in his hands, for example. A Dr Phillips had noted that the contracture was linked to 'a failure of muscle memory'. A person's muscles remember certain basic movements, apparently. Certain motor skills, through repetition, become automatic. But if muscle memory fades, activities that since childhood have required no thought at all – the movements necessary for tooth-brushing, hair-combing, nail-clipping – need to be learned afresh. Satoshi regularly performed hand exercises to try and lessen the impact of his condition, gripping a stone in his fist and working the tendons. Even so, everyday tasks were increasingly difficult. He used to like walking round the gardens in summer, plucking up weeds and tending to flowers, but it was harder now. His body was forgetting. His mind wouldn't, of course. It refused to forget, it lit up his dreams, the eerie sheen of things done and not done.

His eyes weren't so good, but he refused to wear glasses. He was thought to believe that nature should take its course. He ate less each year. His favourite food was fish, preferably salmon, with salty chips that he ate with his fingers. Mostly he spent mealtimes down in the residents' canteen rather than the Sector 1D kitchen. Occasionally one of the staff members took him to a convenience store down the hill, near the fish market. Satoshi bought frugal and simple foods: bags of salad, cheese already grated, carrots, eggs, rice. And biscuits. 'Ya, he likes biscuits, and cold coffee from cans, the aroma as much as the taste.' Sometimes he drank a sherry at the end of the afternoon, and at dinner he liked a glass of white wine if it was available.

Lately he had become frailer and thinner. His wrists and forearms hadn't always been gaunt. Bounce reported that when you put your arm around him these days, you noticed how prominent his shoulder blades felt, even through a heavy jumper. He always wore a heavy woollen jumper, the same one, regardless of the season.

The other residents at Fernhall seemed to consider him thoughtful and prized his background in academia. Some of them called him 'The Prof'. The Shit called him 'The Fucking Prof'. He was famous for his hoarding skills. He couldn't bear to throw anything away. He clutched on to valueless objects as if each one were the key to a precious lock, a lock in a door he hadn't yet come upon. He kept his whole history heaped in cupboards and on his shelves: fat stacks of letters from his parents and old school friends; family photographs dating back to the forties and fifties; boxes crowded with objects whose importance only he knew (beer mats, postcards, a belt buckle, fishing tackle, certain pebbles and stones). He hadn't taken to labelling the boxes, as far as Wendy was aware; he knew only too well what was inside. He had a lot of books, too. Almost as many books as were held in the little reference library on the second floor. Sometimes, when residents couldn't find a particular novel in the library, they asked him. If he had it, he gave it to them.

Before he went silent, which was sometime at the end of his first year in residence, his behaviour had become increasingly erratic. His chess opponents would make a move and he would study the reconfigured pieces with interest, but seconds later his eyes would float elsewhere, fixing on some blank chunk of wall or carpet. He seemed somehow absent; his mind had abandoned the moment. His file revealed that, around this time, he had tried to attack another resident with a felt-tip pen. Later, on the night of 20 July that year, he had attempted to start a fire in his room. Bounce caught him lighting a safety match by the bed.

One or two of his old students at the University of Hokkaidō visited him in that first year. Perhaps one fellow lecturer, too; Wendy wasn't sure. In any event, before their visits tailed off the former students told her about the 'trigger' for him checking into Fernhall, an incident that occurred during an early-morning lecture on a cold bright Tuesday. Satoshi was giving the lecture. But in mid-flow, mid-sentence even, he stopped. He just stood there, behind the lectern, staring out at the audience. It was like he was looking through them, through the fold-down chairs and scribbling hands, at some horrific scene. He raised his hands above his head. Two colleagues from the anthropology department were present. They had noticed that he had been acting strangely recently, but this was where it all came to a head. Satoshi started muttering things under his breath. Then he began to bring his clenched fists down on the thick wad of lecture notes in front of him, lightly at first, but then with greater vigour. It was the final, almighty pummel that sent the lectern tumbling to the floor. One of the two colleagues, a professor, went up to the stage to help him. But Satoshi wanted no help. He swivelled and punched him square on the jaw. The professor went tumbling down, his body flailing hopelessly, his face impacting on a sharp edge of the fallen lectern. Students talked of the sound of tearing flesh, then the thud of the professor's body hitting the floor, purple blood gushing from under the eye.

The wounded professor recovered and tried to hush the whole thing up. He was an ambitious man with his eye on the top job, that of president of the university. He didn't press charges, didn't want to bring further shame on the university and embarrassment on himself, but insisted that Satoshi seek psychiatric help.

I said, 'Was he called Jenkins?'

'Hey?'

'Was the professor's name Jenkins?'

'That might have been it, ya. Dr Jenkins rings some bells. Apparently rumours started going round his department that it wasn't the first time Satoshi had gone crazy, that during the occupation he'd murdered a colleague, one of his own. Something like that. When that kind of stuff gets round, your career in the Far East is over. In my experience the Japanese can forgive most things, hey? But not lack of self-control. And as for Jenkins, it's already hard enough progressing over here when you're Western, especially in an old institution like Hokkaidō University. I myself have come up against prejudice at Fernhall. Ya, even me! But if someone like Jenkins gets in some sort of punch-up, people assume he's an uncultured lout. He's tainted. There's a saying

259

in Japan: "If a nail stands out, hammer it in." The worst thing you can do is stand out from the crowd, hey? If something makes you stand out, cover it up.'

A buzzer sounded. I looked at Wendy Poplar's desktop clock. The digital reading was 21:31.

'Ya,' she said, staring at the numbers. 'It's their bedtime.'

I walked the corridors with her, both of us peering into the rooms through circular windows, her commentary buzzing in my ear. The last few bedside lights died and the rooms filled with instant human gloom.

'This is his room,' she said, rapping her knuckles on the door.

There was no response, but she opened it anyway. We stood in the doorway, her hand on the scuffed doorknob, my hand on the satchel hanging from my shoulder.

'Hey, Satoshi, you have a guest.'

27

I SAW Satoshi in profile. He sat with folded hands in a rocking chair facing a snow-flecked window, his face lit by a lamp on the sill. The pale wood of the chair was highly polished, gleaming as it rocked to and fro. His bed was behind him, tidied in an alcove, so tightly made as to give no sign of human repose.

I said, 'Would it be OK if you left the two of us alone?'

'Why not. Satoshi?'

He looked at us, head tilted to give a clear sightline, and as if in prayer his heavy lids came down with frayed veins across his eyes. His trousers were going shiny at the knees.

'Satoshi, I see you haven't got into bed yet, which is not usually ideal, hey? No. Not usually ideal. But before you go to sleep, which you will, I'm going to leave this gentleman with you. His name's Mr Fossick. He's come all the way from England. Ya. England. To give you something from his mother.'

As his eyelids lifted, I was sure I saw a flicker of recognition in the pupils, a tiny hoop of sunshine. For no longer than a second, perhaps half a second, but I saw it before he turned away, went back to staring straight ahead. He may have been looking out of the window, or he may have been studying his own reflection in the darkened glass. The ceiling above him was mottled with damp stains, grey areas where the outside was seeping in. It seemed only a matter of time before the whole room would disintegrate. The ceiling would go first, then the window frame, then the walls. But as things stood, despite its inevitable fate, the room was holding its own.

'Ya. OK then, good. I'll leave you two gentlemen to it for a few minutes.'

The sound of the door shutting emphasised the quiet it had interrupted. The rocking chair creaked softly, slowly. The only other sound was the sweep of shuffling feet, the rhythms of corridor life behind me. It was strange how, as the chair rocked him, Satoshi was able to sit completely still. He was embraced by the inward-curving arms, caught up in the gentle back-and-forthness. The rocking seemed to occur independently of him.

'You knew my mother,' I said eventually. 'Alice. You were sweethearts once, I think. Before you went to Japan. I think you returned to England in 1946. I don't know whether you got back together then. I guess not, or not for long.'

He carried on rocking, looking straight ahead. On the windowsill in front of him, next to the low-wattage lamp, were his pad and crayon. He made no effort to retrieve them. On a shelf to my right, breaking up a long line of books, was a glass bowl three-quarters full with water. A few silvery fish made laps inside with smooth grace, leaving the surface undisturbed. I moistened my lips.

'She thought a lot of you. That much I can tell, reading

between the lines. No doubt she was hurt, when, for whatever reason, it didn't work out. But it was plain that she cared for you. She was a pragmatic woman. Not the sort to get bogged down in unproductive feelings. Witty, clever. I don't think she would have held bitterness inside her. It's none of my business, of course. None of this is, really. But I thought you would want to know. She mentioned you, and . . . I think she cared.'

The room smelt of biscuits. All kinds of biscuits, jumbled together in a dark cool tin. Rich Teas, digestives, custard creams, bourbons.

'I've come to Japan to give you something. You weren't that easy to find, so I'm afraid it's a bit battered.'

While he carried on rocking, slower than before, I reached into my satchel and took out the package. The ends had begun to unfasten themselves. I let the satchel slump onto the carpet and moved close enough to put the package on his lap, feeling a kind of protective tenderness towards the gift, a need to preserve and restore it even as I gave it away. He didn't touch it at first, but when it started to slip from his knees he clasped hold of it tightly. It sat there, trapped in his hands, his fingernails full of strange lines and looking loose. His hands, his neck, his face: all were embroidered with creases and displaced veins. Looking down at his thinning hair, I found myself trying to put Satoshi in context, to fit the human form to the letters and the story. And it started to work, he began to seem true to my imagination, to resemble the person I had read about, as if I were remaking him in the energy of a lens.

'I don't know how much you know, or how much you want to know.'

He rocked to and fro, back and forth, saying nothing.

'They eventually divorced, but in '59, my mother married my father. He worked in finance. I don't know whether the timing came about by choice or by biology, but she had me very late. 1968. She was a housewife after meeting Dad, then worked at a travel agency. Didn't travel much, nervous flyer. We have that in common.'

He still held the package in his hands as the chair moved him, but his face had changed, if only faintly. A kind of mute strength seemed to have washed over it – a determination, a sense of the limits he might need to exceed in order to match his memories to mine, to my mother's. The wispy brows looked more furrowed now. The cracked lips were rustling into tautness.

'I hope you are happy here,' I said, my throat weak and dry. 'If you're not, if you're not treated well, I will do something about it. I will speak to someone.'

The chair rocked, like a ship on the motion of a wave, transporting and containing him, swaying him between remembering and forgetting. I felt my breathing change, sensed it synchronising with the chair's rhythms, deepening and slowing. It felt familiar yet new. From nowhere, a thought came to mind. The thought of my French teacher at school, Mr Able with the goatee beard that looked somehow optional, stuck on or left off as required, telling me that in French the word 'chair' means 'flesh'.

'My mother died. We had her funeral at a church in Longcross, which is a place in Surrey where she lived.'

Suddenly he stopped still. Completely still. As if frozen by some great shudder of memory. His slippers came to ground on the carpet. The weight returned to his feet. His grip on the package tightened, stubborn knuckles turning white.

I said, 'She didn't suffer. I know people always say that, but I believe it's true.'

I said, 'She fell on the patio in her garden.'

I said, 'She would have died straight away from the blow.'

I said, 'Nothing anyone could have done.'

I felt a lump twisting up my throat, but I swallowed it down. Now that it made no sound, it seemed the chair had been creaking out a rhythmic crying all the time, a measured expression of urgent grief.

His head inclined forward until his chin was drooped on his chest.

'Perhaps I should give you some time alone.'

His hands moved across the package, trembling fingers caressing the paper, unfurling the ends.

'I will give you some time alone.'

It was me saying this, but I found I could not turn away. Our shadows had merged on the thin carpet. He took the three eggshell white envelopes from the bed of flattened brown paper, and he ripped the ends open, one after the other. He tipped the contents of the first envelope into his hand. It was a colour photograph of me as a baby, at the hospital, in my mother's arms. I was familiar with the picture. There had been the larger, framed version on her wall in Finegold, and since clearing out her flat it had been in my wardrobe. There was a small white label stuck on the bottom of the copy that Satoshi held. The label obscured some of my mother's forearm. In her handwriting, it said: 'Robert, my son'. Satoshi held it up to the light and kept it there, trying to shape a response or organise an emotion.

Then he emptied the second envelope. Another photograph slid out. I recognised this image too: a copy had hung on Mum's wall next to the other, the second limb of her strategy to remember 1968, and it too was in my wardrobe gathering dust. A slightly different pose, and this one was in black and white, somehow more out of focus, but once again it was me as a baby in her arms at the hospital.

Except that the label didn't have my name on it. It said: 'Alice, our daughter'.

Satoshi's hands shaking, the fish in the bowl rotating, my eyes slowly turning, taking in the photograph, realising that it was not me caught in the flatness, the gloss, the black-and-white trap.

'But that's. That is. I don't.'

I didn't understand. Alice. My mother's name. Who was this baby in her arms, this other Alice? It made no sense, but it was a strange thing, because although part of me was baffled by this photograph, this label, this name, another part of me felt a surge of familiar heat. Not panic, not fear, not even memory, just a sense of something long ago lost, a lonely abandoned thing, a television left flickering in an empty room.

I didn't leave until he had tipped the contents of the third and final envelope into his hand. Folded letter paper. My mother's handwriting covering several sheets. Strange to see such an expanse of it, the words all crowded together, not broken up on drawers and cupboards.

Bounce, with his hotchpotch facial features, was waiting for me in the dark corridor.

I think I told him I needed water. That must be why he

walked me to the laundry room, handed me a cold paper cone. I don't remember seeing the water cooler itself, just the cone, raising it to my lips and gulping the liquid down in a single swallow. I can picture the watch on Bounce's wrist too: a Rolex, or a counterfeit imitation of one. And I know what happened next, I remember the events that followed. I close my eyes now, and they replay.

Here I am, dazed, thinking about Alice, my sister, counting twelve washing machines, some in sparkling chrome and others in a dirty white. None of them is currently in action, but a dry and heavy heat hangs in the air, the aftermath of earlier activity. The citrus-fresh smell of laundry brings to mind wash-day Mondays in the Longcross house. How my mother would lay out the linen and clothes on drying racks, replacing yesterday's parched laundry with the new and the damp, and then take the dry items and iron them, darn them, sort them, fold them. Having the laundry in front of you is one thing. How you catalogue and codify it is something else entirely.

Such silence. Yet, with all twelve washers switched on, a full orchestra of pistons, pumps and motors whirring and beating at the same time, this room would come to life.

I start to imagine it, the machine music, but something in the atmosphere of the laundry room changes.

Bounce sniffs, his nostrils fanning massively. Then, a beat later, I breathe it too. A chemical fug, the thick warped scent of burnt air. He looks accusingly at the machines. It must be coming from one of them, a fuse gone or a part overheated.

But it is not a fuse or a part. I know this. I know this smell.

28

HE IS creeping lightly toward the laundry room's only door, as if economy of movement and softness of step might keep the danger at bay. The door has a rectangular window and it is clouded over with dim swirls of dust. He reaches a palm out to push, the door swings, the window narrows to the width of an envelope, and pouchy smoke billows in.

Bounce disappears into the corridor. I clench my teeth. My heart is shaking every vein in my body.

Seconds later he returns, his face set in tones of panicked fascination. His eyes are like children's games, full of rolling marbles and jigsaw lines and unmatched colours. He grabs my wrist and takes me toward a sash window at the back of the room. There's a metal bolt screwed into the top panel, clamping the window to the frame. I scan around for a key to open it but Bounce, with a colossal upward jerk, sends the bottom panel crashing over the top. The sheared bolt soars up, strikes the ceiling, arcs downward, clatters, spins, rolls, and with a bristling hiss a wave of icy air bursts into the room.

'You go out,' Bounce says, sweat trickling down his

temples, greasing his delicate lobes. 'Big fire, OK to go out.'

More smoke now, thicker, darker. Suddenly, everything is grey. It is not a room any more but a world, a universe of smoke and ash, a time and space whirring with lost things. The grey mass has no edge or limit and keeps growing.

But I know that we are on the ground floor, and I know that I am right by an open window. If I clamber out blindly, the worst I will end up with is cuts from a thorny bush, a broken ankle from uneven ground. Bounce is right, it's OK to go out, and his hand is pressed against the small of my back as I feel for the windowsill – powdery, thick with dust and grime.

Disembodied voices filter in. Mutterings at first, then high-pitched whimpers, then frenetic shrieks, dancing unnervingly around us, looping through snails of fog. I no longer feel Bounce's hand on my back. I turn and squint. In slow-moving light I make out his bulky form, bent double, heaving. The smoke pulses darker and an alarm finally sounds and Bounce vomits. A wave of colour bursts through the smoke but it has vanished in gritty mist by the time I hear it splash. I can't tell if his sickness is due to nerves, the viscous smoke, or some unrelated stomach complaint. He retches again but this time nothing comes.

'Everyone out, out, out!'

Wendy Poplar's voice snakes in from the corridor. I move away from the window. I grab a clump of Bounce's shirt. I swap places with him. I find myself lifting my right foot awkwardly to try and avoid the invisible puddle of vomit, as if safe ground requires clean shoes, and he crouches by the window, gratefully sucking at the cooler air.

'Fuck! Satoshi's room. It's on fire. Fuck!'

It could be The Shit screaming, I'm not sure, but the mention of Satoshi sends thousand-legged insects running all over my skin. As I swim through the room, currents of sound keep coming, carrying news. It is Satoshi's room that is bilging smoke, it is Satoshi's things that burn, it is Satoshi frozen with fear, unable to get himself out.

I find the door and stumble into the corridor. The smoke is so thick that I frequently have to halt, unable to find a way through the veil. I come across odd shapeless forms edging along walls. Slow motion, stop action, drifting and spinning, in this dark tunnel there are only fragments of noses and eyes and teeth, but for a moment, just a moment, they are all Chloe, lost and lost.

I guide them in twos and threes toward Wendy. She waves a torch, its thin eerie beam sweeping across our faces, marshalling fear with criss-cross energy. She shouts, 'This way out, everyone out!' through a handkerchief spotted with blood.

I talk to her. I tell her there must be an extinguisher, foam thing, somewhere an extinguisher. I talk fast, Bounce through there, window open in there, talk fast in case it helps me think fast, act fast. Each of my words is a crackle of static in the darkness, and I cannot shake the sense that I have said them before, been here before, coughing on the same smoke.

'Satoshi's room,' I say, thick mucus curdling in the back of my throat. 'It's further down there, isn't it?'

'Out,' she says, 'out.'

'Is *he* out?'

'I don't know, fire service coming.'

I shove past her, my forearm finding a way through her breast, soles crunching the glass of exploded light bulbs, legs catching on smouldering furniture.

I can't lose him. I've just found him. I can't let him slip away. There are things I need to know.

Every surface seems to be coated with the crimson embers of paper scraps, curling like prawns on a grill. I start to feel the heat intensify. The air grows dead dry. And then up ahead I see the outline of a person, a stiff little stick with scorched twigs for limbs. He gets brighter as I stagger, turning from black to grey to silver. He stands in an open doorway. In the room behind him there are yellow shapes, orange shapes, a quivering flowerbed of flames.

It is Satoshi. He is not rushing. He is not screaming. He is just standing there. There is something shiny in his hands, a broken shaft of light.

No more than five feet from him, a soft object flattens underfoot. I dip my head and squint. A bag, a satchel, my satchel, with blood gushing out of the flap. I dip lower, squint harder. No, no blood, not yet, just a formless dark cloth. The satchel empty apart from the cloth, no letters, no transcript, no obituary, no documents, only the cloth, the cloth from the Sapporo knife shop. The shiny object in Satoshi's hand is the knife.

'What are you doing?' I shout.

If there is fear in Satoshi's shaded eyes, I can't see it. He holds up the glittering blade and points the tip at my throat.

I whisper, 'What are you doing?'

He stands guard in front of the open door, back-lit by a red-orange glare. I roll my eyes down across the metal, lower my voice even more.

'Why are you standing there?'

Fear has begun its ascent through the wrecked corridor of my throat, swelling it, fattening it, bringing the bulging skin closer to the tip of the knife, and he just stands there, mute, his hand quivering, a tipsy magician waving a wand. The blade moves in shaky circles under my chin. The unsteadiness of fear, or fatigue, or muscle losing memory.

'Is there somebody in there? Is that why you're blocking it? Have you got someone in there?'

He does not deny it. He blocks the entrance. The colours soaking his shoulders and neck become vivid, bold.

The blade winces. I lean back. I give my throat room. He doesn't attempt to follow my Adam's apple with the knife. I raise a clenched fist above my head. I bring it down with all my force. *Whoosh*. His arm, his hand, the knife – they start to fall away in anticipation of the impact. *Crunch, clatter*. The arm folds, easy as paper. The blade finds debris. He starts to roll backwards and as he rolls he grabs, inexpertly, at a clump of hair on the back of my head. I feel an inexplicable flash of hot bliss, sunshine over a dark city, and I clutch his arm, bend it, kick his leg, drag him into cooler corridor, find Poplar, scream at her, dump him at her feet.

And then, alone, running away from them all, the thick air streaming with lost shouts, I burst into his room.

The sensations hit me all at once: the dazzling light, the liquid heat, the madcap crackle. The carpet is disintegrating underfoot, leaving only stone, calcined, a terrifying white, so hot I feel I'm wearing no shoes at all. The skirting board is shivering, the ceiling is moaning, and Satoshi's fish bowl, still in its spot on the shelf, is now a shuddering violent thing. The fish inside whirl and clash, stripped of their silvery skin, grey corpses bubbling to the surface one by one.

There is no one else in here, that much is clear, but I am somewhere else now, I realise that, somewhere long ago lost, the old hymn voices rising up to my ears.

Where is she.

Where is she.

Lost and lost.

I scan the room, shrinking with heat, hypnotised by the rocking chair, the rocking chair still rocking, still swaying from side to side, even with flames licking at the two curved bands of wood that cradle its legs.

Lost and lost.

Where is she.

Where, now, there.

Stinging feet, stinging eyes. A malicious flame growing big by the window. And then the glass explodes, spitting fire drops. Pinpoint pain. Hard to breathe. I hear footfalls on a busy street, a street flooded by light. Bits of desk, chair, shoebox, hardback, falling, all falling. Crumbs of plaster come down on the bed, making no sound, looking like snow.

And now flames are bursting through the ceiling, where the damp stains used to be, revealing a brilliantly illuminated space beneath the building's second level. Lower, closer, graceful amid the chaos, a draught from the shattered window has gathered up a sheet of paper from the floor. It sashays comically as I swipe at it, cuts shapes through the familiar pall, shimmers and ripples as it falls. More pages. Pages of letters, fluttering slowly downward. They relax on a mound of desiccated matchsticks, a heap of small scorched things. My mouth opens, but no words come. Instead of words, a thought: a thought about how the pages crackle with energy and power, the heated life of each new sheet erupting over the embers of the last.

The hissing and the whooshing hit full volume in a split second. The shirt cuffs around my wrists are alight. I smell something but don't know what it is. I lurch face first into the carpetless floor. My eyes inches from withering paper. My fingers sizzling like meat on Teflon. I roll onto my back. I understand the smell is me, my flesh, my skin. Flesh and skin and paper. The words are coming loose, dying. I see them coil around the present and vanish.

Pregnant no she's pregnant no.

I love you, I love you, I love you.

I miss you. I miss you. Oh God I miss you.

I keep thinking that some freak physical phenomenon will save me. A giant tropical wave, a blast of polar ice, something really no more inconceivable than me being here in the first place. I see Chloe, my mother, Chiyoko. All wrapped in a blank sheet of light. An atomic light, familiar yet never seen before, lucid but tiring.

As my body relaxes, I am only dimly aware of the voices calling my name. I barely register the swimming clouds of white foam crowding in on me. The last thing I remember is the hands, glowing with tranquil sweat. A thick bronze hand with an expensive watch around the wrist, dragging me by the belt loops of my jeans. And someone else's hand too, hovering in the middle distance, tattooed with tired veins, clutching unburnt paper.

I remember the feeling, the sense of other people coming near, hope hanging in the plaster dust.

Flat 14
Finegold Mews
Longcross Ave.
Longcross
Surrey
England

1 January 2000

Roppongi World Plaza 9–39
Roppongi 1-chome
Minato-ku
Tokyo 106-0032

Dear Reggie, dear Reginald, dear Mr Satoshi,

It is a strange thing. In my memory you are several overlapping people all at once: my first love, a stranger, a character in a story I may have made up.

Which one of you am I sending this to? Perhaps none. This is a letter I sometimes doubt will get sent, about a secret I sometimes doubt will surface. Yet this little television in front of me says we have entered a new millennium. I never thought I'd live to see one of those. What better time to put the past down on a gaping page.

I am in my new home now, across the road from my last. I am here because I am old and my marbles are slowly rolling away. Perhaps I'll find them again, under the cooker or the sofa, but it does not seem terribly likely. I could not come to the end of things without addressing some words to you. I want to put the words down while the memories still matter.

Five years ago, an extraordinary thing happened. I was not here, I was in my old house. My son Robert was visiting me. Your picture came on the television. I thought I was going mad (and there is some of that, my dear) but it really was you inside the box. You were a respected academic, talking about changes in Japan since the Allied occupation. A little banner at the bottom of the screen said you represented a veterans' organisation based in Tokyo. Your face had certainly changed since 1947. I am sorry to tell you this, but you have not aged at all well. On the screen, under all that saggy skin, you looked like a different person. It took a gesture to convince me: you lifted a glass of water to your lips, sucked up the liquid in a certain way, and you were suddenly you.

I found a phone number for the veterans' organisation. It took me ages to work out how to use the international code, the zeros and whatnot. I used to know how those things worked. Eventually it rang. I suspect the Japanese woman I spoke to was not used to old women calling up from England. She sounded a little scared, gave me your address without any quibble, and I started writing this letter.

That was five years ago. Every now and then, in the time since, I have tried and failed to finish writing. If I ever get round to actually sending it, this version or another, I suppose I will have to ring up the World Plaza and check you're still there. And

I know that you probably won't be. I will find the words to finish the letter, but the address at the top will be useless. I will have to cross it through and stick the envelope in a box, wait to forget about it. That's how life works. If I have learned one lesson, it is that the world is freighted with things that do not quite match.

Robert, the boy I had with my husband, was not my first child. I gave birth to another a long time before him, in October 1947. A little girl who, either out of maternal love or pure vanity, I called Alice. Our daughter: Alice Pickford.

The last time I saw her was 8 November 1947, so ours was a short-lived acquaintance. On Guy Fawkes Night, everyone makes that rhyme: 'Remember, remember . . .' And I always think, it is the 8th of November I will always remember, not the 5th. Silly, but I always think that.

When I found out I was pregnant, you were not there. You had come down from the Lakes, spent those weeks with me in London, and vanished that snowy afternoon without a word. I didn't know where or why you had gone, still don't. I had just got you back from Japan, I wasn't ready to lose you again, to lose you and gain a child. I shut myself away in Freddie's lodgings at Rashleigh House. I made her promise not to tell anyone. It was not difficult; she felt at fault for having let you stay, for having let you into my bed. So on the 8th dear Freddie accompanied me on a train to Clapham Junction. She carried six-week-old Alice, and I carried a bundle of baby clothing. It was a simple plan. We had placed an advert a few days earlier in a local newspaper. We kept it short and snappy. 'Unconditional surrender', it said, as if the decision to give her up came after a long battle. In reality, it took just a few days of quiet thought to decide. From that point on, it was a matter of admin – the advert, the falsely made out birth certificate, and the train tickets.

We gave her away on Platform 2 at 3.35 p.m. They seemed like nice people, the new parents. Nicer than me, no doubt. At this distance from the event, morality is hardly relevant. But there were reasons. I was young, I was alone. I did not want to bring up a child on the parish. Two generations have brought a lot of changes, but the labels for a child back then were hard to shake off. 'Illegitimate', 'out of wedlock', 'bastard'. They were unforgiving labels. It sounds brutal, but lying in Freddie's arms, there was a problem. I suppose, in one sense, I solved it. I must have solved it, because I have never heard from our daughter since.

It is hard to grieve the loss of someone who, God willing, is still out there in the world. With love, there is an awareness of death on the horizon. When the person you love dies, it feels like the final stage, a proper end. The grief is terrible, but your love was true – it has been confirmed by the disappearance of the thing you cared for.

When my mother died, my father helped carry the coffin. As he walked down the aisle, I saw that he had cut his hand on a rivet in the wood. A tiny trickle of blood ran down his wrist and into his shirtsleeve. I was so grateful to see that blood. The blood told me that the pain was real.

When my father himself died, there was no physical injury. But I had a little boy standing next to me by then. I had Robert, my Foss, bleary-eyed as the coffin went past. His tears made the grief tangible.

But with Alice, the grief cannot be expressed or located. There is just shame, and silence. It has been in the air I have breathed for the last half a century. There is a maddening loneliness: not the dramatic, tear-filled solitude I imagined, just loneliness. I expected visceral horrors like those that seemed to haunt your nights, but it is not like that; it is just a quiet, invisible sadness. There is no doctor writing you a prescription and telling you that there will be a period of mourning, that you will 'come out the other side'. There is no 'why don't you take up a new interest?' – perhaps lawn bowls, perhaps bingo, God forbid. There are not people telling you that if you would like to talk about it, they will not be embarrassed listening to your snotty outpourings. There is not even the preordained language of grief to fall back on, the nonsense of expensive cards: my deepest sympathies, my condolences, my thoughts and prayers. I have come to accept that there are a limited amount of thoughts and prayers available for me.

After the transaction on the platform, Freddie took me onto Lavender Hill and bought me a little bottle of Coty Muguet perfume to try and cheer me up. Then the next day, the Sunday, she cooked roast beef with all the trimmings, saying that the banquet was a kind of send-off, a chance to think about the baby but also about all the things I could be thankful for. Freddie was such a good friend, but I found myself sobbing at the table. I sobbed for the longest time, and looked at the only reminder I had – a black and white photograph from just after the birth. Freddie had taken it at the hospital. Nothing else. I wished I had kept an item of clothing, or a strand of hair. I bought more and more of that Coty Muguet perfume and sprayed it around the flat, hoping it would remind me of Alice. But it just reminded me of you, and of my mistakes.

I think about Alice every day. Sometimes, tired of loving someone in black and white, tired of loving someone flat, I conjure her up in my head. I scrunch my eyes shut and try to imagine her as a grown woman in real-life colour. And sometimes it works – a bright picture of her splashes into my mind. But most often there is no picture, just an emotion. Pictures and emotions, emotions and pictures. It is never both at the same time. I cannot send you the emotion, feelings do not travel well. So I have enclosed a copy of my photograph of Alice, and one of my son too. He is a photographer. There are things you and he have in common, and an interest in images is one of them. I surround myself with his photographs these days, and I notice that in his pictures of people he often brings their face and body into sharp focus, but leaves the background scene blurred, isolating the person from the world behind them. He wants every detail of the skin, as though he is trying to inhabit it. Sometimes Robert looks at me with his photographer's eye and I feel like he knows, that he might know there is an absence deep inside me. But there is a limit to what you can see of other people. It is not possible to completely shed your own skin, to climb into some-body else's.

For a while I thought I would go and find her, one day. But, of course, I have not done that. Perhaps, if you receive this, you will gather up the strength that I have lacked. Or perhaps I will get over my shame and tell Robert, let him inhabit my skin, just for a moment. He might want to know his sister. He might want to find her. Freddie has ended up here with me, and she says he should know, that he deserves to. She says she feels burdened with the secret, the question of whether it was the right thing to do all those years ago, but that it is not hers to tell, not hers to answer. Dear Freddie. For years I pushed her away. The best friend I ever had, and yet for decades I avoided her, saw her in the street and turned away, and why? Because something in her eyes, fidgeting in those shallow cups of light, took me back to that day on Platform 2. The thing I am most ashamed of, living tight against her irises. What have I done to those I love?

When I eventually married, it took a while before I could be convinced to have a child with my husband. I almost left it too late. I probably wrapped him too tightly in my arms. I probably made him fearful of the world. The thought of losing him made me sick: every time he left the house as a boy, I worried that a freak gust of wind might throw him off his bike, or that as he daydreamed in a nearby library an unbalanced bookcase would come crashing down on him, or that his tetanus jabs were not up to date, or that he would go into hospital to have his tonsils out and never come back. I worried about all of these things. And now, as I feel my mind going, the thought of forgetting the books he likes to read, or the fact that he used to sleep curled in a ball, or that his first word was 'kettle', or that he cut his toast corner to corner, all those things make me feel queasy too. But he is my son. I will always love him. I think he loves me too, whether or not I forget these things, lose these footholds.

So there is my secret, Mr Satoshi. Our secret. It is disconcerting how quickly a secret can be told, how few words it takes. Every day I forget something. But this secret I have set down, it has been remembered.

I still remember you.

Alice

x

29

A CHEERFUL nurse in white scrubs and plastic shoes unwound the bandages from my arms. Some patches of skin were still wet with blood. It was purple-black, as if a darkness had long coursed through my veins. As it leached from me I released the letter, not wanting to blot out the words. The sheets flapped over the edge of the spindly bed and onto the cleanest floor I've ever seen.

'You look better today, Mr Fossick, recovering very well. Ask your friend, he can see the change.'

She wiped me down with some kind of towelette, bandaged my arms afresh, then carefully rearranged my pillow so that I could tilt my head to the left.

Mr Satoshi was there, tucked up in the only other bed, lying perfectly still on his side. I could tell from the set of his forehead that he had been staring at me for some time. Cotton wool was taped to his ear and his gown was puckered at the shoulders. There was a small window behind him and I could see a sparrow about to alight on the ledge, could hear its beating wings.

He sat up in measured stages, his sharp toes making small gestures under the tight canopy of cotton. The nurse picked up the pages from the floor and, seeing his outstretched hand, gave them to him. He coughed and coughed. You could hear the strands of saliva in his throat, cracking like whips. Then I heard his voice for the first time. Years of silence, yet without ceremony the voice came. It strained and splintered under the weight of the words, full of smoke and out of practice. He drank water and tried to begin again.

'I didn't burn it, the letter, your mother's letter.'

Those were his first words. He said he didn't burn the two photographs either. He burned everything else, all the stuff he found in my satchel, all the things filed away in cupboards, on shelves. He thought they were better burned than not burned.

I tried to keep my eyes open but it felt like weights were welded to the lashes.

'It's all right,' he croaked. 'Why don't you close them now. Close your eyes nice and tight.'

I did it. I closed them as he asked me to do. The ceiling's panelled light left dots under my eyelids.

'Are they closed?' he said.

'They're closed,' I said.

'Good,' he said, 'that's good.'

And he began to read out the letter. I tried to interrupt him, to tell him I had read it all myself, but it seemed he needed to speak the words aloud. He did so hesitantly; the voice came and went and came again. I sensed that his vision was failing, but perhaps because he was scanning for some other detail, something outside the edges of the page. Each time he said 'Alice' his tone became thin and airy, the sound of hands searching through tissue paper.

'That's it,' he said. 'That's what your mother wrote to me.'

I said nothing.

'I left her without a word,' he said. 'I regret that so very much, I really do. She didn't know why, and I don't know why either. I struggle to explain the why.'

'You don't have to tell me anything,' I said, surprised by the quietness of my own voice.

'But I do, you see. I do have to. I need to tell someone, and if it can't be Alice, then, well, it feels right it should be you.'

He started to speak about his time in Japan, telling me things I knew and things I didn't know, the seams of his past slowly opening. With my eyes closed I felt, somewhere deep in my head, the faint pulse of each word. Then, after he'd recovered from another terrible, jagged coughing fit, he came to 20 July 1946. It was the day he left Tokyo to do fieldwork in a nearby fishing village.

'I went with my Uncle George, our colleague Watanabe and one of the servants, a Japanese girl called Kazue. The letters in the satchel, if you read them you'll know, you'll understand who these people are.

'We stayed at a secluded inn and in the evening George, Watanabe and I had some drinks with the owner. Sometime past midnight, probably between midnight and half past, we retired to our rooms. I was sharing a kind of suite with George, and Watanabe and Kazue were sleeping downstairs. I dozed off straight away that night, full of fish and sake. But in the early hours I woke and couldn't get back to sleep. One night you wake from ordinary dreams and every single thing has changed . . . I really believe that can happen, while you are curled up tight, a switch can be flicked and everything is changed for ever. It was a hot, sticky night. The room was quiet. Strange, because George always snored. It took me a while to realise it, the room was huge and his bed, I think his bed was on a raised level by the window, but he wasn't there. Clearly he couldn't sleep either, I thought. He must have gone to get some air. I took a leaf out of his book. I put on some clothes.'

He put on clothes and went downstairs, out onto the inn's veranda which, like the outside walls and the interior and everything else, was made of wood. He stood there looking out at the dark sea taking big breaths of salt air. George was nowhere to be seen. A gentle slope of rocks and pebbles led down to the water's edge. There was a harbour area less than a mile down the coast. Some dim light from the homes and boathouses had spread across the water, mingling with the glow from the moon. That is when he heard a noise. It sounded like a kind of chanting at first. But within a few seconds he became convinced that it was more of a moan.

'A human moan,' Satoshi said, 'a cry of pain, perhaps. I think I . . . I turned back to face the inn, trying to work out where the noise was coming from. The patch of land to the left of the inn, I remember it caught harbour light. To the right of the building there was pure darkness, and all I could make out was a large pyramid of firewood piled close to the wall. So from what I remember . . . I'm sure I explored the left-hand side of the building first. But nothing there. So I walked back around the front of the inn until I got to the stack of firewood. The noise was definitely coming from behind that wood. I remember worrying that George could be in trouble. Perhaps he had been attacked. Wild boar weren't uncommon in the area, though I don't know whether the thought about wild boar occurred to me at the time or has come to me since. I lingered behind the stack, allowing my eyes to adjust to the darkness. Then I reached up and took a heavy piece of firewood from the top. Yes. It was only a foot or so long, but thick, with a sharp end. In one swift movement, holding my breath as I did so, I leapt out into the darkness, piece of wood raised above my head, like some child pretending to be a samurai.'

There was a small pause in Satoshi's speech, already swelling into sound. When he spoke again the words came faster, the mattress groaning under his shifting weight.

'In part, it was as I suspected. There he was – George. At first, all I could see in the gloom was the top of his back. I remember those broad shoulders practically bursting out of the white cotton shirt he had worn to dinner. Then I saw that his trousers were around his ankles. Maybe I thought he was just having a pee against the wall of the inn. I don't know. I must have thought something like that because I brought the piece of firewood down to my side, feeling a bit awkward probably, nothing more. I don't know. But then I saw that there was something between him and the wall, a rag or a rug, and that he was pressing himself against it. But it wasn't a rag or a rug. There, all bent and crumpled, the side of her face pressed against the rough wood, there was, I could see . . . Kazue.

'When George turned round he seemed to look first at the sky rather than me. That's how it happens in my head, at least. Him looking at the sky first. He angles his face upward, towards the moon, and in an instant his features become chalky white. When his jaw comes down, eyes meeting mine, he looks sort of silver, and he says my name, he said my name. I stood there, and Kazue tried to get away, and I remember her rushing between his legs, like something from a cartoon, her bare feet getting caught in the limp cotton of his trousers and pants, and he reached out a hand and grabbed a fistful of her hair, drawing her head back into his body with a jolt, shouting Get lost boy, leave us to it for Christ's sake. Leave you to what, I said, still thinking some reasonable explanation would come, had to come, because the reality of what I could see was too disgusting to digest, too terrible, and in that second it was like –'

'You hit him,' I said, feeling the need to interrupt his words. They were deepening with every vocal beat in their fantasy and fervour, becoming increasingly breathless and grave. Some bond within him had dissolved, some constraint had been removed, and now he couldn't stop amassing tiny details, embroidering memories, reliving that one night in his life.

'As George bent down, trying to pull up his trousers with his free hand, somehow holding Kazue to his hip, I did it. I found myself doing it. I raised the piece of wood high and straight above my head, as casually as though I were going to place it on some imaginary ledge.

'I brought it down, Robert. With all my strength I brought it down on the back of his head. Christ, George screamed, spitting or screaming, maybe both, falling to his knees. He let go of Kazue's hair. The thing that sticks in my mind is that he looked sort of baffled by the blow, by suddenly being on his knees in front of me. As Kazue disappeared behind the logs, I saw that she was wearing a kimono he had bought her when she first became his servant. You could buy them at the PX in Ginza! They had American Stars and Stripes printed on the back!'

'You're shouting,' I said, clenching my eyes tighter.

'I lifted the piece of wood above my head again, I did not even think about it. I brought it down even harder than before, all my strength released, like a length of elastic snapping. Jesus Christ, George said. Something like that. Jesus, God, Christ. I don't know. His voice was all . . . He gurgled the words. He rocked back and forth on his knees, cursing me, looking groggy but also angry. He put both palms of his hands on the ground and there was a chance he was levering himself up onto his feet, so I swung, I swung at him from the side this time, like I was wielding one of those school things, a rounders bat. As the wood struck him on the temple I remember how it sent a shock down my forearm. There must have been a rough rivet or knot protruding from the bark, I don't know, because, because a gash appeared where his eyebrow went thin, just to the side here. It was no more than a pale line in the flesh at first, but it soon became dark and thick with blood, and George was lying on his side now, knees tucked into his ribcage, like a . . . a child, shaken, shaking. But instead of a whimper he let out this deep growl that frightened me. Fear was still on his side even then and my face was hard and hot and tears and sweat were stinging my skin and I went at his legs with a chopping motion, heard his shin splinter and –'

'Enough!' I said, forcing myself – although it hurt – to roll onto my side. I rolled towards him, not away. He was sobbing now, a soft irregular complaint, and I couldn't bear to open my eyes and see his grief. 'It's OK, stay calm, it's OK. If you want to, we can leave it, you can tell me another time.'

I heard him take a drink of water, blow his nose, and I knew then that he would not leave it, that there wouldn't be another time, not for this.

'Afterwards my efforts, my efforts to catch my breath, they were useless. I staggered backwards across the veranda, then back even further, onto the stones, until water soaked my shoes. The sound of the sea poured into me. I looked all around. There was nothing except empty boats in the harbour, lights of houses alongside them. I expected something, but there was nothing. No round of applause. No firing squad. I started to wail like a kid, just like a kid does. My hands were swollen and bloody. I fell to my knees in the water. I stayed there, for a long time, and at some point Watanabe found me. Eventually others . . . they came, took me inside. The next day I was in Tokyo, being questioned.

'What you have to understand is that I was grateful for the questioning, it was a chance to explain it how it was, to free up my conscience and my mind. That's what I thought. Questions will bring answers. I wanted . . . a long prison term, perhaps, and then some closure. I wanted to suffer in solitude, somewhere I couldn't be measured against other people, and come back as the person I was before. But the authorities were only prepared to take things so far. We Westerners were there to democratise the Japanese, to set an example. There was no place for these tales, these tales of child abuse and murder, not in the new Japan. They sent me home. A nice place by a nice lake, as if the sound of soft water was just what I needed. They felt I was insane. I wasn't sure I disagreed. So I went to the Lakes.'

'And then London,' I said, heavy-chested, feeling something twisting deep in my throat, a small knot swelling upward. I was thinking about him, the child he saved in Japan, the child he lost in England, but also about myself.

'London, yes, a few months later. Freddie's lodgings in

Bloomsbury, with Alice. Your mother loved me, but I was no longer there to be loved. We would sit around in the evenings trying to talk, but I would drift away. On her birthday night, when we were supposed to be celebrating, she said this thing I remember. She said, You shouldn't always go back to the past. But, for me, the past, the worst swathe of it, was like a giant curtain cloaking me completely. The present didn't touch me. The more Alice talked of everyday things, of the low gas pressure, of the geyser freezing over, of the cuts putting out the lights in Hyde Park, of the Third Programme being suspended, of us getting married . . . The more she spoke, the more she was Alice. But I was not me. I was not there. No amount of injections, no amount of electric shocks, could jolt me back into life. Do you understand? I kept praying that something would burn up the past, turn that curtain to ash, but nothing did. And it was then, at the point at which I stopped praying, that I realised I would always be on that veranda. Do you understand me? All the time, all the time I could have been with them, could have had . . . a wife, and a daughter, I was there on that veranda.'

I felt tears come now and I gave myself up to them, deep hot sobs like I hadn't felt for years. Scenes, old and new, light and dark, fused under my shuddering lids: the strip-lit cruelty of a smoke-filled room; an evening sun casting pink over Chiyoko's lashes; balletic paper rising and falling; a television screen, dense with images, animated but also still. I was in a room, I knew that. A room in a Hokkaidō hospital. But it didn't feel like I was inside anything at all. I saw myself travelling the world, searching for my sister, countries whirring around me like dead leaves, shorn of their branches but multicoloured. I felt different, somehow, knowing she was out there, that she had been there all along.

'Are you in pain, Robert? Shall I get someone? No? I . . . Well, well, that's it. In the end there are no new memories, only spaces full of stories. Anthropology teaches you this. Some stories are told, some untold. One freezing afternoon in February '47, when I had barely been reunited with your mother a month, I disappeared. She went out to try and get some scrappy meat for our tea. I watched her through the kitchen window. Her hair was speckled with snow. She looked unreal, like a sugar-coated treat my mind had dreamt up. I packed a bag and put on my coat, then walked the opposite way. I never told her how beautiful she looked with the snow in her hair. The number 19 arrived, so I got on it. I went around London on that bus for two hours, maybe three. I never told her that she was the most beautiful thing. I let the bus take me round and round. I stayed with my mother a while. And then I went back to Japan and tried to make new memories where the old ones lived. Does that make sense? I suppose I just . . . I tried.'

Slowly I opened my eyes. I looked through blurry light at the pulsing life signs in his neck, the washed white sorrow on his face. I looked past him, at the window. The glass contained Sapporo. A crane towered over everything. It looked like the anglepoise lamp in my flat. The skyline resembled my toothbrush, upturned, some bristles missing. And yet when I blinked and looked again these comparisons seemed ridiculous. It was a crane. It was a skyline. That was all.

After a long time had passed I said, 'Your story. If it's finished, for now, then I'd like to tell you mine.'

30

THERE IS something about snow, about the way it trembles under a sinking sun, that makes you feel new. The train picked up speed. Stormlight formed around mountains. And the few human trails clinging to the Hokkaidō ground, delicate, slender, arcing in and out, began to vanish in the thaw.

In the dining car, waiting for the jittery neon of Tokyo, reimagining the dazzle of high windows and bright lipstick and fluorescent signs, I sat and watched the white landscape skitter by. I wasn't alone. The passenger next to me, a thick-bodied man with small restless hands, was staring out too. He played with his can of beer, took a double swig and smothered a burp. There was an air of departure in his eyes that made me wonder what he was thinking. Elsewhere in the carriage, dozens of others leaned into the glass, feeling the friction of travel in their teeth, shading their eyes or holding their chins. People of all ages, carried to the capital: parents, grandparents, children; families, young and old, huddled together. Vents hummed with hot air and steam rose from coffee cups, but still they stayed bunched like survivors, staring into the distance. My attention was caught by the largest group, seven or eight men and women standing between chrome bars. They whispered to each other and pointed at branches sleeved with snow. I thought at first that they were all friends, but as they gradually dispersed, one by one, bowing, smiling, I realised they were simply strangers sharing the view.

As the sun became liquid and spread thin across the ground I opened *The Japanese Verb Book*, a parting gift from Mr Satoshi, and prepared to learn. *I go, you go, he goes, we go*. Apparently it makes no sense to teach Japanese that way. The conjugation is the same for all subjects: first person, second person, third person, singular and plural. So I just recited new words in the way the book advised me to do, and closed my eyes to see how much I could remember.

I was trying to conjure up one particularly evasive verb when, rather than words, a picture came. A pale, time-washed picture. It was the image of my sister as a newborn, lying in my mother's arms. She was surrounded by light. And, by the time the tricky verb had revealed itself to me, I had made a decision. There was no need to go looking for Alice. I had a sense that, if she was in a library somewhere, she would manage to avoid any falling books. I couldn't see her succumbing to some exotic disease, or being blown off course by a freak gust of wind. Rightly or wrongly, I felt I knew who she was.

My watch ticked softly, measuring out the evening, the skin around it still looking sore. I hoped we were running on schedule. I wanted to call Freddie from my strange little room on the thirteenth floor. I wanted to sit in the chrome kitchen, yawning, listening to Dolly Parton, the smell of coffee and eggs rising up around me. I wanted to see the shifting planes of Daisuke's face as toast sprang up, water boiled, reflections wavered in dangling knives. I even wanted to see the two dachshunds, wobbling from fridge to freezer and then back, bumping into each other, barely awake and putting on weight. Most of all, I wanted to catch Chiyoko before she left for lectures. A day in Tokyo, perhaps two, perhaps more.

The train made a lovely noise as it struck south, an ambient murmur that gathered up the stray voices of those shuffling through the aisles, muttering to themselves, groping at walls and rails, feeling their way. It was a music that seemed to warp time. I looked back to months and years before and found only traces of myself, images filtering into the present moment, rushing past, leaving a quiver in the trees beyond the glass. I looked back and felt exhausted but at ease.

The man with restless hands had his eyes closed now, oblivious to the tiny thunder of his own snores. Shoulders rolled, he swayed in my direction. He was still in his seat, but only technically. His face was inches from my knees when his body jolted him awake, and he looked astonished by the sight that greeted him, his brows looping high in disbelief. We had been neighbours for some time, but it seemed this was his first glimpse of the bronze trumpet flowers that lay across my lap.

'Winter daffodils,' I said, and he gave me a shaky smile.

ACKNOWLEDGEMENTS

I am indebted to the following authors and works: John W. Dower, *Embracing Defeat: Japan in the Wake of World War II*; John W. Bennett, *Doing Photography and Social Research in the Allied Occupation of Japan, 1948–1951*; David Kynaston, *Austerity Britain: A World to Build*. Any inaccuracies or elaborations are my own.

Very special thanks are due to Clare Alexander, Jason Arthur, Stephanie Sweeney, Emma Finnigan, Laurie Ip Fung Chun, Harvey Marcus, Jennie Rooney, Auden Witter, Marie Bates, Jim Friel, and above all to Amy — without whom, no book.